MURDER IN TRANSIT

MURDER IN TRANSIT

EDWARD MARSTON

Allison & Busby Limited
11 Wardour Mews
London W1F 8AN
allisonandbusby.com

First published in Great Britain by Allison & Busby in 2024.
This paperback edition published by Allison & Busby in 2024.

A CIP catalogue record for this book is available from
the British Library.

10 9 8 7 6 5 4 3 2 1

ISBN 978-0-7490-3017-9

Typeset in 11/16 pt Sabon LT Pro by
Allison & Busby Ltd.

By choosing this product, you help take care of the world's forests.
Learn more: www.fsc.org

MIX

Paper | Supporting
responsible forestry

FSC® C171272

Printed and bound by
CPI Group (UK) Ltd, Croydon, CR0 4YY

CHAPTER ONE

Summer, 1866

As she walked along the platform in the gloom, she was aware that she was being followed. She was a handsome, well-dressed woman in her thirties with a strange dignity about her. When she paused outside an empty first-class compartment, she did not look behind her. Entering, she took a seat beside the window on the far side and held her reticule on her lap. After a few moments, a man opened the door and stepped in. He touched his hat in greeting, but she ignored him. He was a big, broad-shouldered individual in his fifties with an aura of wealth. As he settled into a seat in the middle of the compartment, he was diagonally opposite her with his back to the engine.

He studied her out of the corner of his eye, admiring

her poise, her fashionable attire, and her air of independence. He relished the way that her perfume masked the smell of the oil lamps. Though there was little to see in the darkness outside, she stared through the window beside her. It allowed him to run his gaze over her at will. Ten minutes of close observation slipped pleasantly past. It was then shattered by a succession of noises. A loud whistle was blown, voices were raised, and feet were heard running along the platform. The engine added its own contribution to the swelling chorus. As the train burst into life, a man in the uniform of a naval officer flung open the door and stumbled in, shutting the door behind him. He flopped into a seat and struggled to get his breath back. After noticing the others, he gestured an apology then closed his eyes.

'Wake me when we . . . get to Portsmouth,' he said, slurring his words.

The other man was angry at the sudden loss of privacy. Alone with an attractive woman, the last thing he wanted in the compartment was a drunken sailor only feet away from him. He moved closer to the window, away from the newcomer and opposite the woman. When he showed his irritation by clicking his tongue, she was more tolerant.

'If he has a first-class ticket,' she said, reasonably, 'he's entitled to travel with us.'

'Why couldn't he pick another compartment?'

'I don't think he's in any condition to answer that question.'

'I do apologise,' he said.

'There's nothing to apologise for.'

'I was hoping that we might . . . enjoy some conversation.'

'We can still do that,' she replied. 'Our companion is so drunk that he won't interrupt.'

'The damn fellow is just so . . . inhibiting.'

'He'll snore all the way to Portsmouth. Pretend that he's not even here.'

He glanced at their companion. 'But he is here – and he's in the way.'

'Only if we let him be,' she said, sweetly.

Her manner changed completely. Having ignored him before, she was now meeting his gaze. His interest was kindled immediately. The dozing passenger ceased to exist. Several minutes passed as they stared at each other. It was the woman who eventually broke the silence.

'Tell me about yourself,' she invited. 'When you came into the compartment, you were in a buoyant mood. Where had you been?'

'I dined at my club in Chichester,' he said. 'It was in the nature of a celebration.'

Her eyes widened with interest. 'Celebration?'

'A few days ago, I sold a property on the Isle of Wight for a huge profit. I wanted the opportunity to boast about it. As I'd hoped, my friends were green with envy.'

'What exactly do you mean by a huge profit?' she asked.

'If you want to know,' he said, patting the seat beside him, 'come a little closer.'

'No, thank you.'

'I'll tell you all about my good fortune.'

She gave him a teasing smile. 'You could do that if you sat beside me.'

He needed no more invitation. Standing up, he took off his hat and frock coat then lurched at her. She gave him an uninhibited welcome, letting him kiss and grope her at will. Then he forced her down on the seat and pulled up her dress. It was as far as the encounter lasted. Coming to life, the sailor suddenly leapt to her assistance, producing a length of rope to put around the neck of the older man before tightening it with cruel force. All that the man could do was to flail and splutter for a few excruciating minutes while the life was squeezed out of him. He was then dumped face down on the floor of the compartment.

The woman's nose wrinkled in disgust. She used a handkerchief to wipe her lips.

'Search him!' she ordered.

CHAPTER TWO

There was never a chance to rest for any length of time at Scotland Yard. Demands on the detectives were continual. Whenever they tried to get their breath back, something always came up. Robert Colbeck and Victor Leeming were enjoying a brief chat together in the inspector's office when an urgent summons came from the superintendent.

'Can't he find someone else to take charge of a case?' complained Leeming. 'The moment we sit down, he finds a reason to make us stand up again.'

'Try to see it as a reward for our success.'

'It's unfair.'

'I'd rather view it as a challenge,' said Colbeck, getting up. 'Each case has its individual character. That's what makes our work so fascinating.'

'Every investigation spells danger in one form or another,' said Leeming, ruefully. 'As I know to my cost. Also, it usually takes us a long way away from home. Doesn't the superintendent realise there are such things as wives and children?'

'Family life is an unknown country to him, Victor. Let's find out what he wants.'

He led the way to the superintendent's office and knocked politely before opening the door. Edward Tallis was seated behind his desk, studying a telegraph. He looked up at his visitors. Colbeck was as immaculately dressed as ever but Leeming was in a sorry state. Apart from his routine untidiness, he bore the scars of war. His face was bruised, he sported a black eye and there was a long, livid scratch down one cheek.

Tallis waved the telegraph in the air.

'This is a cry for help from Captain Forrest,' he said.

'I've never heard of him,' said Leeming.

'Your ignorance comes as no surprise to me, Sergeant. Captain Forrest is the Chief Constable of the Hampshire and the Isle of Wight Constabulary. He is also a friend of mine,' boasted Tallis. 'We met at a military reunion. Like me, Forrest saw service in India. He and I talk the same language.' He handed the telegraph to Colbeck. 'A man was murdered last night on a train to Portsmouth.'

'There are few details here, sir,' said Colbeck, reading the message.

'Then you must go to Winchester and find out the full story.'

'Doesn't the Hampshire Constabulary have its own detectives?' asked Leeming.

'The captain wanted the best man for the job,' said Tallis, drily. 'That's why I'm sending Colbeck – and his assistant.' Leeming squirmed. 'What are you waiting for?'

'Nothing, sir,' said Colbeck. 'We'll leave immediately.' He handed the telegraph back to Tallis. 'Please excuse us.'

He led Leeming out of the room and closed the door behind them. Tallis sat back in his chair with an air of satisfaction. He had been able to help a friend in need and to guarantee that the crime would be solved. Reaching for his pen, he composed a reply to Captain Forrest.

'Colbeck never fails . . .'

'But only because I keep barking at his heels,' he murmured.

They could not believe their luck. When their victim had been searched, they found rich pickings. The dead man not only had a wallet bulging with money – as well as a pocket watch and a gold wedding ring – he had been carrying an address book that contained the names of several women. Each one of them had a series of stars beside her name. They came to the same conclusion.

'These are all conquests of his,' said the man. 'He's

kept a record of every time he's shared a bed with them.' He grinned. 'You must admire his stamina.'

She grimaced. 'I loathed the man on sight,' she said. 'I could see from the expression on his face that I'd aroused his interest. The moment I left the ticket office, he followed me onto the platform. What he didn't know, of course, was that you were following him.'

'I waited until the right moment then dived into the same compartment.'

'Thank goodness! I'd hate to have been alone with that dreadful man.'

They were seated at the kitchen table in the house they had rented in Portsmouth. Spread out before them were the spoils from the previous night. He picked up the wedding ring.

'I wonder if he took this off before he got into bed with his mistresses,' he said.

'He certainly kept it on when he tried to ravish me. He was like an animal.'

'That's why I had to kill him. I'm not having you mauled like that. Our other victims were different. In their cases, all I had to do was to pretend to wake up and they pulled away from you. It never occurred to them that you'd stolen their wallets while they embraced you.' He laughed. 'The beauty of it was that they couldn't report the theft to the police because they would be asked about the circumstances in which they'd been robbed.'

'They'd also have had to lie to their wives about how

their wallets had gone astray.'

'I don't feel sorry for Blanchard's wife,' he said.

'Neither do I.'

'In killing her husband, we've done her a favour. She won't see it that way, of course. Mrs Blanchard probably worships him. She doesn't know that she was married to a shameless adulterer.'

'What's our next step?' she asked, picking up the watch to examine it.

'The first thing I must do is to put that naval uniform away for a while. I'm no longer a member of the Royal Navy. Then we must celebrate in some way. Giles Blanchard has been our benefactor. There was well over a hundred pounds in his wallet.' He picked up the address book. 'But this is the real treasure. The women who let him do what he wished to them are in for a very nasty surprise. They'll not only be horrified by his death – they'll discover that it's going to cost them a lot of money.'

Captain John Forrest was alone in his office at the headquarters of the Hampshire Constabulary. Tall, slim, and sharp-featured, he looked younger than his sixty years. When there was a tap on his door, it opened to reveal a uniformed constable who led in two visitors before quietly departing. Colbeck introduced himself and Leeming. Though he was impressed by Colbeck's demeanour, the chief constable's attention was fixed on Leeming's facial injuries.

'You must excuse the sergeant's appearance,' said

Colbeck. 'During a recent investigation, he arrested two men after a lively tussle with them. The injuries they sustained were far worse than the ones before you.'

'I commend your bravery, Sergeant Leeming,' said Forrest.

'Thank you, sir,' muttered the other.

'Not long before you arrived, a telegraph came from Superintendent Tallis. He assures me that, in asking for the pair of you, I have put the investigation in excellent hands.'

'But why did you choose us?' asked Colbeck. 'Are there not able enough detectives in your own ranks?'

'There are none with your reputation, Inspector. For a heinous crime committed on the railway, I felt that you needed to be involved. Fortunately, Superintendent Tallis and I are friends. I knew that he would answer my plea.'

'He's never answered any of mine,' said Leeming under his breath.

'What exactly happened?' asked Colbeck.

Forrest indicated the chairs and his visitors sat down. The chief constable remained on his feet. He was far less intimidating than Edward Tallis. Forrest spoke to them quietly and respectfully.

'Until an hour ago,' he said, 'all I knew was that a man had been strangled to death on the last train to Portsmouth. We had no idea of his name because whoever killed him had emptied his pockets. That seemed to be the motive for the murder.'

'Have you learnt anything to make you question that assumption?' asked Colbeck.

'Judge for yourselves.' Forrest waited while Leeming took out his notebook and pencil. 'We now know that the victim was a Mr Giles Blanchard. He was travelling home to the Isle of Wight. When he failed to turn up, his wife became alarmed. She contacted the police early this morning. Mrs Blanchard was, as you can well imagine, panic-stricken.'

'Where had her husband been?' asked Leeming, looking up from his notebook.

'He'd been to his club in Chichester – it's called The Haven, for some reason. He told his wife that he expected to be home well before midnight. Mrs Blanchard didn't sleep all night.'

'That's understandable,' said Colbeck. 'How was the murder discovered?'

'When the train reached its terminus in Portsmouth,' replied Forrest, 'everyone got out and went on their way. Porters were checking the carriages to make sure that nobody was still on board. One of them saw a man fast asleep, as it seemed, in the corner of a first-class compartment. When he entered and tried to rouse the passenger, the fellow keeled over. There were ugly marks on his neck. The porter summoned the stationmaster, who, in turn, called the railway policeman on duty.'

'What was their response?'

'They were highly alarmed. We're accustomed to crime on our trains, but it's mainly confined to theft, intimidation, wanton damage, and prostitution. Murders are highly unusual. Of the few that have occurred, I can't remember any that featured strangulation.'

17

'How old was Mr Blanchard?' asked Leeming.

'He was in his late fifties. His son described him as fit and healthy.'

'Then it would have needed an even stronger man to overpower him.'

'A stronger man with an accomplice,' mused Colbeck. 'If someone distracted Mr Blanchard, he could have been caught off guard. Well,' he added, 'this sounds like an intriguing case. We are grateful to be involved in it, sir. Thank you for asking for us.'

'You'll have the full resources of the Hampshire and Isle of Wight Constabulary to call upon.'

'How big a force is there on the island?'

'It's smaller than I would wish – and its record is not exactly inspiring.'

'I'm sorry to hear that,' said Colbeck with concern. 'Her Majesty is often at Osborne House. I hope that her security is in no way compromised.'

It was a glorious summer day and Queen Victoria was on her private beach, standing beside her easel in one of the black mourning dresses she always wore. After adding a few brush strokes to her landscape painting, she turned to the woman who stood obediently beside her.

'What do you think of it, Gwendoline?' she asked.

CHAPTER THREE

When he arrived at Portsmouth railway station, Colbeck went in search of the man who had discovered the corpse. He was told that the porter would not be back on duty until that afternoon. The inspector asked for his address and discovered that Alfred Burns lived within walking distance of the station. He set off briskly. When he reached the little house at the end of a terrace, he saw that it was in a bad state of repair. Having knocked on the front door, Colbeck had to wait a few minutes before it was opened by a bleary-eyed man in pyjamas. Well into his fifties, Burns was short, skinny, and inhospitable.

'Whatever you're selling,' he snarled, 'we don't want it.'

'I am Detective Inspector Colbeck and I've been sent from Scotland Yard to investigate the murder that occurred last night on a train. I understand that you found the body.'

'Yes, I did, sir,' said Burns, voice becoming more respectful, 'and it gave me a terrible shock, I can tell you. I couldn't sleep last night for thinking about it. When I finally dropped off, you woke me up by banging on my door.' He stood back. 'You'd better come in, Inspector.'

Colbeck went into the house and found that it was dark, cramped, and musty. Burns led him into a living room and indicated a mottled sofa. As the two of them sat down, the porter tried to wipe the sleep out of his eyes.

'I've no idea who the poor devil was,' he said.

'I can tell you that, sir. According to the chief constable, his name was Giles Blanchard and he lived on the Isle of Wight.'

'I could see he was a toff. A suit like the one he was wearing must have cost a pretty penny.'

'Tell me exactly what happened when you entered the compartment,' said Colbeck, taking out his notebook. 'Every detail is important.'

'Ah, right . . .'

Burns needed a few moments to gather his thoughts. He cleared his throat.

'If you're on the late shift,' he said, 'you sometimes get nasty surprises. People leave all kinds of messes in the carriages and there are always those who forget to take their luggage with them. It's not so bad in first class, mind. People who can afford to travel there usually behave themselves.'

'Get to the moment of discovery,' prompted Colbeck.

'When I saw him through the window, he looked as if he was asleep. That's quite normal. If they've drunk too much, passengers often nod off. I opened the door and reached in to prod him. He didn't move so I got into the compartment and took him by the shoulders to give him a proper shake. When I did that,' said Burns, 'he just fell sideways. I saw these ugly, red marks around his neck. That frightened me so I called the stationmaster. We could both see he wasn't breathing.'

Colbeck waited patiently as the recitation went on, recording only the salient details. When the porter finally ended his tale, he was visibly shaken.

'Had you ever seen the gentleman before?' asked Colbeck.

'It's funny you should ask that, Inspector. At the time, I didn't recognise him. I was so shocked by what I'd found that I couldn't think straight. When I got back here, however, the shock had worn off. I thought about that face of his and them fine clothes.' He snapped his fingers. 'It was then I realised I'd seen him before at the station – lots of times.'

21

'Was he usually alone?'

'No, he was often with a woman.'

'It was probably Mrs Blanchard.'

'Not every time, it wasn't.'

'What do you mean?'

'Well, I saw the same woman twice maybe,' said Burns, scratching his head. 'But I must have seen him with one of three or four younger ladies as well . . .'

The Haven was in a side street in the more affluent part of Chichester. When he got out of the cab, Leeming paid the driver and sent him on his way. The club was in a large, well-maintained building with three storeys. He used the knocker. Almost immediately, the door was opened by a dapper middle-aged man with a practised smile that vanished the moment he saw Leeming's face. He took a step backwards.

'May I help you, sir?' he asked, warily.

'I hope so,' said Leeming.

'Are you interested in becoming a member of the club?'

'I'm afraid not. I could never afford it or find the time to join. I am Detective Sergeant Leeming from Scotland Yard and I'm investigating the death of one of your members.'

The steward was alarmed. 'Who is it?'

'Mr Blanchard.'

'But he was here yesterday evening and looked perfectly healthy.'

'It was not a natural death, I'm afraid. Mr Blanchard was murdered.'

'Heavens!' exclaimed the steward, bringing both hands to his face. 'This is dreadful news. What exactly happened?'

'If you let me inside,' said Leeming, 'I'll be happy to tell you . . .'

Colbeck moved swiftly. When he left the home of Alfred Burns, he took a cab to the headquarters of the Portsmouth City Police. He received a guarded welcome. The police were clearly upset that a murder that had occurred on their doorstep was being investigated by someone from Scotland Yard. Colbeck could see the muted hostility in their eyes. Superintendent Terence Vernon voiced the general feeling.

'We are aware of your reputation, Inspector, and give you the respect due to you, but we feel that we can handle this case just as efficiently in conjunction with the Hampshire Constabulary. Our knowledge of the area gives us a distinct advantage over you.'

'I intend to make use of it, Superintendent,' said Colbeck, briskly. 'May I ask how you got on with Alfred Burns?'

'I've never heard of the fellow.'

'He's the porter who discovered the body last night. You interviewed him, surely?'

'One of my officers would have done so when Burns returned to work today.'

'I couldn't wait until then,' said Colbeck. 'I went to his house and took a statement.'

'Oh, I see,' muttered Vernon, trying to hide his embarrassment. 'Did he have anything of value to say?'

'Yes, he did. It took me some time to get it out of him because he was still dazed by the experience. His mind eventually cleared. Apart from anything else, he remembered seeing the victim at the station before. Mr Blanchard travelled by train to and from Chichester on a regular basis, it seems.'

Vernon was peeved. 'How may we help you, Inspector?' he asked through gritted teeth.

'The first thing I'd like to do is to view the body.'

'I'll take you to the morgue myself,' said Vernon, moving to the door.

'Thank you,' said Colbeck, following him. 'I daresay that there's a lot of press interest.'

'Newspaper reporters have been hounding me all morning. When we finally identified the murder victim, I hoped that they would stop pestering us, but the opposite has happened.'

'It will get worse,' warned Colbeck. 'Mr Blanchard was clearly an important figure in these parts. His death will arouse considerable interest . . .'

Leeming was in the office that belonged to Martin Searle, the club steward. Having told him what had happened, Leeming had to wait while the other man absorbed the information. The news had clearly shaken him to the core.

'This is dreadful,' said Searle at length. 'Mr Blanchard was often at the club. On some occasions, he even spent the night here. He'll be sorely missed.'

'What sort of person was he?'

'He was a delightful man, sir, and very popular with the other members. They all respected him. When he dined here with friends last night, there was a lot of laughter. Mr Blanchard had an endless supply of anecdotes.'

'What time did he leave?'

'It must have been close to ten o'clock. I showed him to the door. There was a cab waiting for him. He'd ordered it earlier. That's the kind of man he was. He planned everything in advance.'

'What sort of mood was he in when he left?'

'He was in good spirits,' said Searle, 'and that was quite normal. When I showed him to the door, he gave me a handsome tip.'

'Would you say that he was drunk and off guard?'

'Oh, no, Sergeant. Gentlemen like Mr Blanchard never get drunk. No matter how much they have, they can hold their wine and spirits. It's a gift.'

'Then he wouldn't have been . . . unstable when he boarded his train?'

'He would have looked as sober as a judge.'

'I see.' He remembered something. 'When you invited me in, I heard a lot of voices. Are some of your members here?'

'A handful of the older ones are in the bar. They've

retired from work, but they'll never retire from The Haven. It's their second home.'

'Is there anyone here who was a close friend of Mr Blanchard's?'

'Oh, yes,' replied the steward. 'Mr Collier is here almost every day. He's close to eighty but is still very spry. He proposed Mr Blanchard as a member many years ago. Mr Collier will be the best person to talk to. Feel free to use my office.' He moved to the door. 'I'll send him in.' He paused. 'Do you want me to tell him about the murder or would you rather do so?'

'I'd prefer it if you left it to me,' said Leeming, 'but you're welcome to spread the news among the other members. Oh, and you might warn Mr Collier that I don't look my best. My face is likely to scare him. When I look in a mirror, it frightens me.'

'Very good, sir.'

When the steward left the room, Leeming checked the notes he had made then looked around the office. It was large, well-appointed, and excessively clean. Photographs of former members adorned the walls. Leeming could see that it was an exclusive establishment for wealthy men. He felt completely out of place there. After a couple of minutes, he heard a walking stick tapping on the hall floor. The door then opened, and Douglas Collier hobbled in. There was no danger of the old man being horrified by Leeming's face. He was virtually blind. Thin, withered, and with a white mane of hair, he looked around the room.

26

'Is there someone here who wants Douglas Collier?' he croaked.

'Yes, sir,' said Leeming. 'Why don't you take a seat? I have distressing news for you.'

'Really? They're not going to raise the membership fees again, are they?'

'Not as far as I know, Mr Collier.'

He held a seat so that it did not move when the old man dropped into it. Collier took a small magnifying glass from his pocket and peered through it at Leeming.

'Do I know you?' he said.

'No, sir. I don't believe that you do. My name is Leeming.'

'Leeming ... Leeming ... You're not one of the Dorset Leemings, are you?'

'I'm a detective sergeant from Scotland Yard.'

'You came all the way down here from Scotland?' said Collier in disbelief. 'Why the devil did you do that? And why on earth did you ask for me?'

Leeming sat down close to him. 'I've got some sad news to pass on to you, Mr Collier,' he said, gently. 'It's about your friend, Mr Blanchard.'

'Splendid chap, Giles. Generous to a fault. He bought dinner here for five of us yesterday evening. His stories had us roaring with laughter.'

'He won't be able to do that again, I'm afraid.'

Collier grinned. 'You try stopping him!'

'Mr Blanchard died last night.' The old man gasped. 'I'm sorry to tell you that your friend was strangled to death on a train to Portsmouth.'

'Giles was murdered?' Collier needed time to absorb the information. 'Who on earth would do such a thing? He was one of the nicest human beings you could ever wish to meet. There must be some mistake, surely?'

'I'm afraid not. I can see that it's been a great shock to you. The steward was the same,' said Leeming. 'There were tears in his eyes.'

'Who exactly are you?' asked Collier, confused.

'I'm involved in the search for the man who killed Mr Blanchard,' said Leeming. 'Since you were close to him, you may be able to help us. I'm told that he had lots of friends.'

'Everyone liked him.'

'He must have had enemies as well.'

'You didn't know Giles,' said the other, angrily. 'He was kind, generous, and wonderful company. How could anyone dislike him? Unless . . .'

'Go on,' urged Leeming.

'Unless . . . it was a jealous husband . . .'

A wicked smirk suddenly flitted across the old man's face. Then he burst into tears as the full weight of his loss became clear to him.

When he viewed the body at the morgue, Colbeck noted the size and muscularity of the murder victim. Blanchard had clearly kept himself fit. Only a powerful man with the advantage of surprise would have been able to strangle him. Unsurprisingly, nothing had been found in the pockets of the deceased. He had clearly been robbed. Colbeck was glad to leave the building and get the stink of disinfectant out of his nose. He took a cab to the ferry terminal so that he could cross to the Isle of Wight. No sooner had he stepped onto the waiting vessel than a familiar voice rang out.

'Bejasus!' yelled Brendan Mulryne. 'That's never Inspector Colbeck!'

'Yes, it is,' replied the other, crossing over to him and shaking his hand, 'and I'm delighted to see you again, Brendan. What the devil are you doing here?'

'I work on this steamer. Sure, it's a grand job. I'm out in the fresh air all day and I get to meet lots of interesting people – like you, for instance.'

'The last time our paths crossed, you were travelling with the Moscardi circus.'

'It was time for a change. I got fed up with the stink of the animals.'

Mulryne was a big, brawny man with an almost permanent grin on his face. When he had served in the Metropolitan Police Force, he had been a fearless and committed constable. Unfortunately, he had been too committed on occasion. Instead of merely arresting criminals, he had pounded some of them into oblivion. Superintendent Tallis had been badgered by lawyers, trying to claim damages for the police brutality used against their clients. Even though Colbeck had spoken up for him, Mulryne had been summarily dismissed.

'Ah,' said the Irishman, realising. 'It's the murder that

brought you here. That Mr Blanchard was strangled to death on a train last night. Strangled and robbed.'

'How do you know?'

'Word travels down here. Secrets don't stay secret for long.'

'You mentioned Mr Blanchard's name as if you knew the man.'

'Oh, I knew that black-hearted devil, so I did. He often used the steamer and treated those of us who worked on it as if we were ignorant peasants. I caught the lash of his tongue more than once. Don't ask me to mourn Giles Blanchard.'

'Other people speak well of him.'

'Well, I'm not one of them, Inspector,' said the other, bitterly. 'When I answered him back one time, he threatened to have me sacked if I did it again. I buttoned my lip after that and suffered in silence. Blanchard was vile. He could never resist the chance to say something nasty about the Irish to me.'

'How did you feel when you heard about his death?'

Mulryne chuckled. 'It made me feel that there was a God, after all.'

CHAPTER FOUR

Victor Leeming had arranged to meet Colbeck at Portsmouth railway station that afternoon. On the train journey there from Chichester, he consulted his notebook. Over a dozen pages had been filled by his spidery handwriting. After speaking to Douglas Collier, he had been questioned by the other members of The Haven who happened to be there. They were desperate to hear full details of the untimely death of their friend. Leeming had talked to them, one at a time, building up a detailed picture of the murder victim.

In the eyes of his fellow club members, Giles Blanchard had been a paragon. Yet what stayed in the sergeant's mind when he left the building was the momentary smirk on the face of Douglas Collier. According to him, Blanchard did not have an enemy in the world – except, perhaps, for a jealous husband. Had the old man been serious? Everything that Leeming had heard from the other members pointed to the fact that Blanchard was a man's man, happiest in male company. He often referred fondly to his wife when at the club, yet he seemed to spend little time at home with her. Evidently, The Haven provided something that she was unable to supply. Leeming wondered if it was a place to hide from a vengeful husband.

Colbeck was delighted to see Mulryne again. The Irishman was clearly doing work he enjoyed in a part of the country he loved. Now that summer had come, he was helping to take large numbers of holidaymakers to and from the Isle of Wight. Mulryne loved to see the excitement of the children who boarded the steamer on their way to one of the island's beaches. There was a secondary reason why Colbeck was pleased to bump into Mulryne. In an emergency, the Irishman would be there to lend a helping hand. Even though he was no longer a policeman, he would do anything for Colbeck. Unbeknown to Edward Tallis, he had already been used by the inspector on more than one occasion and he had always proved his worth.

One eye on the approaching land, Mulryne asked what Leeming was doing.

'He's gone to visit a club in Chichester. We've been told that Mr Blanchard spent the evening there before his fatal journey on the train to Portsmouth.'

'How are Victor's children?'

'They're growing up fast. David is working as a cleaner for the LNWR – much to the delight of my father-in-law. And Albert, who is still in school, has decided that he wants to be a policeman like his father. Do you have any family, Brendan?'

'I might do,' said the other with a laugh, 'but, then again, I might not. Even though I love the company of women, I'm just not the marrying kind.' He saw how close they were to the pier. 'Have to go. Good to meet you again.'

'I fancy that we'll be around for some time so I might well see you again.'

But his words went unheard. Mulryne had already moved to the position he always took up when the steamer was about to dock in Ryde. When the vessel made its first contact with the wharf, Mulryne tossed a rope ashore. Colbeck was soon part of an eager crowd of passengers who surged off the steamer in delight. Unbeknown to him, he was about to walk along the first proper seaside passenger pier in England. Built for the benefit of travellers over fifty years earlier, it took them safely over the mud and sand that previous visitors had had to tramp through.

While the others dispersed in various directions, Colbeck stepped into a cab and asked to be taken to an address just outside Ryde. He was driven through narrow streets filled with quaint houses and clusters of shops. There was a decided elegance about the larger buildings. Ryde had a curious charm, but he was not in a mood to enjoy it. His focus was on the home of the murder victim. Myrtle House, it transpired, was half a mile away from the town. Set in the middle of five acres of land, it was an impressive property that was reached by means of a long winding road. Everywhere he looked, Colbeck saw well-tended lawns and trees. The house itself glowed in the sun. Giles Blanchard had done well for himself.

When they reached the main gate, they were stopped by a tall, strapping young man who was holding a shotgun. He eyed the cab with suspicion. When Colbeck got out to confront him, he was given a gruff welcome.

'This is private property.'

'Who are you?' demanded Colbeck.

'Never you mind that,' said the other with a menacing wave of his shotgun. 'My orders are to keep prying reporters away from here.'

'I can assure you that I am not here on behalf of a newspaper. I am Inspector Colbeck from Scotland Yard, and the chief constable has put me in charge of the investigation. That means I must have access to the house and family of Mr Blanchard.' He took a step forward. 'If you insist on obstructing me, you will be placed under arrest.'

The man gulped. There was an authority in Colbeck's

voice and bearing that made the guard gesture apologetically. Unlocking the gates, he opened them wide. When the cab drove through them with Colbeck inside it, the man doffed his hat in deference. The cab went on its way through an avenue of trees before emerging into the sunlight and coming to a halt in the courtyard. As Colbeck alighted, he saw the front door of the house open to allow the solid figure of a man in his late twenties to step into view.

'Inspector Colbeck?' he asked.

'Yes, sir,' replied the other.

'My name is Paul Blanchard. I was told to expect you.'

'It's a pity that you didn't tell that man at the gates that I was coming. He gave me a distinctly unpleasant welcome.'

'I'm sorry about that,' said Blanchard. 'I'll speak to him.'

'Thank you, sir,' said Colbeck. 'Let me first offer my condolences. It must have come as a profound shock.'

'My mother was the first to hear the dreadful news. She's taken to her bed, I fear. The doctor had to give her a sedative. I did, however, manage to get a full account of my father's whereabouts yesterday so I'll be able to pass on the details to you.'

'That will be very helpful, sir.' He looked up at the house. 'May I ask if you live here?'

'My wife and I have a house nearby, Inspector. In the short term, however, I'll be staying here because Mother needs me.' He stretched out an arm. 'Let's go inside, shall we?'

'Yes, of course . . .'

As he walked past him, Colbeck wondered why the man was so calm and controlled. There was not the slightest hint of pain or grief in his face. During his career as a detective, Colbeck had met the families of many murder victims. They had been uniformly dazed – completely shattered in some cases – by news of their loss. Paul Blanchard, by contrast, seemed to treat a horrifying crime as a minor inconvenience.

'It was Inspector Colbeck's idea,' said the stationmaster, pointing to a large noticeboard.

'I'm glad that you took his advice. Have you had any response?'

'Not as yet, Sergeant.'

'Then I suggest that you put up the same appeal on the opposite platform. The only passengers who see it now are those coming into Portsmouth. Among the people travelling towards London there might well be passengers who were on the last train to arrive here yesterday.'

'Ah, I see what you mean.'

'We must try to reach everyone we can.'

Having introduced himself to the stationmaster, Victor Leeming was pleased to see that a board had been set up, asking passengers who saw anything suspicious on their journey on the previous evening to report it. It might even be, Leeming had argued, that someone had travelled in the same compartment as Giles Blanchard without realising that they were sitting close to the man's corpse.

'We've appealed to the public before,' said the sergeant. 'Thanks to boards we set up on platforms at Bury St Edmund's station, we were given vital information by some passengers about the investigation.'

'Let's hope the same thing happens here, Sergeant.'

The stationmaster was a short, stout, bustling man of middle years who was fascinated by the injuries to Leeming's face. He could not take his eyes off the livid scratch.

'The last time I saw a face like yours,' he recalled, 'it belonged to one of my porters. He had a violent row with his wife and came off worst. He had the same scratch down his cheek.

'Well, it certainly wasn't put there by my wife,' said Leeming with a grin. 'We never have violent rows – just the odd disagreement now and then.' He glanced towards the refreshment room. 'What sort of food do they serve here?'

'It's tasty and filling.'

Leeming rubbed his hands. 'That will suit me perfectly . . .'

Colbeck sat in the drawing room and jotted down information in his notebook. Remaining on his feet, Paul Blanchard explained that his father had been the most successful estate agent on the island and that he was proud to work alongside him.

'Ryde is a small town with fewer than four thousand inhabitants during autumn and winter. Those numbers swell in the better weather. There's a constant demand for accommodation. Father and I help to provide it. As well as selling houses, we bought a construction company so that we can build houses ourselves. Naturally, we operate at the expensive end of the market.'

'I'd already made that deduction, sir,' said Colbeck.

'On your drive here, you'll have passed two of the houses we had built – mansions for wealthy people who like to spend the whole summer here.'

'I'm not sure that this information is altogether relevant, Mr Blanchard.'

'Don't you understand?' said the other with a hint of tetchiness. 'I'm trying to tell you what the killer's motive might have been. Our success has created enemies. There are people on this island who resent the way that we've managed to buy property in which they had a keen interest. Among most businessmen here, my father was admired – but he was despised by a few.'

'Please give me their names,' said Colbeck, pencil poised.

'I'm not accusing anyone of direct involvement, Inspector. All I'm saying is that there are certain people who I believe would be capable of hiring an assassin to kill a hated rival.'

'That's a bold claim, sir.'

'I've given it a lot of thought.'

'Has your father been the target of an attack in the past?'

'One of our new houses was vandalised. We had to hire armed guards to protect it.'

'That's not the same thing as a physical threat,' argued Colbeck.

'My father suffered that as well,' said Blanchard, 'or so I believe. Before we go any further, I must impress upon you that what I am about to tell you is confidential. I would never disclose these details to the press – and neither must you.'

'I give you my word that I would never think of divulging private information to the press. Newspapers are bound to speculate but they'll receive no help from me.'

'That's good to hear.' Blanchard took a deep breath and sat down. 'Six months ago, my father came back from a trip to London with a large bruise on his face. He told my mother that he had been jostled in a crowd and forced accidentally against a pillar. Father hardly noticed the incident at the time.'

'Did your mother believe the story?'

'Yes, she did. It was probably the truth – or so I thought.'

'What changed your mind?'

'A couple of months later, I noticed that he was limping slightly. Father claimed that he had pulled a calf muscle. I urged him to go to the doctor, but he said it was not necessary.' Blanchard bit his lip. 'That afternoon, I went into his office and saw him rolling up his trouser leg so that he could adjust a blood-covered bandage.'

'Did he explain how he got the wound?'

'He claimed that he'd been bitten by a dog.'

'Did you believe him?'

'No, Inspector. I'm afraid that I didn't.'

'Did he report the incident to the police?'

'He told me that it was only a scratch and not worth bothering about.'

'Dog bites can be dangerous. Surely he went to a doctor?'

'Father refused to talk about the incident.'

'What was your mother's reaction?' asked Colbeck. 'She must have seen the wound when they retired to bed.'

Blanchard lowered his voice. 'They slept in separate rooms.'

'Why did he lie to you?'

'I wish I knew, Inspector.'

'I take it that, as next of kin, you were asked to identify the body.'

'Yes, I was. When my mother raised the alarm, I got in touch with the police at once. They told me that the body of an unknown man had been found on a train last night in Portsmouth station. It was only when I got to the police station that they told me my father had been strangled to death. I had to identify his body.'

'I took the trouble to view it myself, sir,' said Colbeck. 'I noticed that your father was well-built and in what seemed to be good physical condition.'

'Put that down to his love of exercise. Cricket was his real passion, but he was also a keen sailor. I reaped the benefit. Father coached me in the finer points of cricket, and he taught me how to sail the family yacht.' He pursed his lips. 'I'm eternally grateful to him for doing that.'

'Consider this, if you will,' suggested Colbeck. 'If he was the victim of an assassin, surely his attacker would think twice about trying to strangle such a powerful man. A knife would have despatched him more easily, or a cosh could have knocked him unconscious and put him at the mercy of his assailant.'

'Yes,' agreed Blanchard, thinking it through, 'you could be right, Inspector.'

'I believe that there were two people involved. One of them distracted your father so that the strangler could attack him by surprise. Also, of course, he'd been celebrating at his club. Drink would no doubt have flowed. He might well have been drowsy.'

'It's possible, I suppose.'

'Give me the name of anyone you consider to be suspects.'

'There is one prime suspect, Inspector.'

'Is he a fellow member of your father's club?'

'As a matter of fact,' said Blanchard, 'he is.'

'Then he might have been aware that your father was due to visit the club yesterday evening. That being the case, he would have known that Mr Blanchard would need to take a late train back to Portsmouth. If an assassin was involved, he would have lurked in readiness at Chichester station and got into the same compartment as your father.'

'That seems to me to be the most likely version of what happened.'

'Who is this gentleman who was a member of the club?'

'Berwyn Rees,' said Blanchard, spitting the name out. 'He's one of those glib Welshmen who is all smiles when he's with you but who traduces you when he's not. The man positively burns with envy at our success. He's a wily character with an uncanny knack of getting what he wants.'

'One last thing, sir,' said Colbeck, making a note of the name.

'What is it?'

'Do you feel that you might also be in danger now?'

'Of course not,' snapped the other. 'What ever put that idea into your mind?'

'Someone might wish to destroy your control over property sales on the island. With your father dead, you are now in charge of the business. That could make you a target.'

'My father was caught off guard and paid with his life,' retorted Blanchard. 'Nobody would ever be able to do that to me. I always take precautions.'

Opening his coat, he revealed a small gun neatly holstered beside his waist.

CHAPTER FIVE

Madeleine Colbeck was in her studio, stepping back to study her latest painting of a railway scene. There was something wrong with it but, to her irritation, she could not decide what it was. Her concentration was interrupted by the sound of laughter from the garden. She gazed through the window to see that her daughter, Helena Rose, was being pushed on her swing by her grandfather. The higher she went, the louder became her squeals of joy. What delighted Madeleine was that her father seemed to be having as much fun as his granddaughter.

The sound of the doorbell took her attention away from both the garden and her painting. Madeleine stepped out to the landing in time to see her maidservant opening the front door. When she heard a man's voice, she immediately used a rag to wipe her hands before she ran downstairs to welcome her visitor. Detective Constable Alan Hinton was stepping into the hallway. Madeleine dismissed the maidservant then took Hinton into the drawing room. She knew at once that he had been sent as a messenger.

'Where has Robert gone this time?' she asked, bracing herself.

'Portsmouth.'

'Oh, that's a relief! I thought it might be York again or even somewhere like Scotland or Ireland. He might be able to get home at night from Portsmouth.'

'Don't bank on that,' said Hinton. 'This letter will give you what little detail he knows. He was summoned by the Chief Constable of Hampshire, who, it seems, is a friend of the superintendent.'

She was surprised. 'I didn't know that the superintendent had any friends.'

'They're few and far between – and they were usually in the army.'

'What about Estelle?' she asked. 'Will someone tell her that Victor is in Portsmouth?'

'That's my job. I'll warn her that he may not be home tonight. I came here first.'

'Thank you, Alan.'

Hinton was a tall, slim, handsome young man who had been promoted from the uniform branch at the recommendation of Colbeck. He was excessively grateful.

'Have you . . . seen Lydia recently?' he asked.

'No, I haven't, I'm afraid. She's been away but, as it happens, she is coming for dinner this evening. You're most welcome to join us.'

'It's very kind of you to ask me, but I have other plans. Please give Lydia my best wishes.'

She smiled. 'Is that all?'

'No, it isn't,' he said. 'Say that I was asking after her . . . fondly.'

'That's better. I'll pass on the message with pleasure.'

'There's something that you can add.'

'What is it?'

He grinned. 'Please tell Lydia that . . . I miss her.'

'I'm sure that she misses you just as much, Alan.'

'I hope so,' he said. 'Well, I must be off. I am on duty, after all, but I'll somehow find time to call on Estelle to tell her where Victor is. As for the inspector, I hope that this investigation will turn out to be a particularly difficult one.'

'Why do you say that?

'It means that he may feel it necessary to call on me once again.'

When he saw Colbeck coming into the refreshment room, Leeming chewed the last mouthful of food and swallowed it guiltily. Colbeck was amused.

'I knew that I'd find you eating something,' he said, sitting opposite him at the table.

'I did my best to hang on, sir, but I was starving.'

'I'm sorry to have kept you waiting. After a visit to the morgue, I took the ferry to the Isle of Wight. But more of that later.' He flicked a dismissive hand. 'First, please tell me how you got on.'

'It was interesting,' said Leeming. 'I not only learnt a lot about Mr Blanchard himself, I may have discovered why he was murdered.'

'Tell me more.'

Without reference to his notebook, Leeming described his visit to The Haven in Chichester, admitting that he felt out of place in such comparative luxury. He talked about the steward and about the club members to whom he had spoken, but he kept his revelation until the end.

'It was the smirk on Mr Collier's face,' he recalled. 'It told me that Blanchard was not what he pretended to be. He might have enjoyed the company of men, but he was attracted to women even more. An angry husband, sir – that's our killer.'

'It's a possibility we must bear in mind,' said Colbeck.

'It's more than that,' insisted Leeming.

'We'll see, Victor. Let me tell you what I've discovered. The first thing is that an old friend of ours is working on the ferry I took to the island.'

'Who is it?'

'Brendan Mulryne.'

'I thought he'd spend the rest of his life with that circus,' said Leeming with a chuckle. 'What brought him to Portsmouth?'

'You'll be able to ask him in person. We're going to be using the ferry quite a lot. Now, this is what I learnt . . .'

He described his meeting with Paul Blanchard and his surprise at the latter's apparent lack of emotion in the wake of his father's death. He also described the rival businessman named by Blanchard as a potential suspect.

'Have you made contact with him, sir?'

'Not yet, Victor. I'm not at all sure that we're after a hired assassin. If such a person did kill Mr Blanchard, he is more likely to be in the pay of an enraged husband. Since you discovered that Blanchard had an eye for compliant ladies, I want you to find out who they were.'

'That may be difficult, sir.'

'You need to talk to Mr Collier again, well away from the club. Point out that we're more likely to catch his friend's killer if we know more about Blanchard's private life.'

'What will you be doing, sir?'

'I'll be looking closely at the man named by the son – and at the son himself, of course. He's behaving strangely. I'd like to know why.'

'Does that mean we'll be staying here overnight?'

'We may be based here for longer than that, Victor. I spotted a pub that could be ideal for our purposes. It's little more than a five-minute walk away. You can book rooms for us at the Hope and Anchor while I have something to eat. What would you recommend?'

'The pies are delicious, sir. I had two of them.'

'Is that all?' teased Colbeck. 'You're slipping.' He

remembered something. 'Oh, by the way, Mulryne gave me an interesting piece of information. Her Majesty the Queen, is in residence at Osborne House on the island. We must make every effort to secure an arrest. We can't have an unsolved murder hanging over Her Majesty's summer home.'

Gwendoline Cardus listened with pleasure to the Beethoven piano sonata. Queen Victoria played it with great feeling. She and her husband, Prince Albert, had played a duet in D Major by the same composer when the latter was still alive. Crushed by his death almost five years earlier, the Queen did her best to carry on without him, but he was always at the forefront of her mind. By playing one of his favourite sonatas, she summoned up fond memories of their life together.

Gwendoline Cardus had been in royal service for many years. She was a full-bodied woman in her early forties with a face that had retained some of its youthful prettiness. Devoted and endlessly patient, Gwendoline regarded working for the Queen as both a joy and a privilege. She relished the way that Her Majesty always turned to her for approval. When the final notes were played, she clapped her hands gently. The Queen smiled.

'Was it really that good?' she asked.

'You played beautifully, Your Majesty.'

'I had to. Somewhere up in heaven, my dear husband was listening.'

* * *

Having been tired out that morning by his granddaughter, Caleb Andrews was glad to hand her over to Nanny Hopkins for the afternoon. The old man was able to relax indoors and to have his habitual nap. Andrews was short, slight, bearded and – as Madeleine knew only too well – possessed of a combative streak. When he awoke, he found his daughter seated beside him. A pot of tea and some teacups were on the little table in front of them.

'I knew that you'd wake up if I ordered tea,' she said.

'How long have I been asleep, Maddy?'

'As long as was necessary.' She poured two cups of tea and added milk and sugar. 'Helena Rose showed you no mercy today. I've tried to explain to her that older people have limited strength and need to be treated carefully. And she should never – ever – pull your beard.'

'I'm as right as rain,' he boasted, 'and she is the main reason. If I didn't have daily exercise with her, I'd start to dwindle. I've seen it happen to friends I worked with. As soon as they retire, they become lazy old men with pot bellies. It's the ones with grandchildren or dogs that still have some life in them. They're kept busy.' He reached for his tea. 'Any word from Robert?'

'Give him time, Father!'

'If he's gone to Portsmouth, he'll have travelled on the London, Brighton and South Coast Railway. That stirs up unhappy memories for me.'

'Why?'

'Don't tell me that you've forgotten, Maddy! I lost a good friend on that line. Frank Pike was driving the

Brighton Express for the first time. Some cruel devils arranged for it to crash into an oncoming ballast train. He stayed bravely on the footplate. His fireman jumped clear, but Frank was crushed to death.'

'I remember him. He used to be your fireman when he worked for the LNWR.'

'Robert will certainly remember the name.'

'I'm sure he will.'

'He led the investigation into the crash on the Brighton. Yes, and he arrested the people responsible for it. Travelling on that line again will awaken old ghosts for him.'

The Hope and Anchor was a large, characterful public house with ambitions to be regarded as a hotel. Since it provided them with adjoining rooms, Colbeck and Leeming were very satisfied with it. Leeming had warmed to the cheerful publican. The man had not turned a hair when he first saw the sergeant's face. Some of the customers, however, were startled.

Leeming and Colbeck met in the latter's room for a private conversation.

'What do we do next, sir?' asked Leeming.

'We take a closer look at Portsmouth itself. Since the killer – or killers – got off the train here, it's more than likely that they live in the town. I daresay that it's a place with lots of hiding places. Let's explore some of them.'

'That suits me.'

'We'll spend the afternoon here,' said Colbeck, 'but

I want you back at the Haven Club this evening. The members will be recovering from the shock of what happened. Find an opportunity to speak to Douglas Collier at length. Ask him why he introduced Mr Blanchard to the club – then probe him about the man's private life. And Victor . . .'

'Yes, sir?'

'Be gentle with him. Let him go at his own pace.'

'It will be very slow,' said Leeming. 'I'm going to be there for a very long time.'

'That's what I'm hoping because I want you on the last train to Portsmouth. As passengers get off it, they'll see that appeal the stationmaster has drafted. One or more of them might have travelled on the train last night,' said Colbeck. 'They may have seen something . . . unusual.'

'I'll draw everyone's attention to the appeal.'

'Good idea.'

'What will you be doing?'

'I'll be finding out a lot more about the Welshman whose name was given to me by Paul Blanchard. He knows the Isle of Wight far better than me because he's at the heart of the business community there. And he feels certain that one of his rivals is involved in the murder.'

'When is he going to start mourning the death of his father?'

'I'm not sure that he ever will. Right,' said Colbeck, rising to his feet. 'let's go and explore Portsmouth. It is, after all, the principal naval station in England. Also, it's a perfect fortress. In my opinion, it houses the man – and his accomplice – who killed Giles Blanchard. Let's see if we can pick up their scent.'

They arrived at the hotel early that evening. Because it was a special occasion, they had dressed accordingly. As they were conducted to the dining room, they collected admiring glances from everyone they passed. They relished the attention. No sooner had they settled down at their table than the wine waiter glided across to them.

'May I get you something to drink?' he asked, looking from one to the other.

'Only one thing will suffice,' the man told him.

'And what's that, sir?'

'Champagne!'

Madeleine Colbeck and Lydia Quayle were also enjoying a drink before dinner. Completely at ease with each other, they were in the drawing room of the house with a glass of sherry in their hands. As they reflected on how they first met, Lydia was full of gratitude.

'My life changed for the better when you came into it, Madeleine,' she said. 'You caught me at a very low ebb.'

'It was Robert who first brought us together. He was leading the investigation into your father's murder and felt that I might be helpful.'

'Helpful! You were much more than that. You were so kind and understanding. I could talk to you in a way that I couldn't do with anyone else. The truth was that I hated my father. It's the reason I left home. But his death made me reel. You were there to steady me. Thank you.'

'I'm the one who should be thanking you,' said Madeleine. 'You started out as a stranger and now you're my best friend. Well,' she added, 'your second-best friend, perhaps.'

'What do you mean?'

'There's someone who adores you even more than I do.'

Lydia smiled. 'Don't you dare start teasing me about Alan.'

'I'm simply telling you what I was told,' said Madeleine. 'When he delivered a message from Robert earlier today, he asked me to pass on his love to you.'

'That's very sweet of him.'

'He's hoping that he might be involved in this latest murder investigation.'

'Every time he's worked with the inspector, Alan has impressed him.'

'Robert is not the only person he's trying to impress. Alan likes to be part of a murder investigation because he wants to catch your eye.'

'I'm very flattered, Madeleine,' said her friend, 'but he is first and foremost a detective. He patterns himself on Robert. I respect that. Now let's put Alan aside, shall we?' she added, before taking a sip of wine. 'I came here for dinner, remember. And I want to hear your news.'

* * *

53

When he got to Chichester station, Victor Leeming took the precaution of slipping into the refreshment room for a bite to eat. He hoped for a welcome at the Haven Club, but he could not expect them to invite him to dine in their restaurant. Besides, the food at the refreshment room was warm and more than serviceable. Since there would be several members at the club, he expected to be the centre of attention but that was not the case. When he arrived there, the steward told him that Douglas Collier had been so upset by the sad news about his friend that he was staying at home that evening. Hoping that he could hear more about the investigation, however, the old man had left word that, if the sergeant returned, he would be happy to see him at his home.

Leeming had seized on the invitation. He needed time alone with the old man to probe his memory. After taking a cab to the address he was given, he found himself outside a large, striking Regency house in a tree-lined avenue. When he rang the bell, he was admitted by a servant. Leeming was soon sitting in a comfortable armchair with a glass of whisky in his hand.

'I prayed that you'd come back,' said Collier, seated opposite him. 'There are so many things I want to tell you about Giles.'

'I'm so glad to hear that, Mr Collier.'

'Some of it is private, mind. I don't want you jotting it down in that notebook of yours.'

'Trust me, sir. I can be discreet.'

'Good.'

Slumping forward, Collier promptly fell asleep. Leeming was not sure whether he should wake his companion or leave him until he recovered. In the event, it was only a short lapse. Collier suddenly opened his eyes, let out a cry of apology, and sat up straight.

'That won't happen again, Sergeant,' he promised.

'I can see you're under great strain, sir.'

'Giles and I were so close, you see. We had . . . similar interests.'

'Were you an estate agent as well, sir?'

'I was a very successful one,' said Collier with pride. 'That's why I ended up with such a lovely house as this. Giles loved it. He stayed here occasionally.'

'Oh!' Leeming's eyebrows lifted. 'I heard that he used to spend the night at the Haven Club.'

'It depended on what had brought him to Chichester.'

'What do you mean?'

'Never you mind,' said the old man with a quiet smile.

Robert Colbeck had been busy. Having sent Leeming off to Chichester, he took the ferry across to the island for the second time. Disappointingly, his old acquaintance, Brendan Mulryne, was no longer on duty. He stepped ashore in Ryde when the town was bathed in evening sunshine, and he began the lengthy walk along its pier. Colbeck then hired a cab to take him to Newport, some four miles away. In the interests of speed, he would have preferred to travel by rail, but no line had been built between Ryde and the island's capital. There was simply no demand for it. Colbeck recalled that the first railway built – between Newport and Cowes in 1862 – had a disappointing start. On the day when it came into operation, the train carried a mere half-a-dozen passengers. Such was the initial response of the islanders to a new mode of travel.

When he arrived at the headquarters of the Newport Borough Police, the most senior officer on duty was Inspector Ruggles, a bear of a man with a full beard. He guessed who his visitor was the moment that Colbeck entered the building.

'Good evening, Inspector,' said Ruggles. 'We were warned that you were coming to the island. As you probably know, we operate separately from the Hampshire Constabulary.'

'I've also had dealings with the Portsmouth City Police,' said Colbeck. 'When you add the railway police, you'll see that I have considerable support to call upon.'

Ruggles invited him into his office and indicated a chair. He was struck by Colbeck's poise and tailoring. For his part, the newcomer was grateful to be given such a warm welcome. As he sat down, he glanced around the office. It was small, cosy, and smelt of tobacco. The inspector's pipe rested in an ashtray. Ruggles sat behind his desk.

'Have you made any progress yet?' he asked.

'It's too early to say.'

'If there's anything that we can do, you only have to ask.'

'Thank you. I really wanted to find out more about the victim, Giles Blanchard.'

'The best person to talk to,' said Ruggles, 'is his son, Paul.'

'I've already done that. All that he did was to boast about his father's success as a businessman.'

'Blanchard made a small fortune. It's no wonder that he was so unpopular with his rivals. They used to writhe with envy when he had another triumph.'

'Did it go any further than envy?'

'I doubt it. Angry businessmen will curse and threaten in private, but they tend to behave themselves in public.'

'Did you ever meet Mr Blanchard?'

'Oh, yes – several times,' said Ruggles. 'I heard him speak at a couple of functions. To be fair to him, he could hold an audience. Other estate agents claimed that he resorted to sharp practice. All that that meant was that he was better at getting what he wanted. Berwyn Rees called him all sorts of vile names. Luckily, they were in Welsh, so I didn't understand them.' He let out a thunderous laugh. 'But the expression on Berwyn's face told that he loathed the man.'

'Do you know Mr Rees?' asked Colbeck.

'I should do. I play bowls with him sometimes. Berwyn is a lucky devil. He usually wins.'

'I saw his name above an estate agency in the high street when we drove past. Judging by the size of his premises, he's a successful businessman.'

'Well, he never talks business to me,' said Ruggles,

'any more than I talk about my work to him. We're all entitled to time off, Inspector. We can't be on duty indefinitely.'

'We have no choice sometimes.'

'How did you get on with the chief constable?'

'We only had a relatively short meeting with him,' said Colbeck, 'but he impressed me. Superintendent Forrest seems to be dedicated to his job.'

'You try talking to those poor devils who work under him.'

'Why? What do they have against him?'

'He behaves as if he's still in the army,' said Ruggles. 'Discipline is important, but Forrest takes it to extremes.'

For a fleeting moment, an image of Superintendent Tallis flashed in Colbeck's mind.

'Were you born on the Isle of Wight?' he asked.

'Yes, I was, and I've spent my whole life here. It's got everything I want. If there's anything you wish to know about this place, you've come to the right person.'

'I'm glad to hear it, Inspector,' said Colbeck. 'You must have seen Giles Blanchard start and develop his business over the years.'

'He did have one setback.'

'Oh?'

'You might not think it to look at him now, but he was a good cricketer in his day. I know that from personal experience.'

'What do you mean?'

'I was a useful bowler as a young man,' said Ruggles,

tapping his chest. 'I once played for the Newport XI against a team from Ryde. Blanchard was their best batsman. When he saw the captain handing me the ball, he grinned like a baboon, thinking he could hit me for miles.'

'And?'

Ruggles slapped his thigh in triumph. 'I bowled him out with my first ball. Blanchard was furious. He just couldn't believe that a skinny young constable like me could get him out. I'll never forget the way he glared at me as he walked off.' Ruggles grinned. 'When he was in company, he was very sociable. What I exposed in that cricket match was his true character.'

The visit to the home of Douglas Collier had been long but thoroughly worthwhile. Without realising it, Leeming had helped the old man to drink through most of the contents of an ornate whisky decanter. It was only when he left the house that the sergeant realised the effect that it had had on him. He lurched and tottered so much that he was lucky to stay on his feet. Collier had been kind enough to despatch a servant in search of a cab. Leeming had great difficulty clambering into it and scolded himself for drinking too much. When they reached Chichester station, the driver had to wake him up. Having paid him, Leeming staggered along with one hand on a wall.

Once on the platform, he dipped a hand into a fire bucket and rubbed cold water over his face. It helped to clear his mind slightly. On the train journey to Portsmouth, he was lucky enough to find an empty compartment, sparing fellow passengers the sight of a drunken man with an unsightly face. He forced himself to stay awake by stamping his feet and pinching himself whenever he was about to drift off. When the train finally reached its terminus, it took him minutes to get himself ready before venturing onto the platform. Other passengers streamed past him. Most of them ignored the board on which the appeal for witnesses had been pinned. They had places to go.

Then one man did stop to read it by the light of the nearby lamp. He spoke to the porter standing beside the appeal. Leeming arrived in time to overhear the passenger say that he had seen something odd as he left the train on the previous night. After taking a deep breath, Leeming stepped in front of the man and introduced himself.

'What exactly did you see, sir?' he asked, trying to sound sober.

CHAPTER SIX

Edward Tallis was always one of the first people to arrive at Scotland Yard in the morning. When he got to his office, he put his top hat aside and sat behind his desk. He then opened the copy of *The Times* he had bought and flicked through the pages in search of a mention of the murder of Giles Blanchard. He soon found it. A whole column was devoted to the crime, giving the basic details before announcing that Inspector Robert Colbeck had taken charge of the investigation. Tallis sniffed in disgust. Why was it that the press always praised the Railway Detective and ignored the superintendent who was responsible for assigning him to his cases? It was monstrously unfair.

He was still bristling with annoyance when there was a knock on his door.

'Come in!' he growled.

The door opened and Captain Forrest stepped into the room. Tallis was on his feet at once, shaking the newcomer's hand and apologising for the brusque command. He indicated a chair and Forrest sat down in it. Tallis resumed his own seat.

'Whatever are you doing here, John?' he asked. 'That's not to say you're not very welcome, but you were the last person I expected to come through my door.'

'Perhaps I should have warned you,' said Forrest. 'I stayed in London last night because I have an appointment this morning with the Home Secretary.'

'Really? Has Mr Walpole sent for you?'

'No, Edward. He acceded to my request for a meeting. That's more than his predecessor ever did. All I got from him was a polite refusal. As I told you, I am celebrating ten years as the Chief Constable of Hampshire and the problems I inherited a decade ago are still largely with us.'

'That's horribly true of us as well.'

'What I will tell the Home Secretary is what any chief constable would tell him. Keeping crime under control is an expensive undertaking. We are hopelessly underfunded. In essence, we need more detectives and even more constables. It can only happen if we offer them more pay.'

'I couldn't agree more, John. I wish you good luck

when you meet the Home Secretary.'

'Thank you.'

'I'm so glad that you're here,' said Tallis, glancing down at his newspaper, 'because I was just reading an article about that murder on the train to Portsmouth.'

'Thanks to you, the right man is in charge. I was very impressed with Inspector Colbeck.'

'Good.'

'But less so with Sergeant Leeming,' added Forrest. 'The man was slovenly.'

'He has his virtues, I assure you.'

'They are certainly not visible.'

'I've taxed him about his appearance many times.'

'Any soldier who failed to dress properly would be severely reprimanded.'

'Quite so,' sighed Tallis. 'Unfortunately, we are no longer in the army.'

'We should maintain the same levels of discipline, Edward.'

'Inspector Colbeck's success is not solely based on his abilities. Some of the credit must go to Sergeant Leeming. He's fearless, hard-working and has the true instincts of a detective. Yes, he has his shortcomings,' conceded Tallis, 'but I choose to overlook them.'

'Is that wise?'

'I don't have a more dedicated officer. The sergeant will never let you down.'

* * *

As he picked his way through his breakfast, Leeming kept wincing at the steady throb inside his head. Colbeck was sympathetic. On the previous night, he had stayed up to wait for the sergeant's return. As soon as he saw him stagger into the Hope and Anchor, he realised that Leeming was in no fit state to give a coherent account of his visit to Chichester. He therefore sent him off to bed and told him that his news could wait until morning. Leeming was certainly in a better condition when they met at breakfast next day, but he kept apologising for what had happened.

'It was all in a good cause, Victor,' said Colbeck. 'Because you and Mr Collier enjoyed some fine malt whisky, you got exactly what I hoped you would get – confirmation that Mr Blanchard was unfaithful to his wife.'

'It took me a long time to draw it out of Collier. His own wife had died years earlier. He not only took pleasure from his friend's behaviour, he was eager to help him.'

Colbeck was shocked. 'Mr Collier was a party to Blanchard's adultery?'

'He has a large house with two or three empty bedrooms. Blanchard had a key to let himself in after dark with . . . whichever woman he brought. Collier never met any of them. When he got up in the morning, his visitors had both left the house.'

'Did he tell you anything about these women?'

'Only that they were always younger than Blanchard. His friend must have had some sort of charm.' Leeming sighed. 'How can a married man behave like that?'

'There's one factor that may have been significant,' said Colbeck. 'Paul Blanchard told me that his parents slept in separate rooms.'

'That's no excuse, sir.'

'I agree.'

'I was disgusted. When I first met Douglas Collier, I was sorry for him. He's old, weary, uses a walking stick and is almost blind. Then I slowly dragged the truth out of him and realised that he was nothing but a—'

'You did well, Victor. You not only discovered something important about Blanchard, you might also have found a motive for his murder.'

'Yes – he was strangled by a jealous husband.'

'Not necessarily,' said Colbeck, pondering, 'but I fancy that a woman might have been involved somehow.' He watched as Leeming had a long drink of coffee. 'How do you feel now?'

'I'm slowly coming alive.'

'Let's move on to the passenger who responded to the appeal.'

Leeming groaned. 'I feel so ashamed about that,' he admitted. 'He was telling me something important, but I couldn't understand what he was saying. However, I did at least do something right. I made a note of his address. He lives in Portsmouth and will be at home today so I can call on him and apologise for the state I was in last night.'

'I'll come with you, Victor. What he has to say might be important.'

* * *

Wearing full mourning attire, Paul Blanchard knocked on the door of his mother's bedroom then opened it. He was pleased to see that she was propped up in bed in her dressing gown with pillows to support her. Catherine Blanchard gave him a tired smile of welcome. She was a short, thin, grey-haired woman in her late fifties but looked much older. Grief had robbed her of what little beauty she had possessed and replaced it with a pale, anxious, haggard face. Her eyes were pools of sadness.

'How do you feel?' asked Blanchard.

'I feel dreadful. How else can I feel?'

'At least you were able to have some breakfast today.'

'I hardly tasted it, Paul,' she said. 'I just keep thinking about what happened to your father. Have the police caught the man who . . .'

'Not yet,' he said, 'but they are working hard to do so. Inspector Colbeck of Scotland Yard has been brought in to lead the investigation. I met him yesterday. He's very experienced. We can both put our faith in him.'

'What faith?' she whispered. 'After what happened, I have none.'

'You heard what the doctor said. Rest is your priority. You must try to stop dwelling on what happened and console yourself with happy memories of the life you shared with Father. Would you like me to bring some photograph albums for you to look at?'

'No, no,' she cried. 'I couldn't bear to do that.'

'Calm down, Mother,' he said, putting a hand on her shoulder.

'Then don't make me look at old photographs. They will only remind me of what I've lost.'

Plucking a handkerchief from the sleeve of her dressing gown, she dabbed at the tears trickling down her face.

'Verity will be coming to sit with you very soon,' he told her.

'That will be nice.'

'We haven't told the children yet. They're far too young to understand. They loved their grandfather so much. They'll miss him. But they still have their grandmother to love,' he reminded her. 'That will be a consolation to them.'

She heaved a sigh. 'I don't feel very lovable, Paul.'

'You will do – in time.'

'Who could do such a thing?' she wailed. 'Your father was a wonderful man. He didn't deserve . . . what happened to him. It's so cruel.'

'His killer will be caught and punished, have no fear.'

'That won't bring my husband back.'

'No,' he said, softly. 'We'll all have to adjust to that.' He heard a knock on the front door. 'That will be Verity. I'll bring her straight up . . .'

The detectives took a cab to an address on the western side of Portsmouth. William Phelps, it transpired, was close to retirement as a lawyer. Now in his sixties, he was a short, stooping man who wore spectacles and had side whiskers. There was an endearing fussiness about him. When they arrived at his house, Colbeck performed introductions and saved Leeming the embarrassment of having to apologise by saying that the sergeant had been unwell on the previous evening. Phelps accepted the explanation without questioning it.

'Where had you been yesterday?' asked Colbeck.

'I'd been to see a client in Havant. In fact, I spent two long days with him. It's a complex case and requires a lot of preparation. On each occasion, my client pressed me to stay for dinner and, having enjoyed the remarkable skills of his cook before, I was glad to accept.'

'Then you caught the last train back to Portsmouth twice in a row?'

'Yes, Inspector.'

'May I ask if wine was consumed during the meals?'

'Not by me,' said Phelps, firmly. 'I am a teetotaller. Neither wine nor spirits touch my lips.'

'I wish I was like that,' murmured Leeming.

'On the first of the two nights,' said Colbeck, 'what did you see at Portsmouth station?'

'I didn't see anything at all there, Inspector. It was at Havant station. At the time,' he went on, 'I dismissed it as something unusual, that's all. I'd forgotten all about it until I saw that appeal on the platform here in Portsmouth.'

'You told me you'd seen something strange,' said Leeming. 'That much I do remember.'

'When the train stopped at Havant station,' resumed Phelps, 'I walked along the platform in the hope of finding an empty first-class compartment. As I did so, two people got out of their compartment, walked a dozen yards, then stepped into another. Why? It was strange behaviour.'

'Perhaps the compartment they were in was crowded,' said Colbeck.

'On the contrary, it had only one other person in it. I glanced at him as I passed. He was a middle-aged gentleman, and he was fast asleep. Not wishing to disturb him, I walked on until I found what I was after.'

'Had the couple found another compartment?'

'Yes, and it had two other passengers in it – a gentleman and a lady.'

'Could you describe the two people who stepped out of the train?'

'I only got the merest glimpse of the lady, Inspector, so I've no idea of her age. It just puzzled me that they'd sought company. Given what the man was, I felt certain that he'd wish to travel alone with his companion.' He smiled shyly. 'They do have a reputation, after all.'

'I don't follow, Mr Phelps.'

'Sailors. The man was an officer in the Royal Navy.'

Instead of working at her easel, Madeleine Colbeck was in the nursery, admiring a painting by her daughter and seeing a distinct sign of talent. Helena Rose was now a boisterous six-year-old, but she did have her quieter moments. Under the direction of Nanny Hopkins, the girl had first drawn a picture of her favourite animals – a dog, a cat, and a horse – then reached for her paint brushes. Madeleine showered her daughter with praise and thanked the nanny, a motherly woman in her fifties with the gift of extraordinary patience. When she heard someone being admitted into the house, Madeleine gave her daughter a congratulatory kiss then went downstairs.

She was delighted to see that Estelle Leeming had called. After ordering a pot of tea, Madeleine took her visitor into the drawing room, and they sat down.

'I know why you're here,' said Madeleine, 'and you've come at a perfect time.'

'I was wondering if you had any news?'

'A letter came from Portsmouth this morning, Estelle.'

'What did it say?'

'They had to stay there last night but they are hoping to come home in a day or two.'

'Will they have made an arrest so soon?'

'I'm afraid not,' said Madeleine. 'All that we get is the pleasure of having our husbands back home for a night, then off they go.'

Estelle was disappointed. 'I see.' She brightened. 'How is Helena Rose?'

'She's decided that she wants to be an artist like her mother. I don't think she realises that it takes years. I had the first five or six paintings rejected before I sold one. But enough about me,' she added. 'How are the boys?'

'Oh, there's good news at last. David has finally decided that he likes working on the railway, after all, and Albert is having second thoughts about being a policeman since he saw Victor's black eye and bruised face. Like his brother, he wants to be an engine driver one day.'

'That will please my father.'

'How is Mr Andrews?'

Madeleine grinned. 'Need you ask?'

'Our boys love him,' said Estelle. 'They still talk about the time when he took them to the engine sheds. It's the reason David works for the LNWR. I just wish that he didn't come home so dirty every day.'

'That's part of his apprenticeship. Even when he was a driver, Father came home in filthy clothes. I know that because I had to wash them.'

'Your life is very different now, Madeleine.'

'Yes, I'm the one who gets dirt all over me now.' They laughed. 'Come on up to the nursery to look at Helena Rose's latest painting. She's always pleased to see you.'

'I love to see her as well.'

'You may not recognise her,' warned Madeleine. 'Most of the paint has gone on her face and hands. She looks as if she has measles.'

Having her daughter-in-law seated beside the bed was a tonic for Catherine Blanchard. She revived slightly and stopped thinking obsessively about her husband. Verity Blanchard was a beautiful woman in her late twenties. She had recovered from the effort of bringing twins into the world four years earlier and had got her figure back. If anything, her mourning apparel showed it off to advantage. Her mother-in-law eyed her approvingly.

71

'I don't know how you keep so slim, Verity,' she said, wistfully.

'Looking after two lively boys is part of the answer. Then, of course, I try to go for a swim, especially in lovely weather like this.'

'Paul was a wonderful swimmer.'

'He hardly goes near the beach now.'

'How can he?' asked Catherine. 'He's like his father. He works all day.'

'I do manage to drag him away from the office now and then. Paul and I play tennis. As I keep telling him, why live in a house with a tennis court unless we use it?'

'When the boys grow up, I daresay they'll be out there every day.'

'Oh, I think Paul has other ideas for them. You know how much he loves cricket. The boys will have cricket bats in their hands before too long. Paul is dying to teach them.'

'Then he's like his father,' said Catherine. 'My husband would have played cricket all day long if he could have done so. He made me sit through so many matches. I could never get the hang of the game somehow. Whenever he looked towards me, I used to give him an encouraging smile. If he scored a run, I always clapped.' Her face darkened. 'Oh, I miss him so much, Verity. This house is empty without him. I still can't believe that he won't walk in through the front door again.'

'You must try to cope without him,' said Verity,

quietly. 'Everything will change when the man who killed him is caught and hanged. Paul is confident that Inspector Colbeck will track him down, however long it takes.'

Catherine was fearful. 'I'm dreading the funeral.'

'But you won't have to go to it, and neither will I.'

'That's not the point, Verity. When the day comes, I'll be acutely aware that the dear man with whom I shared my life is going to be buried in the ground. I'll be like Her Majesty, the Queen. I'll have to spend the rest of my life in mourning for a husband who meant everything to me.'

Queen Victoria, a short, plump lady in black, was seated at her desk. In front of her were over a dozen letters. The one she was now writing was addressed to the eldest of her nine children. When she had finished it, she sat back to read it through. Gwendoline Cardus stepped forward.

'I don't know anyone who writes as many letters as you, Your Majesty,' she said.

'It's both a pleasure and a duty, Gwendoline. Apart from anything else, it occupies my mind.'

She glanced at the newspaper in the other woman's hand. 'Is that a copy of *The Times*?'

'Yes, it is.'

'Let me see it,' said the Queen, holding out a hand.

'Before you read it, I'm afraid that I must pass on some sad news.'

'Oh?'

'Giles Blanchard has died.'

'Never! He's far too young and full of life. Whenever he came to Osborne House, he was bristling with vitality. My dear husband always remarked on it.'

'I'm afraid that Mr Blanchard did not die of natural causes. He was killed.'

'Killed?' The Queen's face blanched. 'Can this be true?'

'I can't give you the full details,' said Gwendoline, 'because I was too upset to read the article in full. I realised that we shall never see him again. I know how fond you and Prince Albert were of him. In the circumstances, it might be better if you don't read the full details of his murder.'

'Nothing will stop me from doing so.' She held out an imperious hand and Gwendoline put the newspaper into it. 'I want to know the truth. When I'm in possession of the facts, I'll write a letter of condolence to his wife and have it delivered immediately. To lose a treasured husband by natural means is painful enough, but to hear that your partner in life has been murdered . . . it must be almost unbearable. Don't you agree, Gwendoline?'

'Yes, I do,' said the other. 'My heart goes out to Mrs Blanchard and her family.'

When he boarded the steamer to take him to the Isle of Wight again, Colbeck was delighted to see that Brendan Mulryne was on duty. The Irishman was ushering passengers on board the vessel. It was only when the steamer set off from the pier that Colbeck was able to talk to his friend.

'I can see why you love this job, Brendan,' he said. 'You get to breathe clean air for a change. There's precious little of that in London.'

'The place stank to high heaven sometimes – and so did the circus.'

'You seemed very much at home there.'

'It was fine for a long while, but you know me. I'm a rolling stone. Anyway,' he went on, 'how is the investigation going? Have you made any headway?'

'It's difficult to say,' replied Colbeck. 'We did gather some useful information this morning, but it doesn't really take us any closer to the killer. I'm going to see Mr Blanchard's son again. He deserves to be kept up to date, and I have a lot of questions to ask him.'

'I wish you the best of luck. Hunting for a killer always used to light a flame inside me. I don't get that sort of excitement when working on a steamer.'

'Have you ever met Paul Blanchard?'

'Yes, I have – once or twice. He's just a younger version of his father. Although, in fairness, he didn't say anything spiteful about the Irish. He just ignored me.'

'He puzzled me, Brendan.'

'Why?'

'His father was killed in an appalling way, yet he didn't show any real sympathy.'

'He's a businessman. The only thing that matters to him is making a profit.'

'In a sense, he's done that,' said Colbeck. 'He stands to take over a thriving business. I thought he might spare a moment to shed a tear for his father.'

'People of that sort never cry,' said Mulryne. 'Anyway, I wish you well. Oh, and I've got a favour to ask you.'

'What is it?'

'Next time you come to the Isle of Wight, can you please bring Victor with you?'

'I certainly will, Brendan,' said Colbeck. 'He's far too busy this morning, I'm afraid. He is trying to identify a suspect.'

Victor Leeming found the Portsmouth dockyards overwhelming. To start with, there were so many people milling about. Timber-built vessels from an earlier era rubbed shoulders with steam-powered ships of the present day. Sailors of all ranks abounded. Leeming had long ago learnt that he was not suited to a naval life. On the few occasions when he'd sailed, he had felt distinctly unwell. He knew that Britain's wealth over the centuries had been created in large part by the skill and daring of its navy. That same navy had also acted in defence of the realm, fighting battles with a mixture of brilliant seamanship and sheer determination. Leeming was in a place of historic significance. He spent the first ten minutes standing there in a state of bewilderment.

Fortunately, there was help at hand. When he saw a uniform that he could identify, he remembered that the Metropolitan Police Force had taken over policing duties at the docks six years earlier. As a result, he was among the sort of men he saw every day of his life. He intercepted the young constable walking past.

'Excuse me,' he said. 'I need to speak to someone about naval personnel.'

'Then you'd best go to Admiralty House, sir.'

'I've been there. They sent me here. What's your name, by the way?'

'Constable Whittle of the—'

'You don't need to tell me that, lad,' said Leeming, interrupting him. 'I wore the same uniform as you do when I first joined the Metropolitan Police Force. I'm Detective Sergeant Leeming and I'm here with Detective Inspector Colbeck.'

Whittle was impressed. 'I've heard of the Railway Detective. He's famous.'

'We're investigating a murder that took place on a train to Portsmouth.'

He went on to explain why he was so keen to meet someone from the navy who could answer the questions he wished to put to him. Whittle was delighted to help.

'I know just the man,' he said. 'I'll not only tell you where to find him, I'll take you there.'

Robert Colbeck called at the house of the murder victim at a time when both Paul Blanchard and his wife were in the drawing room. When he was introduced to her, he found Verity much more affected by the family tragedy than her husband. She was softly spoken and sympathetic.

'I've been sitting with my mother-in-law,' she said, 'and trying to stop her from talking endlessly about what happened. It's only distressing her even more.'

'I'm sure that she appreciates your company,' said Colbeck.

'What news do you have for us, Inspector?' asked Blanchard. 'I can't believe that this is merely a social visit.'

'Far from it, sir. Since we last met, I took the trouble to find out more about Mr Rees. Inspector Ruggles of the Newport Borough Constabulary provided a lot of information about him. And I did notice Mr Rees's estate agency when we drove past. It's quite large.'

'Our premises are even larger,' said Blanchard, crisply. 'What did Ruggles say about him?'

'He had more respect for the man than you did, sir.'

'That's because he doesn't know him as well as I do.'

'Possibly.'

'Have you any idea who was responsible for . . . what happened?' asked Verity.

'We don't have a prime suspect, if that's what you mean . . . but we have two people of interest.'

Blanchard glowered. 'Apart from Rees, who is the other one?'

'We don't know until we identify him. As a result of a public appeal, a man has come forward. Two nights ago, he travelled on the same train as your father-in-law. He was able to tell us about something that struck him as highly unusual.'

'What was that?'

'I can't tell you until we are certain that it's relevant to the investigation. Sergeant Leeming is making enquiries even as we speak.'

Blanchard was testy. 'I do think we should be kept informed of any evidence you gather.'

'You will be, sir – at a time of our choosing.'

'It's our right, Inspector.'

'Paul,' said his wife, 'don't speak so harshly.'

'Keep out of this, my dear.'

'It's kind of the inspector to call on us like this.'

'Thank you, Mrs Blanchard,' said Colbeck. 'I just wished to assure you that we are working hard on this case – and we have plenty of resources to call upon. In my experience, an early arrest is unlikely, so you must not expect it. We may need to toil away for some time. Oh,' he said to Blanchard, 'I had a message for you from Inspector Ruggles.'

'What was it?'

'Your father was an excellent batsman, I believe.'

'He was the best on the island.'

'Inspector Ruggles wondered if you remembered the time when he bowled your father out first ball in a game of cricket?'

Instead of a reply, he was treated to Blanchard's look of utter disdain.

CHAPTER SEVEN

'What rank did this man hold?' asked Shorter.

'I've no idea,' admitted Leeming.

'What uniform did he wear?'

'I didn't see it myself.'

'How old would he have been?'

'Our witness was unsure of his age. He never saw the man's face.'

'What the hell did he see?' snapped Shorter.

'It was dark, Lieutenant. Light on the platform was patchy. But Mr Phelps was certain that the man was in the Royal Navy. Mr Phelps has spent most of his life in Portsmouth, so he knows a sailor when he sees one.'

Luke Shorter sat back in his chair with a look of exasperation. He and Leeming were in an office that was large, well furnished, and caught the sun at that time of day. A breeze blew in through an open window. They could hear the unremitting cries of seagulls. The distinctive tang of the sea drifted into their nostrils. Even when seated, Shorter was an imposing man with a barrel chest and broad shoulders. Having been willing to help a murder investigation, however, he had become increasingly irritated.

'Let me review the facts,' he said, 'few and unsubstantiated as they are.'

'I've told you all I know.'

'But it's second-hand information, Sergeant Leeming. It was provided by a man in his sixties who saw this naval officer from behind and did so in poor light. What am I supposed to do with these few shreds of facts?'

'I hoped that you might identify the officer, sir.'

'Without knowing his rank and without details of his appearance?'

'I thought that you might be able to assist us.'

'Given more information, I'd have been happy to do so.'

'Don't you keep a record of where your officers are at any given time?'

'When ships are in dock,' said Shorter, 'everyone is entitled to leave the vessel, especially if they have been at sea for a long time. Many of them have families here in Portsmouth. They're eager to enjoy some shore leave.

Perhaps that is all that this man you mention was doing?'

'Mr Phelps told us there was something very odd about him.'

'Passengers are entitled to change compartments if they wish.'

'But the one they left contained a dead body.'

'That's purely supposition.'

Leeming sighed. When he had walked into the office, he had been full of hope. It had now almost disappeared. Given such flimsy detail, Lieutenant Shorter was unable to help. Instead of getting the assistance he needed, therefore, Leeming would leave the dockyard empty-handed. He chided himself for having entertained such high hopes.

'I'm sorry that your search ended in disappointment,' said Shorter.

'So am I.'

'The one thing I can do, however, is to make enquiries. Officers take great care of their uniforms. They denote rank. Was the man on the train really in the Royal Navy? Or had he simply stolen a uniform to beguile a lady?'

'I never thought of that, Lieutenant.'

'He wouldn't be the first person to do that.'

'Would it be possible for you to . . . ?'

'Yes, of course it would,' said Shorter. 'I will find out if any officers here are victims of a thief. If, so be it, I learn that a uniform has gone astray, I will contact you at once.'

'Thank you, Lieutenant.'

'Where might I find you?'

'We are staying at the Hope and Anchor.'

'I wish you luck in your investigation. You may have had a setback here, but do not despair.' He bared his teeth in an approximation of a smile. 'Worse things happen at sea.'

They studied the house with interest, noting that only someone with a substantial amount of money would own it. The notebook stolen from Giles Blanchard had given them the address and some interesting details about a woman who lived there. They had discussed a variety of ways in which they might approach her but had not settled on any one of them. In the event, the decision was made for them. The front door opened, and an elderly man was wheeled out in a bath chair by a servant. Moments later, a tall, almost stately woman in her thirties came out and dismissed the servant with a nod. She then pushed the bath chair down the drive.

The couple who had the house under surveillance exchanged a glance. Was the woman pushing her father or her husband? The age gap was significant. When the bath chair got close, they could see that the man appeared to be asleep, and that the woman had a subdued beauty. They watched the bath chair go past, then, having waited a couple of minutes, they followed it. In less than half a mile, they saw their quarry turning into a park and heading for a bench. Before she sat down, the woman bent over the man to adjust his hat to keep the sun off his face. She did so with such tenderness that their relationship became clear.

She was the man's wife.

Colbeck was interested to see how Paul Blanchard's manner had changed in the presence of his wife. The latter was more subdued and less defensive. When Verity eventually went back upstairs to sit with her mother-in-law, Colbeck changed the conversation.

'May I ask how long you have felt the need to carry a weapon?'

'One has to take precautions, Inspector,' said Paul.

'Against whom?'

'The criminal fraternity. Don't be fooled by what you have seen on the island. It may be idyllic for the families who come here in the warm weather to enjoy our beaches, but we have our share of crime. Inspector Ruggles could have told you that. People have been accosted and robbed. Some have been attacked and wounded. I don't need to tell you that prosperity can often make one a target,' said Paul. 'I've had to draw my gun on three or four occasions.'

'Would you have been prepared to pull the trigger?'

'I most certainly would. I'd be acting in self-defence. However, in the cases I mentioned, there was no need. The moment I produced the gun, the men who accosted me fled.'

'Did your father carry a weapon?'

'He felt that there was no need to do so.'

'Yet you believe that he was attacked on two occasions.'

'It didn't stop him from travelling alone,' said Paul. 'When a pickpocket made the mistake of trying to steal his wallet, my father knocked him out and summoned a railway policeman. He was fearless, Inspector. It cost him his life.'

'That remains to be seen, sir,' said Colbeck. 'May I ask if you have ever been to the Haven Club in Chichester?'

Blanchard shook his head. 'I haven't, as a matter of fact.'

'Didn't your father advise you to join?'

'No, he didn't.'

'Why did he spend so much time there?'

'It was another base from which to operate,' explained the other. 'We have an estate agency in Chichester. Father liked to check on it at regular intervals. Also, of course, the Haven Club was a source of potential customers. He had a rare gift of winning people over. In one year, I recall, he helped to sell two or three houses to fellow members.'

'I'm told that he sometimes stayed the night at the club.'

'That's true, Inspector.'

'Did you ever meet a man named Douglas Collier?'

Blanchard stiffened. 'Why do you keep asking me about the Haven Club?' he demanded. 'My father was killed by a stranger on a train, not among his friends in Chichester. Really, Inspector, I find some of your questions quite unnecessary. Instead of badgering me, shouldn't you be searching for the ruthless killer who strangled my father?'

They watched and waited until they were certain that the man in the bath chair was fast asleep. His wife clearly believed that he was. Sitting down on the bench, she took out a book and began to read it. The man nudged his companion. It was time to move in. As she approached the bench, the woman took the trouble of looking into the bath chair. The old man was snoring gently. She therefore sat on the bench beside the woman.

'It's Mrs Lenham, isn't it?' she asked, politely.

'That's right,' said the other, looking up from her book.

'Mrs Agnes Lenham?'

'Why do you wish to know?'

'I have some bad news for you, I'm afraid. Have you read a newspaper this morning?'

'Yes, I have, as a matter of fact. I read extracts from *The Times* to my husband.'

'Then you'll have learnt that Giles Blanchard has been murdered.'

The woman gasped. She checked to see that her husband was still asleep.

'Who are you?' she hissed.

'I'm someone who knows that you and Mr Blanchard were close,' said the other. 'Very close, in fact. That's the bad news I mentioned. You need to buy my silence, Mrs

Lenham, because I'm sure that you would not like your husband to be aware of what you did.'

'It would kill him!'

'Then let's make sure that he never learns the truth, shall we?'

Agnes Lenham shuddered.

Edward Tallis was delighted to see Captain Forrest for the second time that day. Having been to see the Home Secretary, the latter had honoured his promise to call in on his friend again. After giving him a welcoming handshake, Tallis motioned his visitor to a chair. He could see from the grim expression on the man's face that he was not the bearer of good news.

'What happened?' asked Tallis.

'My visit was a waste of time. Walpole kept me waiting for the best part of an hour then invited me into his office. I pointed out that we were desperately in need of more money, and he said that I had to manage somehow.'

'Did he offer no hope of support?'

'He pretended to sympathise and said that he would "look into it". After thanking me for coming, he ushered me out. I was in there for less than five minutes. Frankly, I felt insulted.'

'With good reason.'

'I was entitled to a proper hearing.'

'It's a pity that you were not able to go over his head. Had Viscount Palmerston still been in office as prime minister, you might have fared better.'

Forrester blinked. 'I don't understand.'

'I was thinking of a murder investigation we had in Cambridge. Inspector Colbeck got valuable information from the prime minister himself. Somehow, he contrived a meeting with him.'

'I have no means of doing that with the Earl of Derby, our present incumbent.'

'Quite so.'

'I feel that I was snubbed, Edward.'

'If I remember aright,' said Tallis, pondering, 'there is another Spencer Walpole in government – the Home Secretary's son. He used to have a position in the War Office.'

'What use is that? He has no control over the way that the country is policed.'

'Perhaps not – but at least you'll be talking to someone who respects a former soldier.'

When they met up for supper at the Hope and Anchor to compare notes, Colbeck was in good humour. Leeming, by contrast, was dejected.

'I felt such a fool,' he admitted. 'I went in there with very little evidence.'

'It was an avenue that had to be explored, Victor.'

'The lieutenant pointed out that, just because the naval officer and the lady left that compartment, it did not mean they had killed its other occupant. Had they done so, he argued, they would surely have fled Havant station immediately and disappeared into the night. Mr Phelps led us astray,' complained Leeming. 'All he saw was a man whose uniform he could not identify, conduct a female passenger from one compartment to another.'

'The one they left contained the corpse of Giles Blanchard.'

'They might not have known it, sir. Look what the porter who discovered him told you. The passenger looked as if he was dozing.'

'That's true.'

'The naval officer and his lady probably had nothing to do with the murder.'

'It was a possibility we had to consider.'

'Well, I didn't enjoy considering it. Lieutenant Shorter made me feel like the village idiot.'

Colbeck smiled. 'Village idiots don't solve complex murder cases,' he said. 'You, on the other hand, do and you have an impressive record of success to prove it.'

'Let's forget about me and turn to you, sir.'

'I suggest that we eat some of this food first,' said Colbeck. 'I'm hungry.'

'So am I.'

They savoured a first mouthful before Colbeck gave the sergeant a summary of what he had learnt on his visit to the home of the deceased. Leeming was astounded.

'The son has never been to the Haven Club?' he said.

'My guess is that his father discouraged him from doing so. Blanchard didn't want his son to know what he got up to in Chichester.'

'But they own a business there.'

'Paul works exclusively on the Isle of Wight. Now we know why.'

'Has he never suspected that his father . . . well, had another life?'

'Apparently not.'

'Does that mean we have to conceal it from him?'

'It may be impossible to do so, Victor,' said Colbeck. 'There's no reason for either of us to enlighten him, but the truth about his father may come out another way. It's more than possible that the women with whom he was involved sent billets-doux to him. Giles Blanchard sounds like the sort of man who would treasure such messages. They were proof of his conquests. When his son finds them, he is going to have a terrible shock.'

Leeming forked a sausage into his mouth and chewed it thoughtfully. When the food had disappeared down his throat, he drank his beer before seeking guidance.

'What do we do next?'

'We take the steamer to the island and introduce ourselves to Mr Berwyn Rees. According to Paul Blanchard, the man might well have hired an assassin to kill his father.'

'Was it an assassin in naval uniform with a beautiful lady on his arm?' joked Leeming.

'Anything is possible, Victor.'

After their success earlier that morning, they dispensed with luncheon and celebrated for a couple of hours in bed. Sheer fatigue brought their pleasure to a halt. When she had got her breath back, she remembered her encounter with Agnes Lenham.

'The poor woman,' she said. 'She had two enormous shocks today. Mrs Lenham learnt that her lover had been murdered on a train, then she was forced to come to a financial arrangement with us. She must be reeling.'

'I don't have any sympathy for her,' he said, coldly. 'She betrayed a husband who seems to be barely alive, and she deserves to pay for it.'

'Once a month.'

'She can afford it,' he said. 'She married a very rich man.'

'What if she refuses to pay up?'

'It would never occur to her.'

'How can you be so sure?'

'You've seen that wonderful house she lives in,' he said. 'She's a woman with a position in society. If the truth about her private life came out, she would lose her husband, her status as a respectable wife, and her women friends. In effect, Mrs Lenham would be exiled.'

'That's true.'

'Because of a promise to keep silent, we have earned ourselves a steady income. It means that we can stop using a train as a source of money. In any case, it would be far too dangerous to continue doing so.'

'Why?'

'Our other escapades involved deceiving lustful men. Those crimes went unreported. The latest one will be featured in the newspapers. The one I glanced at this morning announced that Inspector Colbeck has been hired to solve the murder.'

'I've never heard of him.'

'Well, I have. He's had amazing success in catching killers. If he is here, we must go to ground and make no train journeys. The man is uncanny,' he went on. 'He even saved Her Majesty, the Queen on one occasion. But for him, she and other members of the royal family would have died in a train crash. Inspector Colbeck found and arrested those who devised the plan.'

She was back at her desk again, reading the last of a series of letters before writing a reply. When she had finished, she rang a small bell to bring Gwendoline Cardus over to her. Queen Victoria handed her the pile of letters.

'See that these get posted, please,' she said.

'Yes, Your Majesty.'

'I do enjoy dealing with correspondence.'

'It seems to invigorate you,' observed Gwendoline.

'I don't always feel invigorated, I can assure you.' She sat back in her chair. 'I keep thinking of the dreadful news about Giles Blanchard. His wife will have received my letter of condolence by now, but she may not be able to read it yet. Grief makes one feel so confused. The sense of irreparable loss blocks out everything else. Poor Mrs Blanchard!' she sighed. 'The woman is not in the best of health. Well, you've met her when she's attended functions here.'

'Yes, I have, Your Majesty.'

'My greatest fear is that the murder of her husband will take years off her life. Don't you agree, Gwendoline?'

'I do,' said the other, sadly. 'I most certainly do.'

Even though it was only a short crossing, Victor Leeming was not looking forward to a journey on the steamer. He always preferred to have dry land under his feet. When he went aboard the vessel, however, his anxieties vanished at once. The reassuring sight of Brendan Mulryne made him forget his fear of sailing. It was a joy to meet his old friend. He and the Irishman shook hands for the best part of a minute.

'It's wonderful to see you again, Victor,' said Mulryne.

'You don't look a day older, Brendan.'

'Well, I certainly feel it. What's taking you both to the island?'

'We're hoping to meet a gentleman named Berwyn Rees,' replied Colbeck. 'Do you happen to know him?'

'Everyone knows Berwyn Rees. Unlike Mr Blanchard, he's always in such a good mood. I love the lilt of his Welsh accent and he likes my Irish brogue, so he does. Wait a moment,' he added as a thought prompted him. 'You surely can't believe that Mr Rees had anything to do with . . . what happened to Blanchard.'

'No, of course not,' said Colbeck. 'We just thought it would be useful to meet him, that's all. He clearly has a presence on the island and would have known Mr Blanchard well.'

'The two of them hated each other.'

'We hope to find out why,' said Leeming. 'Oh,' he added, clasping Mulryne's hand again, 'it's such a joy to see you, Brendan. I hope that this job of yours doesn't take up all your time.'

Mulryne laughed. 'I could do it with my eyes closed.'

'We'd prefer it if you kept them open.'

'Yes,' said Colbeck, 'it may just be that we need to call on you at some point – if you have no objection, that is.'

'None at all.' Mulryne beat his chest. 'I thrive on action.'

'Then we'll have to see if we can provide you with some.'

'That's a promise,' Leeming put in. 'You'll be back on duty, Constable Mulryne.'

Mulryne frowned. 'What if Superintendent Tallis finds out?'

'That couldn't possibly happen.'

'Besides,' said Colbeck, 'he might not even remember you. It was many years ago when he had you thrown out of the Metropolitan Police Force.'

Mulryne winced. 'It seems like yesterday.'

'Anyway,' said Leeming, 'all you'd be doing was to offer us support during a murder investigation. It shows how public-spirited you are.'

'When you were in uniform,' Colbeck reminded him, 'you loved the work.'

'That's right, Brendan. I'm sure that you'd like another taste of it.'

'As long as I don't bump into the superintendent again,' said Mulryne.

'He's stuck in London,' promised Leeming.

'There's absolutely no chance at all of his turning up here,' affirmed Colbeck.

Edward Tallis cursed the train for being late. It had made the journey from London both longer and more tiresome. Never acquainted with the concept of patience, he was simmering with anger all the way. When he stepped out onto the platform at Portsmouth station, the first thing that caught his eye was the board with the public appeal on it.

'Well done, Colbeck!' he said to himself. 'You've got one thing right. Let's see if you've shown initiative elsewhere. I want results!'

Tea was served in the conservatory. Seated opposite each other, Agnes and her husband picked away at the biscuits. Crispin Lenham was a thin, wasted shadow of the man he had once been. Now in his seventies, he had great difficulty in staying awake for any length of time. There was no hint of the brilliant mind, the restless energy and sense of purpose that had first impressed Agnes. She was married to an empty shell now. Out of it came a hoarse whisper.

'What is wrong, my dear?' he asked.

'Nothing,' said Agnes.

'You haven't said a word for several minutes.'

'I thought that you were still asleep.'

'I rarely nod off during a meal,' he pointed out. 'Do you have something on your mind?'

'Yes, I do, Crispin.'

'Then tell me what it is.'

'It's the care of my dear husband,' she said, manufacturing a smile. 'I embrace the task with pleasure. Whatever happens, I will always be at your side.'

'Bless you, Agnes. I don't deserve such sacrifice.'

After blowing her a kiss, he stifled a yawn then fell gently asleep. All that she could do was to stare at him with an amalgam of love, shame, and sheer desperation.

CHAPTER EIGHT

'I still think that Robert should have made the effort to come home tonight,' said Caleb Andrews wagging a finger. 'You and Helena Rose will start to forget what he looks like.'

Madeleine laughed. 'You say the most ridiculous things sometimes, Father.'

'It's not funny, Maddy. I'm serious. A man should keep his word. You told me that Robert promised he'd be home tonight.'

'All that he promised was that he would try. The letter that came today warned me not to expect him. He and Victor have far too much to do.'

'Then he should send for young Hinton.'

'Robert will do what he feels is best.'

'That should include an occasional visit to his family.'

'Stop exaggerating!' said Madeleine.

They were in the drawing room. Through the window, they could see Helena Rose playing with Nanny Hopkins, throwing a ball to each other. Whenever Nanny Hopkins dropped it, the girl would shake with laughter. Andrews beamed.

'Look at her,' he said, fondly. 'She's an angel.'

'No, she isn't, Father. Angels behave themselves and Helena Rose is very naughty. When she tosses the ball, she makes sure that it's out of Nanny Hopkins's reach.'

'Robert should be here to enjoy seeing his daughter at play.'

Madeleine was sad. 'I don't remember that you took time off from work to watch me playing in the park.'

He was affronted. 'I had a job to do, Maddy.'

'So does Robert.'

'Yes, but he has more control of his time,' argued Andrews. 'I didn't. When you're stuck on the footplate of a steam engine all day long, you have no freedom of movement. I regret that. I've told you a hundred times how painful it was to miss watching you grow up.'

'I know,' she said, kissing him on the cheek.

He fell silent for a while as old memories began to surface. Then he turned to her.

'We went to the Isle of Wight once.'

'I don't remember that.'

'It was before you were born, Maddy,' he told her. 'Your mother had always wanted to go so I saved up the money and we had a whole day there. She loved it and said that she'd be happy to live there. But we could never afford that. I was only a fireman. Money was scarce. We had to be very careful.'

'Couldn't you have worked there?'

'How?' he asked. 'There were no trains on the Isle of Wight in those days. And they still don't have a proper railway network there. It's something Robert will have found out. The Isle of Wight is still stuck in the past.'

They found Berwyn Rees at his estate agency in Newport. He was a striking individual of middle years with a shock of red hair above a mobile face. The moment they entered the premises, Rees rose from his seat to give them a welcome, pumping their respective hands in turn. His low, melodious voice seemed to ooze out of his mouth. Colbeck noticed that, though the man had a broad smile, his eyes were darting from one to the other as he weighed his visitors up.

'I had a feeling that you'd pay me a visit, Inspector,' he said. 'You are both welcome on the island.' He indicated seats and they sat down. 'This is a distressing business,' he went on, resuming his own chair. 'Giles will be a great loss to the business community here.'

'It's his family who bear the greatest loss, sir,' Colbeck pointed out.

'You don't need to tell me that. As soon as I heard the news, I sent my condolences to them and offered to help in any way I could.' He shrugged his shoulders. 'Unhappily, my offer will be ignored. Paul Blanchard will dismiss it with contempt.'

'You and his father were sworn enemies, I hear.'

'There was nothing personal about it, Inspector. We were in competition, that's all.'

'I'm led to believe that there might be more to it than that, sir.'

Rees laughed. 'Don't listen to Paul,' he warned. 'He doesn't like the Welsh. His father was the same. Giles seemed to consider us an inferior species. Yet look at the difference I've made on this island. I've not only started a male voice choir here and paid for a children's playground to be built in Newport, I founded a summer festival that attracts a huge audience every year.'

'That's very commendable, Mr Rees.'

'Giles claimed I only did such things to attract attention, but that's not true. I have a big heart, Inspector. I like others to share in my good fortune.'

'You sound like a true Christian, sir,' said Leeming.

'Yes,' added Colbeck. 'May I ask which church you attend?'

'No, you may not,' said Rees, chortling. 'Few Welshmen here go to church on a Sunday. They flock

100

to a Baptist chapel like me. It supplies all my spiritual needs.'

'Where did Mr Blanchard go?'

'Where else, Sergeant? He went to St Thomas's Church in the centre of Newport. It was rebuilt ten years or so ago. But I don't think that Giles had a religious bone in his body. He only went there to be seen whereas I go to chapel out of a deep conviction.'

'Have you any idea who might have wanted to kill Mr Blanchard?' asked Colbeck.

'Well, it certainly wasn't me, Inspector,' replied Rees, cheerfully. 'Though I daresay that Paul probably accused me of being involved in the murder somehow. I'd be surprised if he didn't.'

They continued to ply him with questions, but the Welshman was far too adroit to give anything away. At the probable time of the murder, Rees pointed out, he had been asleep in bed with his wife. As for the suggestion that he might have hired an assassin, he burst out laughing.

'What did I stand to gain?' he asked. 'All I'd be doing was to replace one Blanchard with another. Giles may have gone, but his son would replace him, and Paul is even more determined to suppress his rivals than his father. Also,' he added, 'Paul carries a loaded weapon.'

'How do you know that?' asked Colbeck.

'I make it my business to gather information about my rivals.'

'You're a member of the Haven Club, I understand.'

'Yes, I do put in an appearance there occasionally,'

said Rees. 'Unlike Giles, I never stay the night there. I prefer a bed with my wife in it.'

'I daresay that you met Mr Douglas Collier at the club,' said Leeming.

'Impossible not to, Sergeant. Doug haunts the place like a resident ghost. Because he was a close friend of Giles's, I never had much to do with him. Yes,' he went on, 'it was Doug Collier who got Giles elected to the various committees. For some reason, Doug worshipped him.'

'Do you have any idea what that reason was?' asked Colbeck.

'No, I don't,' said Rees. 'Giles was at the heart of the club, you see. It meant a lot to him. For me, it was just a nice place to spend a few hours now and then. I was an occasional member, but he spent far more time in Chichester.' He beamed at them. 'Is there anything else I can tell you?'

'Not at the moment,' said Colbeck, rising from his seat. 'Thank you for your time, Mr Rees. We may need to speak to you again.'

'There's a question you forgot to ask, Inspector.'

Colbeck raised an eyebrow. 'Is there?'

'Yes,' said Rees. 'Will I be going to the funeral?'

'Will you?'

'Most certainly. Believe it or not, I liked Giles Blanchard – to some degree, that is. I will certainly be there to pay my respects. It's the decent thing to do.'

* * *

Agnes Lenham felt so desperate that she was unable to eat more than a few items on the plate. She wished desperately to be alone but, in front of her husband, she had to appear as if everything was quite normal. He thanked her for helping to feed him with her customary care, then let her push him to the drawing room where he always had his afternoon nap. Once off duty, Agnes was able to withdraw to her bedroom to consider her situation. It was frightening. She was the victim of blackmail at the hands of a cruel woman. A stranger had somehow learnt her secret. Her friendship with Giles Blanchard had brought her a love and happiness she had never tasted before, and she had savoured every moment they spent together. They were special to each other. That, at least, was how it had seemed at the time.

Now that someone knew about her clandestine lover, the whole thing appeared in a very different light. She had, she now confessed, betrayed her husband at a time when he needed her most. The doctor had warned her that he might have only a few years to live, and she promised to make them as fulfilling as she could. He relied on her for almost everything. What he loved most was his morning visit to the park – even though he usually slept through it. Today there had been a terrifying break in her routine. Instead of sitting quietly on a bench and reading a novel, she was approached by a woman who knew about her adultery and who threatened to reveal it. There was no escape. Reporting the woman to the police was out of the question. If the truth came out, Agnes would be reviled by her family and her friends. The shock would certainly kill her husband.

She was at the mercy of a woman with no name. Agnes was being forced to pay a sizeable amount of money to her once a month. The first payment had to be handed over on the following day. Because her husband had trusted her completely, he had given her the key to the safe and told her to take out as much money as she wished whenever she needed it. Taking the key from the drawer of her dressing table, she went furtively off to the safe in what had been her husband's study. After locking the door so that nobody saw what she was doing, she used the key to open the safe and reached out a wad of banknotes. After peeling off the amount demanded, she put the rest of the money back into the safe and locked the door. Her heart was pounding.

Agnes was now both an adulteress and a thief.

'What did you think of him?' asked Colbeck as they headed for the pier in their cab.

'I rather liked him,' admitted Leeming. 'Berwyn Rees has worked hard to build up his business yet found time to do things for other people. Since I can't sing, I wouldn't have joined his male voice choir, but I like the sound of his summer festival.'

'I thought he was rather too fond of himself.'

'Maybe he was just delighted that his main rival was dead.'

'That will certainly be to his advantage,' said Colbeck,

'but I don't believe that he was in any way linked to the murder. If he had been, he'd have been less open with us.'

'He'll only go to the funeral so that he can gloat.'

'You're being unfair, Victor. One thing I can guarantee.'

'What is it?'

'Mr Rees will sing the hymns beautifully. He might even feel a pang at the loss of Mr Blanchard. After all, they'd been involved in a tussle for many years.'

'Blanchard has not really gone,' Leeming reminded him. 'He's still there in the shape of his son. In fact, Rees fears Paul more than his father.'

'I wonder why.'

'Paul may be even more ruthless.'

'I'm not sure if that's possible.'

'Businessmen are always at each other's throats. It's a case of dog eat dog. I'd hate to work in their world.'

'Chasing criminals is far more dangerous, Victor.'

'Yes,' said Leeming with a grin, 'but there's nothing like the thrill of catching them, is there? That's why we do it.'

Edward Tallis had been doing his own detective work. Knowing where his detectives were staying, he booked a room at the Hope and Anchor, and asked the landlord where Colbeck and Leeming might have gone. The man scratched his head.

'I overheard them talking about a visit to the island,' he said.

'What are they doing there, I wonder?'

'Well, they're not going to build sandcastles on a beach, sir. I can tell you that.'

Tallis gave him a stern look then stalked off. When he reached the pier, he was in luck. A steamer was minutes away from docking. He accepted that it might not have his detectives aboard, but he felt certain that they would return to the mainland in due course. Meanwhile, he had to keep one hand on his top hat so that the stiff breeze did not blow it off. As the steamer came in to dock, he saw a burly man throw a rope to someone on the pier. Once the vessel had been secured, passengers were allowed to leave. They came out in droves.

When he spotted them, Tallis was delighted. He moved across to intercept his detectives. Leeming was startled by the sight of him, but Colbeck reacted as if he had been expecting a visit from the superintendent.

'It's good to see you again, sir,' he said, warmly.

'Yes,' mumbled Leeming.

'I had a visit from Captain Forrest early this morning,' said Tallis, 'and I was embarrassed by the fact that I had so little to tell him about the investigation.'

'I should have thought that someone as experienced as the Chief Constable of Hampshire would know that a case like this will take time,' said Colbeck. 'Time and endless patience.'

'That's why we're staying a second night, sir,' explained Leeming.

'I will be staying with you,' warned Tallis.

'Oh!'

'That will give us an opportunity to bring you up to date, sir,' said Colbeck, smoothly. 'Let's walk back to the Hope and Anchor.'

'Before we do that,' said Tallis, gazing at the steamer. 'When you arrived, a man threw a rope from the vessel. I could have sworn that it was Brendan Mulryne.'

'You must be mistaken, sir.'

'I've got good eyesight, Inspector.'

'There was a vague similarity, I suppose, but it could not have been Mulryne.'

'No,' said Leeming, 'he still works for that Italian circus.'

'That's the best place for him,' growled Tallis. 'He should be kept in a cage with the other wild animals. Mulryne was uncontrollable.'

'Forget about him, sir,' suggested Colbeck. 'We have lots to tell you. First, however, I'd like to know what Captain Forrest was doing in London.'

'He had an appointment with the Home Secretary.'

'May we know why?'

'It's none of your business,' said Tallis. 'Why were you on the Isle of Wight?'

'We were gathering intelligence, sir.'

'Was it a successful visit?'

'We believe so,' said Colbeck. 'You will hear all about it at the Hope and Anchor.'

'Over a drink,' added Leeming. 'I need it.'

* * *

They were relaxing together in their drawing room. The man was using a pencil to write something on a sheet of paper. His companion was troubled.

'Do you think that we asked too much?' she said.

'No, I don't.'

'Where will she get it at such short notice?'

'Men like her husband tend to keep ready cash at home – locked up in a safe.'

'What if Mrs Lenham loses her nerve?'

'That won't happen, believe me. She'll do exactly what you told her. Otherwise, her whole world will come tumbling down around her. Mrs Lenham will do anything to prevent that.'

'How could a woman of that quality get involved with someone like Blanchard?'

'He had a lot more to offer her than that skeleton of a husband.'

'I found Blanchard revolting,' she said, pulling a face. 'If you hadn't been there, he'd have taken me by force.'

'Nobody will ever do that, my love,' he assured her, 'because I'm always within reach. It wasn't the first time I've had to save you from an overzealous gentleman. But it may well be the last.'

'What do you mean?'

He indicated the sheet of paper. 'I've just been totting up the figures. Apart from the money we found in Blanchard's wallet, we now have a regular income of two hundred pounds a month. If Mrs Lenham tries to wriggle out of paying it, you must tell her that we'll increase the amount. That will bring her to heel.' She pursed her lips. 'What's the matter now?'

'I feel almost sorry for her.'

'Well, don't,' he insisted. 'My guess is that she married a much older man in the hope that he'd soon die and leave her to inherit everything he owned. Agnes Lenham may look sweet and respectable but, in essence, she's cold and manipulative.'

'If you say so.'

'I do. That woman will rescue you from having to attract lecherous men on late trains. We'll have a steady supply of money from her – and Mrs Lenham is only the first of our victims. Once we've pocketed two hundred pounds tomorrow, we'll go in search of our next benefactor. Blackmail is a lot more profitable than anything else we did.' He spread his arms wide. 'Enjoy it.'

When she was certain that her mother-in-law was asleep, Verity Blanchard got up from the chair beside the bed and crept out of the room. After breathing a sigh of relief, she went downstairs. Her husband was in what had been his father's study, a rectangular, book-lined room with a desk, chair and two high-backed leather armchairs. On a small table between the armchairs was a copy of a brochure advertising houses for sale.

When she entered, Paul was kneeling behind the desk. He looked up at her.

'How is Mother?' he asked.

'She fell asleep.'

'Thank you so much for sitting with her, Verity.'

'It's no effort. I just wish that I could offer her some comfort.'

He rose to his feet. 'I've been trying to open some of these drawers,' he complained, 'and they won't budge. Where on earth did Father keep the keys? I need access to every scrap of paperwork – contracts, correspondence and, most important of all, his will.'

'The keys must be in the house somewhere.'

'I'm afraid not, Verity. I've searched high and low. Father was very secretive. I fancy that he kept the keys with him.'

'Where are they now?'

'His killer must have stolen them. He stole everything else as well. When I went to identify his body at the morgue, they told me that his pockets were empty when he was found.'

Verity was shaken. 'Does that mean the house key will have gone astray as well?'

'Almost certainly.'

'Then someone could let himself in here at will.'

'I thought of that, Verity,' he said. 'It's the reason I arranged for a locksmith to call in tomorrow. I want the locks changed on the front and back doors of the house. Please don't tell Mother. She has enough to worry about.'

She bit her lip. 'Is it going to get any better, Paul?

'Better?' he repeated.

'The last couple of days have been filled with misery

and fear. I feel as if we're groping our way through a fog of despair.'

'That's an illusion,' he said. 'Father's death was a savage blow, but it was not without its advantages to us. I am now in charge of the business. Remember that. It means I can make the changes that Father always opposed. We will be able to grow and prosper.' He put an arm around her shoulders. 'Be patient, my love. All will be well in due course. Once the killer or killers are caught, this tragic episode in our lives will come to a halt.'

'When will that be, Paul?'

'Fairly soon, I hope. Inspector Colbeck is working hard on the case.'

By the time they returned to the Hope and Anchor, the inspector had adjusted to the fact that Edward Tallis had come to check on the progress of the investigation. Victor Leeming, however, regarded the newcomer as an intruder, arriving out of the blue with the express purpose of catching them out. When the three of them sat around a table in a quiet corner, the sergeant vowed to say as little as possible. Colbeck gave a succinct account of their movements in the past two days. Tallis's frown soon disappeared. He even rose to a smile of approval.

'I knew that you would leave no stone unturned,' he said. 'This revelation about Mr Blanchard's private life is significant. It's a pity that you don't have more details about his amours. If you did, then the respective husbands of these women would have to be regarded as suspects.' He turned to the sergeant. 'In acquiring the information about Mr Blanchard's adultery, you've opened up a whole new dimension to the investigation.'

'Thank you, sir,' said Leeming.

'That evening you spent with Mr Collier was fruitful.'

Yes, thought the other to himself. It gave me the worst headache of my life.

'What about this Welshman?' asked Tallis.

'I don't believe he had anything whatsoever to do with the murder,' said Colbeck.

'Yet Blanchard's son named him as a suspect.'

'Having met Mr Rees, I'd exonerate him of any involvement, sir. He was a fierce rival of the deceased, but he would not stoop to murder.'

'Then who would?'

'There are many possibilities. Chief among them, as you suggested, are the cuckolded husbands. We must try to find their names. Then there are the two passengers known to have shared a compartment with Blanchard that night.'

'The naval officer and the lady,' said Leeming.

'Mr Phelps found their behaviour strange. I trust his instincts.'

'I'm not sure that I do,' said Tallis. 'Can you imagine an officer in the Royal Navy strangling a man to death in front of a respectable woman?'

'Yes, I can,' suggested Colbeck. 'What if Blanchard had been pestering her?'

'We know he had an interest in women,' Leeming pointed out.

'So her companion would have felt compelled to rescue her,' said Tallis.

'But would he have had a ligature in his pocket?' asked Colbeck. 'It's hardly standard issue for naval officers. Why was he carrying it? Unless . . .'

An idea began to blossom in his mind.

CHAPTER NINE

After a sleepless night, Agnes Lenham felt ill with fatigue and haunted by fear. Hidden under her bed was a bag containing banknotes to the value of two hundred pounds. They felt like a bomb about to explode and destroy her. Her whole existence was at stake. After forcing herself to get up and go through her daily routine, she had to muster her strength to face her husband and their servants. Breakfast was served in the dining room but the very sight of it made her feel queasy. She asked her husband the usual questions about his health, and she told him that he was looking better. Crispin Lenham could not say the same about her. She was so tense and drawn that he became worried.

'Are you not well, Agnes?'

'I had a headache, that's all,' she replied.

'But you never have headaches. You're the healthiest person I know.' He reached out to touch her arm. 'It's one of the reasons I married you.'

'Just give me a little time to recover, please.'

'Have as much time as you wish, my dear. You clearly have no appetite for food. That's proof positive that you are feeling unwell. Right,' he went on, 'you'll be spared the task of taking me to the park this morning.'

'No,' she cried. 'I have to go there.'

'One of the servants can push me just as well.'

'I won't even hear of it, Crispin. It's my duty and I love taking you. Besides,' she claimed, 'I'm starting to feel hungry. That's a good sign. As soon as I have a full stomach, I'm sure that I will be fine.'

'We could always miss our visit to the park,' he told her.

'That's out of the question,' she insisted. 'Please stop arguing about it and simply keep to our routine. It's a lovely day, Crispin. The fresh air will do you good.'

'I'm hoping that it will do the same for you, my dear.'

As she nodded her head, Agnes contrived a weak smile.

Breakfast at the Hope and Anchor was a more enjoyable occasion without the superintendent there. Tallis had risen an hour earlier, eaten a hearty meal, and left to catch a train to London. Leeming felt a sense of profound relief. Once again, they had a free hand.

'I wish he hadn't turned up like that,' he said. 'It gave me a real fright.'

'I should have thought that you'd be used to the superintendent's unexpected visits by now, Victor,' said Colbeck. 'You should be able to take them in your stride.'

'We work best without him, sir.'

'His job is to keep our noses to the wheel, and he does that well. Besides, that chat we had with him about the case was very productive. I'm daring to believe that we now have a clearer idea of who killed Blanchard.'

'It was that naval officer and his friend.'

'They are certainly people of interest to us, Victor.'

'It's them, sir. They did it. All we need to do is to get posters printed offering a reward for information that leads to the arrest of that man and his female accomplice.'

'I disagree.'

'Why?'

'If they really did murder Blanchard, we'd only frighten them away. I have a strong feeling that they live in Portsmouth. Why else would they have been on that last train here? If we launch a public appeal, we'd be warning them that they are in danger.'

'How else can we catch them, sir?'

'In the same way that we caught other criminals,' said Colbeck. 'We remain patient, collect evidence, and sift it with care. It's a procedure that's much easier to follow on a full stomach.' He looked down at his plate.

'That's why we must eat every piece of this excellent breakfast.'

'It's not as good as the one that Estelle makes every morning,' said Leeming, wistfully.

'Nothing can compete with a family breakfast.'

'I miss it so much. When can we go back home, sir?'

'When we deserve it, Victor.'

Leeming ate his food for a few minutes then broke off. 'What do you want me to do today?' he asked.

'I'd like you to have another chat with Mr Phelps. Now that he's had more time to think about it, he may recall some details about his train journey that night.'

'What if he's gone to that client of his in Havant?'

'I had the feeling that his dealings with the man were over for the time being,' said Colbeck. 'Call at his home here in Portsmouth. He's our one link with those two people on the train.'

'Where will you be going?'

'I intend to pay another visit to Paul Blanchard. His behaviour interests me. Since he and his father were so close,' said Colbeck, 'why does he show no signs of grief? It's unnatural.'

When there was a loud knock on the front door, one of the servants went to see who it was.

'Leave this to me, Jenny,' said Blanchard, coming out of the drawing room. 'It will be the locksmith I'm expecting.'

'Very good, sir,' said the woman, retreating into the kitchen.

117

Blanchard opened the door to reveal a tall, thin, sinewy man in his forties who was carrying a large tool bag. He gave a deferential smile.

'Good morning, sir,' he said. 'I'm Dan Jewitt.'

'I'm pleased to see you, Jewitt. This is an emergency.'

'That's why I came so early.' He peered at the lock on the front door. 'Is this one of the ones you want changed?'

'Yes, it is. Before you tackle this and the lock on the back door, I've got a much easier task for you. Follow me.'

When he stood aside to let Jewitt in, the man removed his hat and looked around. After closing the front door, Blanchard took him down the passageway and into his father's study. Jewitt let out a whistle of appreciation.

'That's a beautiful desk, sir,' he said, running his eyes over it.

'My father settled for nothing but the best.'

'I love to see real craftsmanship.'

'I didn't bring you here to admire the desk. I just want you to unlock the drawers.'

'Say no more, sir,' said Jewitt, bending down to tug at the drawers in turn. 'This won't take long.' He straightened his back and turned to Blanchard. 'I'm very sorry to hear what happened to your father, sir. It must be a bad time for you and—'

'Just do as you're told,' snapped Blanchard. 'Call me when you've finished.'

'Yes, sir. Of course . . .'

But the words went unheard. Blanchard had gone out.

They arrived in the park early so that they could take up their positions. They had a clear view of the bench on which their victim routinely sat. The woman was nervous.

'What if she doesn't turn up?' she asked.

'She has no choice.'

'Perhaps she was unable to get the money in time.'

'She'll have it,' he said, confidently. 'You put the fear of death into her.'

'I did. She turned white.'

They stayed in their hiding place for twenty minutes, then Agnes Lenham came into sight, pushing the bath chair in which her husband was reclining. She looked fearful, glancing nervously around as if in danger of attack. When she reached the bench, she first checked that her husband was asleep, then adjusted his hat to protect him from the sun. They watched as she took out a small bag and placed it behind the bench. The woman then opened her book and pretended to read.

The man, meanwhile, moved quickly and silently across the grass towards her. Snatching up the bag, he ran back to the hiding place. He opened it and took out the banknotes, counting them quickly.

'I told you that she'd pay up,' he said.

'Is it all there?'

'Every penny. Let's go.'

'She doesn't even know that the bag has gone,' she said.

'What she will know is that it was over quickly. She won't be so scared next time.'

Leeming arrived at Phelps's house to find that he had gone to his office in Portsmouth. Having made a note of the address, the sergeant walked briskly in the direction indicated, grateful that the lawyer had not travelled to Havant again. When he was admitted to Phelps's office, the latter rose to his feet with a smile on his face.

'I'm so glad to see you again, Sergeant Leeming,' he said.

'Why?'

'I've been thinking about what happened that night.'

'I was hoping you might have done that, sir. Any detail, however small, might be critical.'

'Sit down and I'll tell you what I remembered.'

'Thank you,' said Leeming, lowering himself onto a chair and taking out his notebook.

'At my age,' admitted Phelps remaining on his feet, 'the mind can play strange tricks. I have these sudden lapses of memory. My wife keeps pointing them out to me.'

'Did you have a lapse when we first spoke to you?'

'I believe so.'

'What was it?'

'Well, I missed out something that may be important,' said Phelps. 'I told you that a man and a woman got out of a compartment and went in search of another. I walked behind them.'

'I have your exact words here,' said Leeming, flipping to the relevant page in his notebook.

'What I didn't tell you was that the man was doing something rather . . . unusual. If they had been man and wife, she would surely have been on her husband's arm. Then again, if she was a woman of loose morals, he would have put his arm around her and pulled her close. In other words, his intentions would have been clear.'

'What did the man do?'

'He supported her,' said Phelps. 'She was clinging to him. It was almost as if he had to carry her along. I assumed that she might have been drinking and was unsteady on her feet, but there might be another explanation.'

'She was in distress?'

'Exactly. Something had happened to upset her. I can't think what it was. When I passed the compartment in which they had been travelling, I glanced in and saw a man fast asleep – at least that's what I thought I saw. I now know that he was dead.'

'He'd been strangled,' said Leeming, 'and we can now be almost certain that the naval officer was the killer. It's no wonder that the woman was frightened. She'd witnessed a murder.'

'That never occurred to me at the time, Sergeant Leeming. And how could I forget that he was helping her along like that?' asked Phelps. 'I suppose the truth is that I didn't get a close look at them. Also, of course, I was searching for a compartment to get into myself and was distracted.'

'You've remembered it now, sir, and I'm so grateful that you did.'

'I'll try hard to recall if there's any other detail I forgot.'

'That's quite unnecessary,' said Leeming, closing his notebook and getting to his feet. 'You've told me something of great significance and I'm very grateful.'

It took Dan Jewitt longer than he had predicted but he did finally unlock all the drawers in the desk. He got no thanks for his efforts. When Paul Blanchard entered the study, he was more interested in getting the locksmith out of the room than in listening to his explanation for the delay. While Jewitt went off to assess the next task, Blanchard closed the door of the study then locked it. Fishing out the documents in the desk drawers, he began to go through them, sorting them into piles. It was in the last drawer that he made an unexpected discovery.

Inside a box was a collection of letters, held together by a blue ribbon. When he pulled one of the letters out, there was a faint whiff of perfume. The missive was short, loving, and unnervingly explicit. Blanchard could not believe what he was reading. Before he could examine a second letter, knuckles rapped on his door.

'Yes?' he shouted.

'There's an Inspector Colbeck at the front door, sir,' said Jewitt.

'Oh, I see . . . Ask him to wait in the drawing room, please.'

'Very good, sir.'

Blanchard was still quivering with shock at his discovery. Thrusting the letters into their box, he dropped it back into the drawer from which they came. Then he slammed the drawer shut and put both hands to his face in horror. For several minutes, he was unable to move.

Back at their house, they spread the banknotes out beside those found in their victim's wallet. They had never had such a large amount of money before. He gave her a warm hug.

'Didn't I tell you that it would be easy?' he asked.

'I was so nervous,' she confessed. 'I was afraid that Mrs Lenham would turn around and see you. But she didn't even realise that you were there.'

'She did as she was told. That's the main thing. She'll do the same in a month's time.'

'What do we do before then?'

'We'll enjoy spending some of this money.'

'Does that mean I can have that new dress I saw?' she asked, hopefully.

'You can have whatever you want, my darling. Before we do that, however, there's a more important job for us.'

'Is there?'

'Yes,' he told her, picking up the notebook stolen from Blanchard. 'Find me the next lovesick woman we can torment.' He handed her the notebook and she opened it. 'Well?'

'Don't rush me. I need time to think.'

'I chose Agnes Lenham because I liked the sound of her name. Also, she had more stars beside her name than any of the others. I fancy that she was Blanchard's favourite.'

'I daresay that the woman is regretting that she ever met him now.'

'Who is our next target?'

'Christina Falconbridge.'

'That's a name with a real ring to it. How many times did they have a rendezvous?'

'It was only once.'

'Then pick another name,' he advised. 'We want someone who was so foolishly in love with that repulsive man that she gave herself time and again.'

'How little you know of women!' she teased. 'The first time is always the best. It's a bold step into another world. My guess is that Christina Falconbridge is still dreaming about the event. When she learns of his murder, she will be heartbroken.'

'Heartbroken and supremely vulnerable,' he said. 'Then let's track her down.'

When Blanchard finally came into the drawing room, he shook Colbeck's hand and showered him with apologies.

The inspector waved them away.

'I see that you're having locks changed,' he said. 'A wise precaution.'

'Somebody has my father's keys. I'm taking no chances.'

'In your position, I'd assign one of the servants to keep watch at night.'

'I hadn't thought of that,' said Blanchard.

'Burglars prefer the dark, sir. Anyway,' said Colbeck, 'this is not a courtesy visit. You'll be wondering what we have been doing.'

'Have you made any progress?'

'We believe that we have, sir. A witness has come forward. On the night in question, he joined the train at Havant and noticed that a man and a woman alighted from a compartment in which a male passenger was, it seemed, fast asleep. That man,' said Colbeck, 'was your father.'

'Was he dead at the time?'

'In all likelihood, he was.'

'Then the two people who left the compartment must have been his killers.'

'It's a strong possibility, sir.'

'Where did they go? Did they leave the station?'

'No, Mr Blanchard. They climbed aboard the train further down the platform.'

'Forgive me, Inspector,' said Blanchard, confused. 'I can see how a man might have taken advantage of my father if he was caught off guard. But would he do so in front of a woman? It's almost inconceivable.'

'Not to us, sir. My guess is that the woman might have been used to lure your father into that compartment. If that were the case, all his attention would be on her. I need to ask you a sensitive question, sir. I hope that it won't embarrass you.'

'Have no qualms on that account, Inspector.'

'I know that your father was a respectable married man and a pillar of the church, but he had been drinking at the Haven Club. Could you imagine that he might be . . . tempted by a woman?'

'Certainly not!'

'The woman in question would no doubt have been . . . very skilful.'

'That's enough, Inspector,' shouted Blanchard, face reddening. 'I find your question both intrusive and insulting. My father was a man of impeccable integrity in every way. Please don't even raise the subject again.'

'As you wish, sir,' said Colbeck, raising both palms. 'Please accept my apology.'

Madeleine Colbeck was about to descend the stairs when she happened to glance through the window. To her delight, she saw Lydia Quayle walking towards the house. The sight made her hurry downstairs, and fling open the door.

'That's what I call a welcome!' said Lydia, laughing.

'I wasn't expecting you today. Oh, I'm so pleased to see you, Lydia.'

'To be honest, it was Helena Rose who brought me here.'

'Why?'

'I have something for her,' said Lydia, holding up a small parcel.

'Come inside and show me what it is.'

When her friend stepped into the house, Madeleine hugged her then led the way into the drawing room. They sat beside each other on the sofa.

'I was in a bookshop this morning,' said Lydia, 'and noticed this little book about animals. They're so beautifully drawn, and there's a little poem about each one. I just couldn't resist it.'

When she took it out of its wrapping, she handed it over. Madeleine opened it at once and, as she glanced through the pages, she was excited by the quality of the artwork. She also found the poems delightful.

'Helena will learn these by heart. Oh, thank you, Lydia. You're so kind.'

'What's the point of being a favourite aunt if you can't buy your niece presents?'

'This will be a welcome distraction for her,' said Madeleine. 'At the moment, she keeps asking me the same question – when will Daddy come back home?'

'Is there any answer to that question?'

'Not yet, I fear. I'm still waiting for the postman to come. Yesterday's letter warned me that there was a lot to do. Robert said that he needs to make repeated trips to the Isle of Wight.'

'What makes people live in such a small place?' asked Lydia.

'It sounds wonderful.'

'Well, it wouldn't suit me. I prefer London. There's something about a big city that makes me feel alive. It's so full of adventure.'

'I'm sure that the Isle of Wight has its attractions, Lydia.'

'I daresay that it has. We used to have holidays on the Isle of Man. When we were children, it was lovely. We played all day. As we got older, we noticed that the people there were . . . well, very different to us. Some of them seemed almost foreign.'

'Have you ever been back there?'

'No,' said Lydia. 'I've outgrown it. That's the trouble with islands.'

Madeleine laughed. 'You still live on an island. It comprises England, Scotland, and Wales.'

'There's still so much to explore here. My heart goes out to Robert,' she said. 'If he keeps visiting the Isle of Wight, he'll soon have seen all that it has to offer.'

While he listened to Colbeck's report, Paul Blanchard was tense and uncomfortable. His face was impassive, but his mind was on fire. The discovery that his father had been unfaithful had shocked him to the core. What added to his distress was that, no sooner had he learnt the hideous truth, than the inspector arrived to ask him a question that was like the thrust of a sword. Blanchard tried hard to persuade himself that his father was wholly committed to his wife and family, but the evidence against him was too strong.

As he explained the steps that he and Leeming had taken, Colbeck was conscious that his host was only half-listening. In the past, Blanchard had fired endless questions at the inspector, but he hardly said a word this time, resorting to a series of nods and grunts. Colbeck tried to jolt him into a conversation.

'I'm afraid that I disagree with your estimate of Mr Rees,' he said.

'What's that?' asked Blanchard, finally paying attention.

'I took the trouble of calling on him, sir. It was unfair of you to call him glib. He was friendly. I sensed no malice in him. Mr Rees guessed that you would blame him for the murder of your father but denied any involvement in it.'

'He would,' snarled Blanchard. 'I'd expect nothing else of him. Berwyn Rees is a proven liar, Inspector. I could give you dozens of instances of it. That fluent tongue of his might have deceived you, but I still believe that he was involved somehow.'

'What did he stand to gain?'

'Revenge.'

'I'm not convinced of that, sir,' said Colbeck. 'As he pointed out to me, he would never consider being a party to the murder of your father because it made matters worse for him.'

Blanchard frowned. 'Worse?'

'One powerful rival might have died, but he's been replaced by another. Namely, you, sir. Mr Rees considers you to be even more of a threat to him than your father. It's a potent argument.'

'Don't listen to a word that Berwyn Rees says.'

'The man is entitled to defend himself.'

'You're taking his word over mine, are you?' said Blanchard, angrily.

'I'm making an impartial judgement.'

'Rees was somehow involved in my father's death, Inspector. I feel it in my bones.'

'It's not a feeling that I share,' said Colbeck. 'However, I accept that you know the gentleman far better than I do, so we will look more closely at him.'

Blanchard glowered. 'I insist that you do.'

CHAPTER TEN

It was not quite so easy this time. They watched the house from a safe distance, but nobody came out or went in. After almost two hours, the man resorted to another plan. Seeing an elderly couple coming down the road, he intercepted them to ask a polite question.

'Excuse me,' he said, 'but I wonder if you would help me.'

'Yes, of course,' said the old man. 'What do you wish to know?'

'I wondered if, by any chance, you know where Mr and Mrs Falconbridge live?'

'They live at number twenty-three. But it's not "Mr

Falconbridge". It's Major Falconbridge. If you're hoping to speak to him, you're out of luck. He's in Wiltshire with his regiment.'

'Oh, I see.'

'They're a charming couple,' said the man's wife. 'Not that we see them together very often, mark you. Marrying a soldier means that a wife spends a lot of time apart from him.'

'Yes, I suppose that it does. Thank you for your help.'

He waved them off then returned to the point from which he and the woman had been watching the house from a concealed position. He told her what he had discovered.

'Mrs Falconbridge is a lonely wife, is she?' said the other.

'It's a possible motive for her to go astray.'

'How could she have met Blanchard?'

'I suspect that she and her husband bought the house from him,' he suggested. 'These are all expensive properties – the kind that he sells. If he'd sold them the house, he would certainly have met the wife. We know for certain that Blanchard had a wandering eye.'

'And it may have alighted on Mrs Falconbridge.'

'Let's not get too carried away,' he warned. 'All that we know for certain is that her husband is rarely here. That must be a huge relief to her.'

'Why?'

'Well, she must surely have heard about the death of

Giles Blanchard. It was in all the newspapers. Even if she didn't read about it, someone must have mentioned the murder to her. It will have caused a lot of overexcited gossip.'

'When she heard about the incident, she would have been devastated. Mrs Falconbridge must be so grateful that her husband is with his regiment,' she said. 'Otherwise, he'd have been suspicious about the way that she reacted.' She turned to him. 'What do we do now?'

'We stay right here.'

'For how long?'

'As long as is necessary,' he told her. 'The woman is bound to come out at some point.'

Colbeck was patient. Having told Paul Blanchard what they had discovered, he had managed to elicit a grunt of approval from the man. Colbeck made no further mention of Berwyn Rees. The name was clearly anathema.

'May I ask why your father does not have a safe in the house?' he asked.

'We have one in our main office,' replied Blanchard. 'It's a highly expensive Chubb safe. Everything relating to the business is kept in there.'

'Then why were you so anxious to open his desk?'

'I wanted to find his will, Inspector.'

'His solicitor would have a copy of that, surely?'

'What I was after was the initial draft in my father's own hand.'

'But you were unable to open the drawers in the desk.'

'Really, Inspector! said Blanchard, irritably. 'Why do you keep on about the desk?'

'I'm sorry, sir. It's a nasty habit of mine. I come from a family of cabinetmakers. Desks always fascinate me. As a boy, I was given the job of trying to find where the secret compartment was. My grandfather was a genius at concealing the mechanism. Sometimes it would take me half an hour or so to locate it.'

Blanchard was surprised. 'Do all desks have a secret compartment?'

'If they are of sufficient quality, sir, they often do. And I daresay that your father's desk would be of the highest standard.'

'All the furniture in this house is the very best that was available.'

'Did you ask the locksmith to find the secret compartment for you?'

'No,' said Blanchard, uneasily. 'I didn't, as it happens.'

'Would you like me to show you where it is?'

'That won't be necessary, Inspector. Jewitt can find it. I'm paying him enough.'

'I will do it at no expense,' volunteered Colbeck. 'I relish a challenge.'

'Then get out there and find the man who killed my father!' urged Blanchard. 'Don't rest until the killer is safely behind bars!'

* * *

Victor Leeming was pleased. After what he felt was a profitable visit to William Phelps, he went to the railway station and caught a train to Havant. Gazing through the window of his compartment, he watched it slowly appear. It was a small market town with a church at its centre. Colbeck had told him that, for centuries, its chief industry had been parchment-making. Water from the local springs was used in the process. Tanners and cloth-makers also relied on it. Leeming wondered what sort of employment he would have had back in the olden days. There would certainly have been no organised police force. He decided that he would have been a miller or an innkeeper.

When he left the train in Havant, he was lucky enough to find a porter who had been on duty at the station on the night of the murder. Eric Dobson was a short, fat, middle-aged man with a walrus moustache. He seemed delighted to be talking to a detective involved in the murder hunt.

'That's right, sir,' he said. 'I saw that train come in and go out.'

'Did you notice anything odd?'

'I noticed that two passengers got out and headed for the exit. Another two – a man and a woman – stepped out of a first-class compartment and walked along the platform. That seemed funny to me. What was wrong with the one they'd been in?'

'Was there also a man waiting to get on the train?'

'Yes, there was. He walked behind the couple and

glanced in the compartment they'd just left. That made me curious, so I went to look for myself.'

'What did you see?'

'There was a man propped up in a corner. He was fast asleep.'

'Did you wonder why the other passengers had left the compartment?'

'Of course,' said Dobson, stroking his moustache. 'My guess was the man had probably had too much to drink and been sick all over the floor. Imagine the stink in there. It was no wonder that the other passengers got out.'

'Why didn't they report that there was a mess in the compartment?'

'They were in a rush to get back on the train, sir. The woman was very upset. Well,' he added, 'she would be if someone had left a pile of vomit only feet away from her. The man was helping her along.'

'What about the other passenger?' asked Leeming.

'He was just behind them. When they got into a compartment, he walked past and found one to get into himself.' Dobson shrugged. 'The train then pulled away and I thought no more about it. Until I heard that a murder had been committed, that is. The man I thought was fast asleep had been strangled. The killer had to be the person I saw helping the woman on to the platform.'

'How far away were you from the incident?'

'Twenty yards or so, I suppose.'

'Then you didn't get a good look at either of those passengers.'

'I saw enough of the woman's face to notice something. When she looked in my direction, she was dabbing at her eyes with a handkerchief. Then she took it away and I saw her face for a second. She was lovely. Even though she was crying, she looked . . . beautiful.'

Their wait was eventually over. The front door of the house opened and out stepped a tall, slender woman in her late thirties. Turning to the left, she walked quickly along the pavement as if anxious to get somewhere.

'Follow her,' said the man.

'Are you sure that it's Mrs Falconbridge?'

'I'm certain that it is.'

The woman came out of her hiding place and went in pursuit of her. It was not a long walk. After less than five minutes, Christina Falconbridge turned a corner and headed for a church. Once there, she let herself in and closed the heavy door behind her. The woman who had trailed her waited over five minutes before letting herself into the cool church. Sitting at the rear of the nave, she saw that the other woman was kneeling at the altar rail. The contrast in the latter's appearance was marked. When striding along the street, Mrs Falconbridge had looked proud, confident, and handsome. Head bowed and shoulders hunched, she was now in a position of abject submission. She was also oblivious to the fact that someone else was in the church with her.

It was a long time before she hauled herself to her feet, bowed to the altar then turned to walk back up the aisle. Lost in her thoughts, she did not see the woman step out to intercept her. At the very last moment, she became aware that she was about to bump into the stranger.

'Oh!' she cried. 'Do forgive me. I didn't see you there.'

'I understand, Mrs Falconbridge,' said the woman, softly.

'How do you know my name?'

'Oh, I know a lot more about you than that. I'm just wondering what brought you to church. Did you come to mourn the death of Giles Blanchard – or to repent of your sin?'

'Who are you?' gasped the other in alarm.

'I'm someone who knows your guilty secret, Mrs Falconbridge. What would your husband say if he realised that you had betrayed him?'

'He must never know!'

'Then we need to talk,' whispered the woman. 'Let's step outside, shall we? It would be improper to have this conversation on consecrated ground.'

Paul Blanchard was in a quandary. While he'd been anxious to know every detail of the progress of the investigation, he was thrown on the defensive. Colbeck kept offering to find the secret compartment in his father's desk. If he did so, the inspector would find out what had been hidden there. Having already made one uncomfortable discovery in the desk drawers, Blanchard did not wish to repeat the experience in front of someone. He therefore hurried his visitor on his way and summoned the locksmith.

'I haven't finished the front door yet, sir,' said Jewitt.

'Something else takes precedence. Come into the office.'

'But I've already opened those drawers for you, Mr Blanchard.'

'There's something we forgot.'

'Is there, sir?'

'Yes,' said the other leading him into the study. 'Desks like this tend to have a secret compartment, don't they?'

'They do,' agreed the locksmith.

'Could you see if you could find it?'

'Of course, sir.' Jewitt knelt beside the desk. 'My guess is that it may be here.'

Feeling under the desk, he pressed various parts of it but to no effect.

Blanchard was impatient. 'Get on with it, man!'

'I need a few moments to find it, sir.' He moved to the other side of the desk and explored it with his finger. Without warning, there was a ping as the secret compartment opened. 'There you are, sir. It's all yours.'

'You can get back to the front door now.'

'Don't you want to see how it closes?'

'Just get out.'

Jewitt left at once and Blanchard locked the door behind him. The secret compartment contained a silver box with a small key beside it. Pulling the box out, he used the key to open it and saw what was inside. At first, he was bemused. When he realised what he had found, however, he was absolutely horrified.

Eager to pass on his news, Leeming was pacing up and down the pier. When the steamer docked, he waited until Colbeck appeared out of the throng of passengers. After an exchange of greetings, they headed back towards the Hope and Anchor.

'Did you speak to Mr Phelps?' asked Colbeck.

'Yes, I did, and he told me something that had slipped his mind.'

'What was it?'

Leeming explained that, when Phelps had walked behind two passengers who left their compartment at Havant, he noticed that the woman was in distress. Her companion was supporting her.

'If he'd strangled Blanchard in front of her,' said Leeming, 'it's hardly surprising that she was upset. After leaving Mr Phelps, I took a train to Havant station.'

'That was enterprising of you.'

'I managed to find a porter who'd been on duty that same night. Everything he said supported Mr Phelps's evidence.'

'You did well, Victor,' said Colbeck.

'All I confirmed is what we suspected, sir. The naval officer must have strangled Blanchard.'

'It certainly looks that way.'

'How do we find them? That's the question.'

'My guess is that they're still here but keeping clear of the railway. Don't forget that they stole Mr Blanchard's wallet. He might have had other things of value on him as well. Whatever the case, they'll be happy to disappear for a while. We'll have to be patient until they give themselves away.'

'What if they don't do that, sir?'

Colbeck frowned. 'Then we may be here for quite some time, I'm afraid.'

When she returned to the spot from which they had been watching the Falconbridge house, she was so pleased that she began to gabble. He took her by the shoulders.

'Calm down, calm down,' he urged. 'You're too excited.'

'I'm sorry.'

'Tell me what happened when you went into the church.'

Speaking more slowly, she described the conversation she had had with Mrs Falconbridge, and how shocked the woman had been when her secret had been revealed. Unlike Agnes Lenham, she did not have an aged husband who was close to the end of his life. She was married to a major in the army, a man who trusted his wife implicitly. The prospect of having her secret revealed had reduced the wife to a gibbering wreck.

'Before I even asked her,' said the woman, 'she was offering to pay for my silence. The woman was desperate. She's not able to get the money immediately but promised

141

that she would have it by the end of the week.'

'Good. Where will she hand it over?'

'Outside that church.'

It took Paul Blanchard a long time to recover from the shock. Seated in the study, he tried to control his disgust. His father's murder had shaken him, but he did at least stand to gain from the crime in due course. The empire they had created would belong entirely to him. Instead of being able to remember his father fondly, however, he now viewed him as cruel and loathsome, living a hidden life at the expense of his wife and family. Finding the letters in the desk had been a harrowing experience. But the discovery of the silver box tore away the last few remnants of love and respect that he still had for his father.

What made his suffering worse was that there was nobody with whom he could share his pain. The ugly truth about her husband simply had to be hidden from his mother. It would shatter her fond memories of a happy marriage. Blanchard's own wife also had to be kept ignorant of the truth because Verity held her father-in-law in high esteem. Were she to learn of his adultery with a string of women, she would be at once hurt and outraged. Blanchard would never dare to tell her what he had found tucked away in the silver box.

The more he brooded, the angrier he became. In a fit of rage, he suddenly leapt up from his chair and ran to the fireplace. A fire had been laid but was never used in the warmer months. Blanchard grabbed the box of Vestas tucked away behind the clock on the mantelpiece and used one of them to light the fire. After waiting until it began to blaze, he grabbed the letters from a drawer, tore them up and tossed them onto the flames. The silver box felt the full sting of his fury. Snatching it up, he rushed to the fire and poured the contents of the box into it, staring at them until the last shreds had vanished up the chimney.

When he slumped into a chair, Blanchard was quivering with shame.

Helena Rose Colbeck had been delighted to see Aunt Lydia again and thrilled to receive the book. When she flicked through the pages, she was laughing with joy. It was the painting of a pony that really caught her eye. After staring at it for a minute or more, she grabbed a pencil and began to copy the one in the book. Madeleine nudged her friend and the two of them left the nursery.

'I told you that she'd love it,' said Madeleine. 'As it happens, she keeps asking for a pony.'

'A real one?' asked Lydia.

'I'm afraid so.'

'I didn't learn to ride until I was nine.'

'Well, I never had the chance to ride at all,' admitted Madeleine. 'The closest I ever got to a horse was when the baker let me feed an apple to the one that pulled his cart. Oh, I'm so glad that my daughter can enjoy having treats that never came my way.'

'What about the time your father sneaked you on to a steam engine? That was a treat, surely?'

'Yes, it was very special, Lydia.'

'It's no wonder you choose to paint railway scenes. It's in your blood.'

'That's true. I've had a lifelong romance with railways.'

'And it still continues,' noted Lydia. 'Except that you're now also having a romance with the famous Railway Detective. When is Robert going to appear in one of your paintings?'

Over a meal at the Hope and Anchor, they were able to discuss their progress. Having been excited by what he had learnt during his respective meetings with William Phelps and a porter at Havant railway station, Leeming was now less enthusiastic about the information he'd gathered. He felt strangely disappointed.

'We seem to take one step forward and two steps back,' he complained.

'Don't be so pessimistic, Victor. I feel that we're on the right track.'

'But we're nowhere near making an arrest, sir.'

'Our work – as you well know – is slow but sure. Every day brings new information.'

'I'd rather it brought us closer to the killers.'

'Oh, there was only one killer, I fancy,' said Colbeck. 'His female accomplice was duly horrified by it. That's why she wanted to leave the compartment at the next station.'

'Havant.'

'What does it tell you about the woman?'

'It was the first time she'd witnessed a murder.'

'But not the first time she'd travelled on that train. I believe that she and that man have gone in search of victims during a journey before. When I questioned the railway police at Portsmouth station, I was told that the most frequent crime on the line was theft. Pickpockets were active,' recalled Colbeck. 'What if the couple we've identified were plying the same trade?'

'It's possible, I suppose.'

'The woman distracted people so that the man could pick their pockets.'

'Yes, that porter told me how beautiful she was. She would distract anyone.'

'Beautiful but deadly,' said Colbeck. 'Well, they won't be a menace on the late train for quite a while, I'm sure. They know that the railway police will be more vigilant now. Also, they will have plenty of money. Blanchard's wallet probably contained a fair amount and there'd be a pocket watch and other items to sell. That's your next task, Victor.'

'You want me to visit the jewellery shops in Portsmouth?'

'Start as soon as you've finished your meal.'

'Very good, sir.' Leeming ate another potato then recalled something. 'Oh, you haven't told me about your visit to Paul Blanchard.'

'It was rather puzzling,' said Colbeck.

'In what way?'

'His behaviour was quite strange. He couldn't wait to get me out of the house. It was almost as if I'd called at the wrong time.'

Paul Blanchard was still in his father's study. He was so preoccupied that he didn't hear the knock on the door or the attempt to open it. A second, louder knock brought him out of his reverie.

'Paul!' called his wife. 'Are you in there?'

'Yes, yes,' he replied, getting up to unlock the door and open it.

'Why did you lock yourself in?' she asked.

'I wanted some privacy.'

She peered at him. 'Are you all right?'

'I'm fine, Verity.'

'Well, you don't look it. Your face is white, and you're shaking. What's upset you? Is there something on your mind?'

'Of course, there is,' he snapped. 'My father has been murdered and I've been forced to take control over the business. Can't you see that I'm under intense pressure?'

'Yes,' she said, hurt by his tone, 'and I'm trying to offer you my full support.'

'Why did you want me?'

'I only came to tell you that luncheon is served. If I'd known you were in this mood, I wouldn't have bothered.'

After taking a deep breath, he managed a gesture of apology.

'I'm sorry, darling. It was very rude of me.'

'And why is it so warm in there?' she asked, putting her head around the door, and seeing the fire. 'What on earth made you light that? We don't need a fire in summer.'

'I . . . needed to burn something.'

'What was it?'

'Never you mind.'

'But it's such a strange thing to do.'

'I was acting on impulse.'

'Why?'

'It doesn't matter now, Verity.'

'It does to me.'

'Has Jewitt finished yet?'

'That's the other thing I came to tell you. He's put new locks on both doors and wants your approval of his work.'

'I daresay he wants to be paid as well.'

'What's happened?' she asked, worriedly. 'Inspector Colbeck was here earlier. Did he bring bad news?'

'It's nothing to do with him, Verity.'

'Well, I won't press you. I just want you to know that I'm ready to share any burden you have. We've had such a happy life together. Let me help you through this darker period.' He took her in his arms and hugged her. 'That's better. I'm your wife, Paul.'

'I couldn't be more grateful.'

'A trouble shared is a trouble halved.'

'It's not as simple as that.'

'Then I won't press you. I know that you're under great strain. Apart from anything else, you're worried about your mother. So am I, to be honest. She's hardly eaten anything today.'

'I'll speak to her.'

'She told me that she'd rather be alone for a while.'

'Oh, I see.'

He stepped out of the study and locked the door behind him. She was surprised.

'Why did you do that?' she asked. 'Nobody else would dare to go in there.'

He bristled. 'Stop criticising me, will you?'

'I'm just trying to understand why you're acting like this. There's no need for a fire in the study, and no point at all in locking the door. What's going on?'

'It's none of your business,' he said.

'You're hiding something from me, aren't you?'

'Don't be ridiculous!'

'I've never seen you like this before. It frightens me, Paul.'

'That's your problem,' he said, coldly. 'Now you'll have to excuse me. I must go and deal with the locksmith.'

Turning on his heel, he walked off down the corridor. All that his wife could do was to stand there in dismay, wondering exactly what she had done to upset her husband.

CHAPTER ELEVEN

Queen Victoria was seated in the drawing room of Osborne House, reading a book, and enjoying a rare moment of leisure. There was a tap on the door and Gwendoline Cardus entered.

'I'm sorry to disturb you, Your Majesty,' she said.

'No apology is needed, Gwendoline,' said the Queen, setting the book aside. 'I was just reading some of Mr Tennyson's poems. They bring me such pleasure.'

'It's about Mr Tennyson that I came.'

The Queen's face clouded. 'There's no problem, is there? I enjoy his visits so much.'

'He sent word that he may be a trifle late – half an

hour at most.'

'How kind of him to warn us! It's so typical of the man. What about Mrs Scott-Siddons?'

'As far as I know,' said Gwendoline, 'she will be here at the time agreed.'

'Excellent! I don't know which gives me the greater thrill – reading the poems myself or listening to them being read by the great-granddaughter of the famous Sarah Siddons. Which would you prefer?'

'In my opinion, Your Majesty, nothing can compare with hearing them being read aloud in the presence of the poet himself. I find Mr Tennyson's work so moving.'

'Having him as a neighbour is one of the many delights of coming to Osborne House.'

'I agree.'

Gwendoline was about to excuse herself when the Queen raised a hand to detain her.

'Is there any more news about the investigation?'

'All that I can tell you, Your Majesty, is what the morning newspapers say. They have great faith in Inspector Colbeck. It is only a matter of time, they claim, before he solves this appalling crime.'

'And what of Mr Blanchard's family? They must be in a complete daze.'

'Your letter of condolence will no doubt have brought them comfort.'

'Writing it was the least I could do,' said the Queen. 'I still fail to understand the mentality of anyone who felt impelled to kill Giles Blanchard in such a brutal way. It was unnecessarily cruel. He was such a complete gentleman in every way.'

'He was robbed as well, Your Majesty. According to the police, his wallet, watch, and even his wedding ring were stolen.'

'How dreadful!'

'We must hope that the culprit is caught very soon.'

'Yes, indeed. As you know, we have cause to be eternally grateful to Inspector Colbeck. He once saved our family from a potential disaster on the royal train. I remember how modest he was when my dear husband and I thanked him in person. Oh,' she sighed, 'I do hope that he can work his magic once again.'

Berwyn Rees was surprised to see him. After giving Colbeck a warm welcome, he took the inspector into his office, and they sat down.

'I didn't expect a second visit,' said Rees.

'I just wanted to ask you a few more questions, sir.'

'What about?'

'Your relationship with Mr Blanchard.'

'Father or son?'

'Well,' said Colbeck, 'I suppose that it concerns both. Why would Paul Blanchard feel certain that you were somehow involved in his father's death?'

'He blames me for any setback.'

'A murder is rather more than a setback, Mr Rees.'

'Yes, yes, of course. I chose the wrong word. The fact is that I've locked horns with the Blanchard family

151

for over a quarter of a century. They see me as a hated foreigner, trespassing on their territory.'

'You are in direct competition with them.'

'So are other estate agencies, but they don't get the abuse that I suffered at the hands of Giles and Paul Blanchard. I won't bore you with the details. Suffice it to say that they've blocked my appointment to various committees on the island, and they had the gall to lure away some of my best employees.'

'Did they offer them more money?'

'Yes – it was a direct attempt to undermine us.'

'That sort of thing must happen all the time in business,' said Colbeck. 'Have you never poached employees from your rivals?'

'Of course,' admitted Rees, 'but I've never gone to the lengths that Giles Blanchard did. He and his son launched a systematic attack on my agency.'

'You seem to have survived it quite well, sir.'

'That's because I was prepared to fight fire with fire.'

'What do you mean?'

'I stood up to their bullying. Other estate agents caved in.'

Colbeck saw the glint in the Welshman's eyes. His business activities might be conducted with complete propriety, but Berwyn Rees was at heart a warrior. There was a vengeful streak in him, not completely hidden behind his disarming smile.

'Let me ask you something else, if I may,' said Colbeck. 'Did Mr Blanchard enjoy a happy marriage?'

'He showed all the signs of doing so, Inspector. At public events, his wife was always on his arm, and he treated her with the greatest of respect.'

'Then why didn't he spend more time at home?'

'It's too late to ask him that question.'

'What's your answer?'

'If truth be told,' said Rees, 'I always wondered why he went to the Haven Club so often. I enjoyed an occasional visit there, but I'm not entirely at ease in exclusively male company. I'm a family man. It's in my blood. I always felt slightly out of place there.'

'We're looking at the possibility that Mr Blanchard may have been distracted by a woman, making him vulnerable to an attack from behind by a man. When I mentioned our theory to his son,' said Colbeck, 'he treated it with utter contempt.'

'He would do.'

'Why do you say that?'

'Because he would never believe that his father would go astray. Giles had gone to such lengths to create the image of a perfect family. It was an image that fooled me for years.'

'What stopped you from continuing to believe in it?'

'Eluned.'

'I beg your pardon.'

'Eluned is my niece from Brecon, as pretty and pure a young woman as you could wish to meet. She has the bloom of youth allied to a touching innocence. Unfortunately, Eluned has not yet learnt the effect she has on men.'

'Did she have an effect on Giles Blanchard?'

'Oh, yes,' said Rees with feeling. 'Eluned didn't notice it, but I did. We were at a garden party with friends. Among the other guests were Giles and his family. He behaved with his usual mixture of civility and condescension. Then he caught sight of Eluned.'

'How did he react?'

'The mask was suddenly whisked off. Instead of a doting husband, he became a man with darker urges. When I saw the way that he stared at her, I moved across to Eluned and blocked her from his sight. I was not going to let him ogle her like that. It was indecent.' He sat back in his chair. 'Does that answer the question you came here to put to me?'

'Yes, it does,' said Colbeck, thoughtfully. 'Thank you, Mr Rees.'

When Leeming had first explored Portsmouth with Colbeck, he had been amazed at the number of pubs in the city. On his second tour, he discovered that it was also replete with jewellery shops. They ranged from small establishments tucked away in a quiet corner to larger businesses in prime positions on major streets. Leeming worked his way through them systematically. He came to one that was owned by Jeremy Hargreaves and Son. When he entered the premises, the elderly, bald-headed man behind the counter recoiled from the sight of his face.

'May I help you, sir?' he asked, guardedly.

'I hope so. I'm Detective Sergeant Leeming and I've come from Scotland Yard to investigate the murder that took place recently on a train.'

'Then you're most welcome,' said the other, relaxing. 'I'm Jeremy Hargreaves. If there's any way in which I can help you, I'll be glad to do so.'

'The murder victim was robbed of everything he had on him. Among the items stolen was a gold pocket watch and a gold wedding ring, both of which we understand were of the very best quality. We suspect that the killer might try to sell the items.'

'Well, he didn't attempt to do so here, Sergeant.'

'Oh, I see.'

'Thieves have come here in the past,' recalled Hargreaves. 'When they've asked for a valuation, I've deliberately given them such a low figure that they've gone elsewhere. I, meanwhile, have sent word to the police station that someone is trying to sell what is patently stolen property. As a result, more than one criminal has been caught in the act, so to speak.'

'I wish that all jewellers were as helpful as you, sir.'

'We have standards to maintain. Others in the same trade are not quite so careful with whom they do business. Their sole aim is to make a profit on everything they buy or sell.'

'Yes,' said Leeming. 'Of the six jewellers I've visited so far, you're the only one who will turn a thief away, then report him to the police. I'd like to shake your hand, sir.'

'It's my pleasure, Sergeant.'

After a warm handshake, Leeming left the shop and paused to consider his situation. He put himself in the position of the killer and wondered what he would do with the stolen items. Trying to sell them so soon after the crime would be a mistake, he decided. There was an intense search for the man who strangled Giles Blanchard, and it was led by a famous detective. Any sensible criminal would bide his time until it was safe to offer the items to a jeweller. Having reached that decision, Leeming abandoned his search and headed back to the Hope and Anchor.

When he entered the pub, he was disappointed that his efforts had been fruitless, but his spirits soon lifted. The landlord handed him a letter from Lieutenant Luke Shorter. The frown on Leeming's face was soon replaced by a hopeful smile.

Madeleine Colbeck was still in the drawing room with Lydia Quayle when there was a knock on the front door. As soon as she heard the door being opened by a servant, she recognised the voice of the visitor. Excusing herself, she went quickly into the hall to welcome Alan Hinton. She could see from the smile on his face that he had brought good news.

'Has Robert sent for you?' she asked.

'No,' he replied, 'but the superintendent decided that I was needed. He went to Portsmouth himself and saw the scale of the problem.'

'Congratulations, Alan!'

'It has lifted my spirits, I must confess. Since I will be seeing the inspector . . .'

'Yes, yes, I'd love you to take a letter from me. I'll write it at once.'

'Keep it short, please. I must be on my way.'

'Wait in the drawing room,' suggested Madeleine. 'You might find that you have more time than you imagined.'

She waited long enough to hear Lydia's cry of delight then she slipped away.

An incident on a train late at night had changed their lives. Having set out to rob an unwary passenger, they had ended up instead with his dead body. The man had adjusted swiftly to the situation, but his companion was still haunted by what had happened.

'I'll never forget that terrible noise he made,' she confessed.

'I had no choice. If I hadn't been there to rescue you, imagine what would have happened.'

'That very thought has been keeping me awake at night.'

'The memory will soon fade, my love,' he promised.

'I don't think that it will ever disappear.'

'Console yourself with the thought of what we've gained. Thanks to the notebook we stole from him, we have a new way to make money – a new and much safer way. You don't have to entice a stranger now.'

'That's true. I hated those guzzling kisses I had to put up with.'

'Forget that period of our lives,' he advised. 'We have an easier way to make money now.'

'I know and I'm so grateful.'

'Two hundred pounds is already in our grasp, and we'll have the same amount from Mrs Falconbridge each month. What could be simpler?'

'It doesn't stop me thinking about Mr Blanchard. You murdered him.'

'He deserved it. So let me never hear you speak of that vile man again. Yes, we're being hunted by the police, but they have no idea who we are or where we are.' He hugged her. 'Didn't you enjoy that meal we had to celebrate?'

'I loved it.'

'We can dine in style more often from now on.'

'Yes – we've earned it.'

'Always remember that. I promised you that we could have a good life together,' he said, 'and I've kept that promise, haven't I?'

'Yes, you have,' she agreed, kissing him softly on the lips. 'It's the reason I love you.'

Robert Colbeck had been on the Isle of Wight a few times, but he had still not set eyes on the royal residence, Osborne House. He took a cab to a position from which he had a good view of the property. It was an arresting sight and he got out to study it. Colbeck knew that it had been designed by Prince Albert and Thomas Cubitt in the style of an Italianate villa.

The fact that the royal family had elected to spend time on the island increased its popularity, and brought visitors in their thousands.

Letting his gaze drift from one aspect to another of the house, Colbeck admired it for a long time, noting that, for all its quirky magnificence, it was essentially a home and not a palace. His attention was then diverted by the sound of an approaching carriage. He caught a glimpse of the passenger in the vehicle and felt a thrill of recognition. It was Tennyson, a dark, bearded man in his fifties. As a great admirer of his, Colbeck was delighted to see the Poet Laureate in the flesh, clearly on his way to Osborne House.

'Thank you for your message,' said Leeming as they shook hands. 'Is it true that someone's uniform was stolen?'

'Yes,' replied Shorter. 'The victim was Lieutenant Whiting. He was very angry when he discovered the theft.'

'When did it take place?'

'Four or five days ago.'

'Did someone break into his lodging?'

'He wouldn't give me the precise details. Whiting was still pulsing with anger. Uniforms are expensive items to replace. He wanted the thief to be keel-hauled.'

'You have to catch him first, sir.'

Leeming was delighted with the news. Having left the dockyard dejected after his earlier visit, he now had grounds for optimism. There was no guarantee that it was Blanchard's killer who had stolen the uniform, but Leeming felt that it was a strong possibility. The man they were after was not a genuine naval officer. He was an impostor in a stolen uniform.

'Is it possible for me to meet Lieutenant Whiting?' he asked.

'No, it isn't,' said Shorter.

'But it would be helpful to know where he was when his uniform was stolen.'

'Really, Sergeant! You're a detective, aren't you? When is the best time to steal someone's uniform?'

Leeming snapped his fingers. 'When he's not wearing it.'

'Exactly.'

'In that case, the lieutenant must have been at home with his wife.'

'He is not married.'

Leeming's heart sank. 'Oh, I see.'

'But he had been at sea for months,' said Shorter. 'When he stepped ashore at the start of the week, he might have felt the need for female company.'

'Do you mean that he . . . ?'

'Don't even think of searching the brothels of Portsmouth. There are far too many of them, and, in any case, you might be led astray.'

Berwyn Rees had confirmed what Colbeck already knew. Giles Blanchard was a man with a keen interest in the opposite sex. It had prompted him to be unfaithful to his wife on more than one occasion. His son's denials were based on a natural urge to protect his father's reputation. Colbeck felt that it was time to confront him on the issue. Driven back to the house, he was admitted by a servant and went into the hall. Paul Blanchard came out of the drawing room in surprise and glared at his visitor.

'What brings you back here, Inspector?' he demanded.

'If we could have a moment alone, sir, I'll be happy to tell you.'

'Let's go into the study.'

Colbeck noticed that the door had to be unlocked. Evidently, the study was out of bounds to anyone but Blanchard's son. When they went into the room, the man turned to confront him.

'Do you really have to bother us again?' he asked.

'I wanted to give you an opportunity to correct the lie you told me earlier, sir.'

'What lie?'

'You were outraged at the suggestion that your father might have taken an interest in other women.'

Blanchard was livid. 'Do you dare to question my word?'

'I have proof that it was a barefaced lie, sir.'

'It was the truth, Inspector, and I stand ready to defend my father against the blatant falsehoods of his detractors.'

'Actually,' said Colbeck, 'the proof I'm talking about was provided by one of his best friends. Sergeant Leeming had a long talk with Douglas Collier at the man's home. He admitted allowing your father to make use of his house whenever he had a . . . companion for the night.'

'That's arrant nonsense!'

'We are inclined to believe the gentleman.'

'Mr Collier is a whisky-sodden old fool,' said Blanchard. 'If he is trying to blacken my father's name, I'll have him sued for slander.'

'As a former barrister, sir, I would advise against it. You would certainly lose the case.' He lowered his voice. 'I do not blame you for trying to defend your father's reputation, sir, but it's a stance you must abandon.' He glanced at the pile of documents on the desk. 'Since you needed the services of a locksmith to open the drawers in your father's desk, something of importance was hidden away. You had sight of it. My guess is that you were duly shocked and refused to believe the evidence of your own eyes.'

'My father was a man with high moral standards.'

'Whenever he was with the family, I'm sure that that was the case. But his fondness for the Haven Club took him to Chichester on a regular basis. He had more freedom there.'

'I don't have to listen to this,' said Blanchard, turning away.

'Then you weaken our chances of solving your father's murder. Your father's attitude towards women is a crucial element in the investigation. Until you accept that he was not a species of saint, we will be hampered.'

'I fail to see how.'

'That's because you don't want to see it, sir. All the evidence that we have gathered points to the fact that Mr Blanchard was the victim of a woman's charms. My belief is that you already know that in your heart. Indeed,' said Colbeck, pointing to the documents on the desk, 'you may have discovered the uncomfortable truth – discovered it and destroyed the evidence.'

'It's none of your business.'

'If you refuse to help us, sir, please don't hinder us.'

'What I learnt about my father was . . . irrelevant.'

'Did you find the names of any . . . female friends?'

'No, Inspector.'

'Would you swear to that on the Holy Bible?'

'Yes!' affirmed Blanchard.

Colbeck met his gaze and held it. He saw the anger in Blanchard's eyes slowly die away.

The man's head fell to his chest. The Bible would not be needed.

After apologising to the Queen for his lateness and for the absence of his wife, Tennyson was taken into the drawing room by Her Majesty. Chairs had been set out in rows for the guests. Queen and poet sat beside each other in the front row. Other rows were filled with friends who loved the occasional entertainments at Osborne House. The Queen leant slightly towards the Poet Laureate.

'We are to be favoured with a new and exciting young actress,' she said. 'Her name is Mrs Scott-Siddons. I leave you to guess from which theatrical family she is descended.'

'Might she be related to the illustrious Sarah Siddons?' he asked.

'She is indeed, and she follows in her great-grandmother's footsteps. Earlier this year, her debut as Portia in *The Merchant of Venice* was well received by audiences and by critics. I felt impelled to invite her to read your poetry in front of a select audience.'

'I look forward to hearing her, Your Majesty.'

It was not long before the actress appeared to a polite ripple of applause. She curtseyed in response then took up her position. Mary Frances Scott-Siddons was a beautiful woman with a trim figure, a melodious voice, and a surprising confidence for one so young. After opening the book, she began to read *The Lady of Shalott*, investing it with great poignance. Tennyson was entranced.

He knew that the poem was a favourite of the Queen and could see how moved Her Majesty was by the recitation. The closing stanza plucked at his heart.

Who is this? and what is here?
And in the lighted palace near
Died the sound of royal cheer;
And they cross'd themselves for fear,
All the knights at Camelot
But Lancelot mused a little space;
He said, 'She has a lovely face;

God in his mercy lend her grace,
The Lady of Shalott.'

The applause was long and well deserved. There were tears in the eyes of the Queen and the poet himself was moved and astonished. He had never heard his work read with such clarity of interpretation. At the rear of the assembly sat Gwendoline Cardus, doing her best to hide the swirl of emotions inside her.

CHAPTER TWELVE

When he caught the steamer back to the mainland, Colbeck was able to talk to Brendan Mulryne once again. As a result, the crossing seemed to be over in seconds. Musing on what he had learnt on the island, the inspector walked briskly back to the Hope and Anchor. He was pleased to find Victor Leeming there, seated at a table and consulting his notebook.

'I hope that you're reviewing the valuable evidence you've gathered,' he said, sitting down opposite the sergeant. 'How did you get on?'

'Not as well as I'd hoped, sir.'

'Why not?'

'After calling on several jewellers to no avail, I stopped to wonder if the killer would try to get rid of the stolen items so soon. If he did so, he'd be taking an unnecessary chance. I think that he's much more likely to wait until the crime had faded in the memory.'

'Or,' said Colbeck, 'he'd try to sell the watch and the ring in a different city.'

'That's a possibility, of course.'

'You may have to go further afield, Victor.'

'But there's been another development.'

'Tell me more,' invited Colbeck.

'I had a summons from Lieutenant Shorter . . .'

He went on to describe his second visit to the dockyard and how it had raised his hopes.

After listening carefully, Colbeck voiced his doubt.

'It's possible that the killer stole the lieutenant's uniform, but it's by no means certain.'

'Where else would he get that uniform except from someone in the navy?'

'I can think of one obvious place – a theatre.'

Leeming sagged. 'I never thought of that.'

'On that walk we had in the city, we went past the Theatre Royal. I daresay that they keep costumes of all sorts there – including those of naval lieutenants.'

'You're right, sir.'

'I still think that you are more likely to find a jeweller who bought a gold wedding ring and pocket watch. He might give you a description of the person who brought the items. You won't get that sort of information at the theatre. If they have had a naval costume stolen, they will have no idea who the thief was.'

Leeming was deflated. 'Oh – that's true.'

'Don't be disheartened, Victor. I feel that we've made a small advance today.'

'I wish that I felt that. What did you discover?'

'I heard about a pretty young Welsh girl named Eluned.'

'Who?'

'She is Mr Rees's niece.'

He told Leeming about his second visit to the estate agent and how Rees had confirmed that Giles Blanchard was not the contented married man he seemed. On the strength of what he'd learnt, Colbeck had returned to the home of Giles Blanchard and challenged his son about his father's private life. After outright denials, Paul Blanchard had finally been forced to admit that his revered father had been unfaithful to his wife. The confession was an important step forward.

'What do we do next, sir?' asked Leeming.

'We eliminate one possibility.'

'How can we do that?'

'By going to the theatre this very evening.'

'But there'll be a performance there.'

'We are going to watch it, Victor. Before it starts, I'll ask the manager if the company has had the uniform of a naval lieutenant stolen from their wardrobe. In short, we will be mixing work with pleasure before returning to supper here.'

'What play are we going to see?'

'It's Mr Sheridan's delightful comedy, *The Rivals*.'

'I've heard of that.'

'I can't promise you any naval costumes,' said Colbeck, 'but you will see a member of our gallant army. The hero of the play is Captain Jack Absolute.'

The performance at Osborne House had been a great success. Mrs Scott-Siddons was given an ovation. As the guests filed out, they were able to thank the Queen for their invitation and praise the poet whose work had given them such pleasure. When they had all departed, the Queen was left alone with Gwendoline Cardus.

'I think that her great-grandmother would have been delighted with her, Gwendoline. She was quite faultless.'

'I agree, Your Majesty,' said the other. 'She didn't simply read the poems, she brought out their full meaning. There were times when she lifted her eyes from the book and delivered whole stanzas she had learnt by heart.'

'Mr Tennyson was delighted with her – and he was our guest of honour.'

'All in all, it was a splendid occasion in every way.'

'It will be difficult to match it,' said the Queen. 'Mrs Scott-Siddons told me that she would be more than happy to perform here again, but with talent such as hers, she will be in constant demand in the theatre.'

'Quite right, Your Majesty.'

The Queen looked at her closely for the first time and noticed something.

'Your eyes are rather red, Gwendoline,' she said. 'Are you unwell?'

'No, no, I feel fine.'

'You look as if you've been crying.'

'Mine were not the only tears shed this afternoon,' said Gwendoline. 'Everyone of us was deeply moved by what are sublime poems. It's a tribute to Mr Tennyson that his work can provoke such a reaction, Your Majesty. It had a powerful effect on me.'

Paul Blanchard and his wife dined together that evening. Verity had tried to persuade her mother-in-law to join them but the latter had turned down the invitation, preferring to mourn in private.

'Why did Inspector Colbeck come back a second time?' asked Verity.

'There was something he wished to check. I forget what it was.'

'I find that surprising.'

'Why?' he asked.

'Well, his second visit obviously had a profound effect on you.'

'You're quite mistaken, Verity.'

'I could see it in your face – and hear it in your voice. It worries me.'

'There is no need for you to worry. The inspector and I had a brief chat then he went on his way. His second visit was something of a nuisance, but it didn't upset me.'

'I know you too well, Paul. When you are troubled, I recognise the signs.'

He was evasive. 'Let's talk about something else, shall we?'

'I'm curious about what happened, that's all.'

'Well, you've no reason to be curious,' he said, sharply. 'Please change the subject.'

'There's no need to speak to me like that,' she said, offended by his tone. 'I'm entitled to ask a simple question, surely. What's going on, Paul?'

He needed a few moments to calm down. When he spoke, he was apologetic.

'I didn't mean to snap at you like that, but I'm mourning the death of my father and his murder is always at the forefront of my mind. Even though he is trying to solve the crime, the inspector somehow unnerves me. He keeps prying into our family history in a way that has no relevance to the investigation.' He offered his hand, and she took it. 'But that's no reason to speak harshly to my dear wife, who has been such a wonderful support to me through these dark days.'

'I forgive you. I should be more understanding.'

'And I should be grateful for the immense help you've given me.' He smiled at her. 'Please forgive my occasional lapses, Verity. From now on, I'll try to keep my temper under control.'

Victor Leeming felt extremely uncomfortable in the foyer of the Theatre Royal. People looked at his bruised face and decided that he had been hired to throw out unruly patrons. Robert Colbeck, by contrast, was completely at ease. He loved to watch plays, and, in his limited free time, he tried to fit in an occasional visit with his wife to a theatre. What troubled Leeming was that the inspector had left him alone while he went off to speak to the manager in the latter's office. The sergeant was grateful when he reappeared.

'Well?' he asked.

'They have had things stolen from here,' said Colbeck, 'but the uniform of a naval officer is not among them.'

'So there's no reason for us to be here, sir.'

'There's a very good reason, Victor. Ever since we've been here, we've worked hard for long hours. I think that we deserve a rest. It will take our minds off the case that brought us here and enable us to enjoy the sheer pleasure of laughter.'

'I'm not in the mood for laughter,' said Leeming, gloomily.

'You soon will be.'

'How do you know?'

'Because you're about to see one of the finest comedies ever written. Also, you will do so in a darkened theatre and will therefore not feel so self-conscious about your appearance.'

'I'll be grateful for that, sir.'

'Look out for Mrs Malaprop.'

'Who is she?'

'You'll soon find out,' said Colbeck. 'If she doesn't

make you roar with laughter, then I'll apologise for dragging you here. Oh, and keep an eye open for Sir Anthony Absolute.'

'Why?'

'He's a peppery old man who might remind you of someone you know very well.'

Alan Hinton whiled away the train journey by thinking about his chance meeting with Lydia Quayle. Having expected to stay for minutes at the Colbeck residence, he had been there for over two hours. It meant that he caught a much later train than planned, arriving in Portsmouth in the evening. When he reached the Hope and Anchor, he was hoping to find his colleagues there, but the landlord told him that Colbeck and Leeming would not return until later. Hinton therefore left his luggage in his room and went out to explore the city. Since his mind was still fixed on Lydia, he saw very little of it.

After the earlier argument with his wife, Paul Blanchard was on his best behaviour. He was quiet and attentive during the meal, allowing his wife to do most of the talking and agreeing with the various suggestions she made. For her part, Verity was careful to keep away from any subject that might be contentious, talking instead about details of the funeral.

'When can we decide on the date?' she asked.

'When the police give us permission,' he told her, 'and that will be soon. Once it's in our possession, we can start to make plans. I've already made a preliminary list of people who need to be contacted.'

'I'll be happy to write the invitation cards for you, Paul.'

'Thank you.'

'And, of course, I'll expect to look after your mother on the day itself.'

'That will take a great load off my mind.'

'Have you spoken to the vicar about the service?'

'Not yet,' he said, 'but I've arranged to see him early next week.'

'Good.' She heaved a sigh. 'I'll be so glad when it's all over.'

'So will I, Verity. But the funeral is only one ordeal we must face. There's still the wait for the arrest of the man who murdered my father. Inspector Colbeck is confident that he will soon be identified and caught, but I don't share his optimism.' He clenched a fist. 'I want a clear sign of progress.'

On their walk back from the theatre, Victor Leeming could not stop laughing. He kept repeating some of his favourite lines from the play, and telling Colbeck that he thought Mrs Malaprop was the funniest woman he'd ever seen on a stage.

'It was an excellent company,' said Colbeck. 'Sheridan would have loved the performance.'

'Not as much as me!'

Leeming was still chuckling when they got back to

the Hope and Anchor, and found Alan Hinton waiting for them.

'What on earth are you doing here, Alan?' asked Leeming.

'The superintendent felt that you needed another pair of hands.'

'We could certainly do with another pair of feet,' said Colbeck. 'There's a lot of leg work to do before we solve this case. Welcome to Portsmouth, Alan!'

'Thank you, sir.'

'Join us for supper and we can discuss the case.'

'The superintendent has already given me the bare bones.'

'I'll put some flesh on them,' Colbeck promised.

'Talking of the superintendent,' said Leeming, 'we've just seen someone very like him in a play. Sir Anthony Absolute was bristling with anger. Does that remind you of someone?'

Hinton grinned. 'Yes, it does.'

'Superintendent Tallis sometimes has good cause to be angry,' Colbeck reminded them.

'Nothing sparks his rage so much as a failed investigation. Let's do our best to avoid that by getting up early tomorrow and tackling this case with renewed energy.'

When he walked into the bedroom next morning, she was combing out one of her wigs with an almost wistful expression on her face.

'You won't be needing that, my love,' he said.

'It's a pity in some ways. This was my favourite. I miss wearing it.'

'Those days are behind us. Thanks to Blanchard's address book, we have an easier way to make money now. There's no physical danger involved.'

'That is a relief,' she agreed. 'Who is our next victim?'

'Mrs Emily Venn. She lives on the Isle of Wight, so we won't have to travel by train.'

'How did such a repulsive man attract so many women?'

'I suspect that his bank balance had a lot to do with it,' he said. 'Perhaps he showered them with gifts or actually paid them.'

'The first two were married and so is Mrs Venn. Why did he always pick on someone's wife?'

'He looked for women who were vulnerable. Mrs Lenham's husband was very much older than her, and clearly not in good health. Blanchard supplied an excitement that his wife did not get at home.'

'That's a possible explanation, I suppose.'

'Mrs Falconbridge had an absent husband, so she must have felt very lonely.'

'I watched her kneeling in prayer in that church,' she recalled. 'I didn't get the impression that she was confessing her sins. What I saw was a woman who had lost someone very close to her. Imagine the shock she must have had when she discovered her lover had been murdered.'

'Don't waste any sympathy on her.'

'I won't. She betrayed her husband.'

'And she now lives in fear that he will find out – unless she guarantees our silence, that is.'

'What sort of woman will Mrs Venn be, I wonder?'

'A very foolish one. She let that ogre share a bed with her – several times, according to his notebook. Blanchard probably had a beautiful wife,' he said. 'Why on earth did he have to prey on other women? And there's another question to ask. What will his family think of him, if they ever learn the sordid truth?'

After the shocking discovery he had made the previous day, Paul Blanchard entered his father's study with some trepidation. He glanced down at the grate where he had burnt the letters which had destroyed his faith in a man he had worshipped. He looked at the framed photographs that stood on the desk. They showed his father playing cricket, beaming at his wife on their wedding anniversary, and staring at the camera with his grandchildren. That was the man whom everyone thought they knew. His son had discovered his father's secret life and been repelled. One question now tormented him.

What sort of face could he possibly wear at the funeral? He would have to listen to a long line of mourners, telling him what a wonderful man his father had been. It would put him under immense pressure. The funeral would be a continuous ordeal.

* * *

Victor Leeming and Alan Hinton walked to the railway station together, but they caught trains that went in opposite directions. Colbeck had decided that they were more likely to trace a gold ring and pocket watch than a stolen naval uniform. He ordered both detectives to visit jewellery shops in places that could be reached by rail, reasoning that the killer would, in all probability, dispose of the items by catching a train to somewhere within easy reach. Leeming went off with happy memories of his visit to the theatre on the previous evening while Hinton was still excited by the idea that he was now part of a murder investigation.

Colbeck, meanwhile, took the ferry once more to the Isle of Wight. It meant that he had the pleasure of another chat with Brendan Mulryne.

'Bejasus!' said the Irishman, laughing. 'You're on this steamer more often than I am.'

'The difference is,' Colbeck pointed out, 'that you get paid for being here, while I need to buy a ticket. That's not a complaint, mind you. If I can run a killer to ground, I don't care how many times I sail to and from the island.'

'You've got the patience of Job.'

'It's something I've had to develop over the years.'

'How long before you make an arrest?'

'It will be sooner rather than later, I hope.'

'Well, I wouldn't like to be in the killer's shoes. I bet that he started sweating the moment he learnt that Inspector Colbeck was on his tail.'

'I disagree, Brendan. I fancy that he and his accomplice

believe they are quite safe. It's the reason that I know they are still living in Portsmouth.'

'I wish I had instincts like yours.'

'They rarely let me down.'

'What's Victor doing this morning?'

'He's hunting for some items stolen from the murder victim,' said Colbeck. 'He and another detective are trawling through a long list of jewellery shops.'

'I still think that we could have got more money for that ring and the pocket watch,' she said. 'You accepted the first amount you were offered.'

'It was the best thing to do,' he argued. 'I got rid of items that were of no use to us, and we received a reasonable price for them.'

'I'm not so sure about that. We should have gone to three or four other jewellery shops for an estimate.'

'I disagree. It's not as if we're short of cash. Blanchard was very generous to us.'

'He was a rich man. Look at the money he lavished on his women.'

'I daresay that he had to buy their favours. We'll reap the benefits.'

'What do you think Mrs Venn will be like?' she asked.

'I think she'll be as weak and stupid as the others,' he predicted. 'Imagine how she must feel now that Blanchard is dead. She'll be in mourning.'

* * *

Emily Venn was a rather plain, fleshy woman in her thirties who wore a corset to disguise her bulk. After waving off her husband, she went upstairs to the master bedroom. Once inside, she locked the door behind her. She then moved to the bed and reached under the mattress to take out an envelope. Folded up inside it was a page from a local newspaper. With trembling hands, she unfolded it and winced involuntarily when she read the headline MURDER ON THE TRAIN. Emily had read it dozens of times, but its impact had not faded. She felt the same dizziness and the same searing sense of loss she had experienced the first time she saw the news. Giles Blanchard had been cruelly strangled to death. The consequences for her were frightening.

If her husband ever found out how she had betrayed him, he would throw her out of the house and stop her from having any contact with the children. Her friends would also shun her, and she would be a social outcast. There was nothing in her own home that would give her away, but she had less certainty about her lover's abode. When she sent him a letter of thanks for the magical times they shared together, she assumed that he would destroy it. What if he did not do so? Supposing his son found the letter? Emily had foolishly signed her name, and he might work out who she was. It would be a calamity for her. She felt sick at the very thought.

Her husband had already noticed slight changes in her appearance and behaviour. He suggested that she should see a doctor, but she would not hear of it. Emily had made a conscious effort to appear and sound like her old self, forcing a smile and treating her husband with more than her usual care and concern. It was only when she was alone that she could brood on what had happened. Giles Blanchard had noticed that there was something missing in her life, and he had stepped in to provide it, giving her an excitement that she had never known with her husband. When they had been alone together, nothing else mattered.

Everything mattered now.

'You'd better come into the study, Inspector,' said Blanchard, leading the way.

'Thank you, sir,' said Colbeck, following him into the room.

'Do you have any news?'

'I'm afraid not.'

'Then why are you pestering me again?'

Blanchard closed the door and waved his visitor to a seat. He himself sat behind the desk.

'I'm sorry that you feel I am pestering you, sir,' said Colbeck. 'It's not my intention. All my efforts are focussed on the search for your father's killer. That should at least earn me a degree of politeness when I happen to call.'

'Of course, of course,' apologised Blanchard. 'Please forgive me.'

'Yesterday, you made a discovery that must have hit you like a punch. You learnt about an aspect of your father's life that made you look at him in a very different way.'

'I was stunned, Inspector.'

'That's understandable, sir.'

'I refused to believe it at first – then I read those letters he'd hoarded.'

'It's about those that I came.'

'You're too late. I burnt every one of them.'

'But not before reading them, I hope.'

'I forced myself to read every single word.'

'Then you will also have seen the names of the women who wrote those letters.'

'All that they used were their Christian names – though anything less Christian than that type of missive is hard to imagine.'

'Yet they must have been written with love,' suggested Colbeck.

'There was more lust than love, Inspector. It was revolting.'

'Can you remember any of the names?'

Blanchard was puzzled. 'Why on earth would you want to know?'

'Because one of those women might give me valuable information about what happened on the night of his murder. Had he spent time with one of them before he got on that train?'

'I've no wish to know!'

'Well, I do, sir. If we can identify any of these women, I need to warn them.'

'I'd much rather that you arrested the hussies.'

'They might be in danger,' Colbeck pointed out. 'If your father kept their letters, he might also have kept a record of their addresses. The killer stole everything from him. If he gained access to the names of those women, he would be able to blackmail them. Are you following me, sir?'

'I think so,' said Blanchard.

'If we can trace one or more of them, these women might lead us to the killer. We can lay a trap for the time when he comes to receive payment for his silence.'

'Those women deserve to be blackmailed! Let them suffer.'

'Don't you want your father's killer to be caught?'

'Of course, I do.'

'Then we need to seek help from wherever we can find it. Now,' said Colbeck, 'try to recall the names, please. It's vital for you to do so.'

'I suppose that it is,' muttered Blanchard.

'Think hard, sir. You may have important evidence.'

He got his first glimpse of Emily Venn through a telescope and was unimpressed. Even from that distance, he was able to see that she lacked any obvious allurements.

'What is she like?' she asked.

He handed her the telescope. 'See for yourself.'

She studied the woman for a full minute then clicked her tongue.

'That's not her,' she decided.

'Yes, it is.'

'But she's as plain as a pikestaff.'

'Not everyone can be as beautiful as you,' he said. 'When I first saw her, she was giving orders to a servant. That's why I'm certain that she's Mrs Venn.'

'It doesn't say much for Blanchard's taste in women.'

'Be fair to him. Mrs Lenham was pretty, and you said that Mrs Falconbridge had a kind of bruised charm. Clearly, he chose them for their looks. Mrs Venn obviously had other qualities that appealed to him. I'll be interested to find out what they are.'

'What are we going to do?'

'First, we must get closer. It looks as if she is going to stay in the garden for a while.'

'That's good. I may get the opportunity to approach her.'

'Show no mercy,' he urged. 'Make her pay.'

CHAPTER THIRTEEN

When he arrived at the house that morning, Caleb Andrews was given a warm welcome. His daughter opened the front door to let him in, then she kissed him on the cheek. Before he could even speak, Helena Rose came running down the stairs with whoops of joy and threw herself into his arms. After hugging her, he stepped back and saw the book in her hand.

'What have you got there?' he asked.

'Auntie Lydia gave it to me,' she replied, excitedly. 'It's got poems in it. I've already learnt some of them.'

'Clever girl!'

'Would you like to hear one?'

'I'm sure that he would,' said Madeleine. 'Grandad would love to listen to every poem you know by heart. But not just now, sweetheart. Give him time to get his breath back. Grandad will come up to the nursery very soon.'

'That's a promise,' he added.

'Don't be long,' said the child.

As she scampered off upstairs, Andrews looked fondly after her.

'She's growing up so quickly,' he observed. 'I don't remember you being as tall as that at the same age, Maddy.'

'No, I shot up when I was a bit older.'

'Any word from Robert?'

'The post hasn't been delivered yet,' she said, 'but I have some news. Alan Hinton called in yesterday. He is joining the investigation.'

'About time, too!'

'It was the superintendent's idea.'

'Robert will make good use of him. Alan is a real asset.'

'He was so delighted to be sent off to Portsmouth,' said Madeleine. 'He always finds that working with Robert is so exhilarating.'

Having visited six jewellery shops in succession, Hinton's earlier excitement had faded slightly. But he pressed on regardless, hoping that he would soon find a place where the stolen items had been offered for sale. As he entered the next shop, he was given a welcome smile by the owner, a slim, elegant man in his fifties with thinning hair.

'Good morning, sir,' he said. 'What can I do for you?'

'With luck,' replied Hinton, 'you might be able to assist a murder investigation.'

'Heavens! How on earth can I do that?'

Hinton explained who he was and why he was trawling jewellery shops. The owner was intrigued by the idea that he might be instrumental in helping to track down a killer.

'As it happens,' he said, 'I did have someone in here yesterday, offering to sell something.'

'Was it a man or a woman?'

'It was a woman, actually.'

'And what did she wish to sell? Was it a gold wedding ring and a pocket watch?'

'No, it wasn't,' said the man. 'It was a ruby necklace belonging to her late grandmother.'

Hinton sighed with disappointment. 'But if someone turns up to offer me the items that you mentioned, I'll get in touch with you at once. Tell me where I can find you.'

Because it was such a sensitive matter, Colbeck was patient. For several minutes, he watched Blanchard trying to remember the names of the women who had signed the letters sent to his father. The effort was telling on the man. Forced to acknowledge his father's rampant adultery, Blanchard was torn between embarrassment and disgust. He jotted a few names on a pad then crossed one out and wrote a similar name in its place.

'This is the best I can do,' he muttered. 'I was so keen to get rid of them that I didn't memorise the names. All I can give you are vague guesses.'

'That's a starting point,' said Colbeck, taking out his notebook. 'What's the first name?'

'I'm not sure, Inspector. It began with "A" but the rest of the signature was a squiggle. I suppose that "A" could stand for . . . Alice? Anne, maybe?'

'It could equally well stand for Abigail, Adelaide, Agnes, Andrea and so on. Can you think of any woman in your father's circle with a name that begins with "A"?'

'No, I can't, I'm afraid.'

'What else have you remembered?'

'There was one that began with "C" and looked like Chris.'

'That might be Christine, I suppose,' said Colbeck. 'Do you know anyone of that name?'

Blanchard shrugged. 'No, I don't.'

'Think hard, sir. Might she be a client of yours, perhaps?'

'Very few women buy a house, Inspector. Some of our clients do bring their wives with them, but, for obvious reasons, the purchaser tends to be a man.'

'Yes, of course.'

'I find this so painful,' confessed Blanchard. 'I just

wanted to get those letters out of my sight and out of my mind. That's why I burnt them.'

'You weren't to know that you might be destroying valuable evidence, sir. The women who sent those letters did so out of love. I daresay that you despise every one of them, but I have some sympathy for them. What they did was wrong,' said Colbeck, 'but they are paying a heavy price for it. Imagine how they must have felt when they heard about your father's murder.'

'I don't give a damn for their feelings, Inspector!'

'That's understandable, sir.'

'Those women led my father astray. I despise them.'

'I see that you jotted down two other names,' said Colbeck, peering at the pad.

'It's the two signature that were actually legible.'

'What are these women's names?'

'The first one is called Marigold,' said Blanchard. 'She had an educated hand.'

'What about the other woman?'

'Her name is Emily.'

Emily Venn was seated on the veranda in her garden, oblivious to the breeze that disturbed the curls on her head. Lost in contemplation, she was unaware that someone had just let herself into the garden and was approaching her. It was only when the newcomer's shadow fell across her that Emily realised that she was not alone.

'Mrs Venn?' asked the visitor.

'That's right.'

'Mrs Emily Venn?'

'Yes, that's my name. Who are you?'

'You don't need to know my name,' said the woman. 'I've come to discuss your friendship with Giles Blanchard.' Emily's jaw dropped. 'We know how close you and he were, Mrs Venn. In fact, we know the exact number of times that the two of you slept together.'

'Who are you?' she asked, eyes full of terror.

'I'm someone who can keep a secret – at a price, that is.'

'What do you mean?'

'I mean that, unless we can come to an arrangement, your husband will become rudely aware of the fact that his wife was in the arms of another man on eleven different occasions.' She smiled. 'True or false?'

Emily was trembling with fear. Someone knew her secret. She was helpless.

'How much do you want?' she gulped.

While Hinton had travelled east by train, Leeming had gone in a westerly direction. The latter was full of confidence at the outset, certain that one of them would have a successful search. After barren visits to a sequence of jewellery shops, however, his optimism had slowly drained away. Travelling on to Southampton, he took a cab to the main street and went into a jewellery shop without any real hope of success. His arrival caused an upset. Seeing his face, the middle-aged man behind the counter backed away in fear. Leeming reassured him.

'Don't be frightened, sir,' he said. 'I am Detective Sergeant Leeming from Scotland Yard, and I am hoping that you will be able to help us with our murder investigation.'

'Oh, I see.' The man relaxed. 'Are you talking about that case in Portsmouth?'

'That's the one. The victim's name was Giles Blanchard.'

'How can I possibly help you?'

'Am I speaking to the owner of the shop?'

'Yes,' said the other. 'My name is Cyril Underwood.'

'Has anyone come in here in recent days and tried to sell you items of jewellery?'

'Yes, they have, Sergeant. Two people came here to sell and three wanted an estimate for the jewellery they brought with them.'

'Tell me about the customers who brought something to sell.'

'The first one's name was a Mr Farrar. In the wake of his wife's death, he wanted to sell her necklace, and use the money to purchase something for their daughter. Everything was above board. He accepted my valuation and spent the money on a beautiful brooch.'

'What about the other customer?'

'His name was Mr Cullen. I've done business with him before. He brought a bracelet that his wife no longer

191

wore. I'm sorry, Sergeant,' he added. 'I'd have loved to be instrumental in the capture of a killer, but I simply can't help you.'

Colbeck was gently persistent. While he recognised how painful it was to discuss Paul Blanchard's father with him, he was compelled to do so. Until they could make direct contact with one or more of the women involved with the older man, they could not get the vital details they needed. Though he found the whole exercise distasteful, Blanchard searched his memory for the names of those who had written to his father.

'I've remembered something at last,' he said, slapping his thigh. 'One of the women was not called Christine at all. I'm almost certain that her name was Christina.'

'Thank you, sir,' said Colbeck. 'We now have an Emily, a Marigold, a Christina and someone whose name begins with 'A' to find.'

'I know nobody with any of those names. They're complete strangers. When the desk drawers were finally unlocked, I found a lot of documents hidden away in them but no address book.'

'In all probability, your father had it on him, hence my concern for the women listed. In the wrong hands, it could make them easy targets. I suppose that the address book couldn't be hidden somewhere else in the house?'

'No, Inspector. I searched.'

'What about the safe at his office?'

'I've been through that as well.'

'Then we must assume that the address book is in someone else's hands. The women listed in there are in danger. After the loss of a man they loved, they will now have to contend with someone making financial demands on them.'

'It serves them right!'

'Your attitude is understandable, sir,' said Colbeck with diminishing patience, 'but I can't make any moral judgements about these individuals. I simply want to rescue them from the danger of blackmail and arrest the man who strangled your father to death.'

'I'd be grateful if you could do that soon, Inspector.'

'The only promise that I can make is that we will work tirelessly to get the result that we all desire. Meanwhile,' said Colbeck, 'please continue to think hard about the names you saw on those letters. We simply must identify them.'

'They led my father astray!' howled Blanchard. 'They deserve to suffer.'

'That depends on how you choose to view them, sir. Were these women predatory females who lured an unsuspecting man – or were they instead his victims? Before you answer that question,' he warned, 'I suggest that you remember the number of women involved.'

Emily Venn was in a state of panic. At a time when she was mourning the death of her lover, a nameless woman had let herself into the garden and issued a demand. Unless Emily obeyed her orders to the letter, the woman threatened to make Emily's husband aware of the fact that his wife had betrayed him on several occasions. There seemed to be no escape. Confessing the truth to her husband was not even considered. He would, literally, throw her out of the house. The only way to keep her blackmailer at bay was to pay her the amount of money demanded. Emily went into the house to collect her handbag, then she set off on foot towards her bank.

'I was wrong,' she admitted.

'About what?'

'Mrs Venn. When I first saw her, I thought she was almost ugly. At close quarters, however, I could see why she had attracted Blanchard. She was a full-bodied woman with beautiful, pale skin. It almost glowed.'

'Will she do what she is told?' he asked.

'Oh, yes. I put the fear of death in her.'

They were on the steamer, making their way back to the mainland and discussing their trip to the island. It had been short but effective. They had now frightened three different married women into paying them money. It was the start of a whole new career for them.

'And there are still other names in that address book,' she recalled.

'We'll do what Blanchard himself did,' he said, putting an arm around her shoulders. 'We'll work our way through the whole lot of them.'

After fruitless hours of visiting a succession of jewellery shops, Hinton moved on to Chichester and allowed himself a break in the refreshment room at the railway station. After a light meal, he felt ready to begin his search once more. Hinton went off into the beautiful old town but saw none of its glories. He did not even permit himself a glimpse of its cathedral. When he was on duty, he had eyes for nothing else. The first jewellery shop he found was unable to help him, and the next one also turned him away with an apology. When he entered a third shop, he expected the same result.

'Can I help you, sir?' asked the manager.

'I sincerely hope so.'

'What are you looking for?'

'I'm looking for two items that were stolen from a murder victim.'

When Hinton introduced himself, the manager immediately took him to an office at the rear of the shop, leaving an assistant in charge. Wilfred Weekes was a solid man of middle years with rubicund cheeks. He peered at his visitor over the top of his pince-nez.

'What exactly was stolen, sir?' he asked.

'A gold wedding ring and a pocket watch.'

'I see.'

'Have either of those items been offered to you, sir?'

'As a matter of fact, they have. But I had no reason to question their provenance.'

'When were they brought in?'

'Two days ago.'

'May I see them, please?'

'Yes, of course.'

Weekes used a key to open a safe and withdrew a tray of items. He selected a gold ring and a pocket watch before handing them over to Hinton. The detective was delighted.

'These were stolen by the killer,' he said.

'I doubt that very much.'

'Why?'

'Because the person who sold them to me vouched for their origin. Both had belonged to his late father, who had left instructions that they could be sold to raise money for the repairs.'

'What repairs?'

'Those needed on the church roof,' said Weekes. 'The person who brought the items here was the Reverend Horace Latimer, the vicar of St Andrew's in Oving. He struck me as a deeply religious man who had pledged his life to his parishioners. I'm sorry,' he went on, 'but there's been an extraordinary coincidence. A wedding ring and a pocket watch were sold to me, but they have no connection whatsoever with the crime that brought you here.'

Hinton was crestfallen.

When he left the Blanchard house, Colbeck took the opportunity to call on Berwyn Rees once more. He remembered that the Welshman was very much involved in events on the island and would therefore know many of the people who lived there. It was possible that he might identify one of the women whose names had surfaced. When the inspector called, Rees was pleased to see him again and eager to help in any way. He took Colbeck into his office.

'What can I do for you?' he asked.

'I'm trying to trace a woman who might possibly live here.'

'Who is she?'

'All I have is her first name – Christina. Does that ring a bell with you?'

'Yes, it does. Christina was a pretty girl with pigtails who went to school with me.'

'Does she still live here?'

'I'm afraid not, Inspector. Christina's mother was from Scotland. When her father died, they went to live in Dundee. Heaven knows what happened to her.'

'I'm after a Christina who might still be here.'

'Then I can't help you, I'm afraid. I know two Christines, and there's a Chrissie Hopkirk who lives in Brading, but that's it. Why are you after this woman?'

'She may be able to help us,' said Colbeck. 'That's all I can tell you. Let me try a second name. Do you know of a woman named Emily?'

'The honest answer is that I don't, but I've got a vague memory of having met a woman of that name. I'm afraid that she didn't make much of an impression on me. How old would she be?'

'Emily would be middle-aged.'

'And you think that she lives on the island?'

'It's a reasonable deduction, Mr Rees. There's also a woman named Marigold.'

The Welshman's eyes twinkled. 'Is there a reward for finding these woman?'

'Yes, sir,' said Colbeck, smiling. 'You'll have the satisfaction of knowing that you made an important contribution to a murder investigation. It's impossible to put a price on that.'

Having visited every jewellery shop in Southampton and its suburbs, Victor Leeming decided that it was time to abandon his search. Pangs of hunger were reminding him that he had not eaten since breakfast, so he had a meal in The Merry Harrier before heading for the railway station. When he consulted his notebook, he saw that he had been to almost thirty jewellery shops in vain. A few reported having dubious customers who had tried to sell suspicious items to them, but a wedding ring and pocket watch were not among them.

Closing his notebook, Leeming hoped that Alan Hinton had had more luck than him. By way of consolation, he reached for his pint of beer. The first sip revived his spirits.

During the times he had worked with the inspector, Hinton had been taught the importance of checking everything carefully. If the slightest doubt arose regarding information received, then it was vital to take a second look at it. Hinton therefore took a cab to the village of Oving. He did so without high expectations. Jewellers like Wilfred Weekes seemed to have a second sense for any customer trying to unload stolen items on them. Hinton had therefore resigned himself to finding that the vicar of St Andrew's was indeed the Reverend Horace Latimer, and that the transaction he had had with Weekes was perfectly legitimate.

When he reached the village, he was impressed by its many charms. Chief among them was its sense of rural contentment. The pace of life was slower. People found time to stop and enjoy conversations with friends. There was none of the bustle, the abiding stink and the overcrowding found in London. Dominating the village was the church of St Andrew's, first built in the thirteenth century yet still standing proudly on its original site. Hinton looked at the board outside the church. It announced that the vicar was indeed the Reverend Horace Latimer. While Hinton studied the times of the services, a white-haired old man came out of the church and walked towards him. When he reached the detective, he gave him a warm smile.

'Welcome to Oving,' he said.

'Thank you,' replied Hinton.

'I can see that you're interested in churches. What brings you to ours?'

'Curiosity.'

'If you'd like to see inside, you're most welcome. I'm Percy Webber, one of the wardens. Do you want me to give you a brief history of St Andrew's?'

'No, thank you,' said Hinton, stepping back to look

upwards. 'I'm more interested in the roof than in the inside of the church.'

'Really? Why is that?'

'I heard that it's in a state of disrepair.'

'Who told you that?' asked Webber with a throaty chuckle. 'We had it repaired only last year. It cost a small fortune.'

'I thought it was in a dreadful state. That's why the vicar's father wanted to leave some money towards the repair in his will.'

'You're behind the times, young man. The vicar's father died donkey's years ago. He did leave money for the church, but it was not for the roof.'

'I see,' said Hinton, trying to conceal his astonishment. 'Where might I find the Reverend Latimer?'

'He'll be in the vicarage,' said Webber. 'You've caught him just in time.'

'What do you mean?'

'He's retiring at the end of this year. Having him at St Andrew's has been a real blessing. He's looked after us for nigh on forty years.'

Robert Colbeck had had a rather frustrating time on the Isle of Wight. Even with the assistance of Berwyn Rees, he had been unable to identify any of the women he was keen to trace. After leaving the estate agent, he went to Newport to renew his acquaintance with Inspector Ruggles.

While he was more than willing to help, the inspector

was unable to do so. He knew nobody with either of the names given by Colbeck.

Ruggles was inquisitive. 'Are these women connected with Giles Blanchard?'

'They might be.'

'It doesn't surprise me.'

'Why not?'

'Over the years, I saw him at various functions. He loved to be the centre of attention and was always well behaved. Until, that is, he felt that nobody was looking at him.'

'What did he do then?'

'To put it politely,' said Ruggles, 'he sized up the women. I watched him do it time and again. I've seen that look in a man's eye, Inspector. He was on the prowl.'

'That accords with what we've discovered about him.'

'I always felt sorry for his wife.'

'Yet she adored him.'

'Only because she was unaware of his interest in other women. Mrs Blanchard will mourn him as the devoted husband she believed him to be.'

'I very much doubt that,' said Colbeck, sadly.

'Oh?'

'By the time of his funeral, she may know the harsh truth about him.'

After bidding farewell, he left the police station and climbed into the waiting cab. On the journey back to Ryde, he regretted that they had made such little progress. They might have learnt how and when the murder took place, but they seemed to be no closer to making an arrest. It was dispiriting. Colbeck was not looking forward to sending his next telegraph to Superintendent Tallis.

He began to sift the evidence once again, searching for something they may have missed. He was so preoccupied that he did not even feel the slowing down of the cab when they reached the ferry, or hear passengers disembarking. Only when the cab came to a sudden halt was he shaken awake. He paid the driver and walked towards the steamer.

Then he realised that someone was blocking his way. Leeming and Hinton were standing side by side, arms outstretched. Colbeck came to a halt.

'What are you two doing here?' he asked.

'We've brought you good news, sir,' said Leeming. 'Or, at least, Alan has.'

'Couldn't you wait until I returned to the mainland?' asked Colbeck.

'No, sir. You still have business on the island.'

'Yes,' added Hinton. 'My search of the jewellery shops finally yielded a dividend.'

'I wish one of mine had,' moaned Leeming.

Colbeck was puzzled. 'What's this all about?'

'See for yourself, sir,' said Hinton, taking a box from his pocket.

'What is it?'

'I'll show you.'

Opening the box, Hinton held it up in front of him.

Colbeck's eyes lit up with pleasure.

'You found the wedding ring and the pocket watch,' he said, opening the box to examine its contents. 'Well done, Alan!'

'Thank you, sir.'

'Now do you see why you can't board the steamer just yet?' asked Leeming.

'I do, indeed,' said Colbeck.

'You'll be able to show those items to Paul Blanchard. He'll confirm that they were stolen from his father. Alan not only found them, he has a good description of the man who sold them to a jeweller in Chichester.'

'That's right,' said Hinton. 'When he murdered his victim on the train, he was dressed as a naval officer. At the jewellery shop, he was posing as a clergyman.'

CHAPTER FOURTEEN

When they returned to their house in Portsmouth, they were still congratulating themselves on their success. They had contacted three of their chosen victims in a row and arranged for a payment from each. There had been no resistance from the three women and no sense of danger in the transaction. That was the element that had most appeal for the woman.

'We took too many chances before,' she recalled. 'We flirted with danger.'

'I found that rather exciting,' he admitted.

'You weren't the one who had a complete stranger groping you.'

'Yes, I know. But I was always there to rescue you.'

'Thank goodness!'

'That life is behind us now, my love. We have a steady income at last. If it goes on like this, we can think about buying a larger house.'

'Who is next in line?'

'Let's reel in the money from the first three wives first,' he said. 'Mrs Lenham paid up at once and you've arranged to collect the first instalments from Mrs Falconbridge and Mrs Venn. Each of them is married to a rich husband and they probably have money of their own. I daresay that Blanchard rewarded them in some way as well,' he decided. 'He may have bought each of them a treasured piece of jewellery, for instance.'

'What's the point of that? They wouldn't have been able to wear it.'

'Yes, they would – when they were in bed with him.'

She laughed. 'I never thought of that.'

'Can you imagine Mrs Venn, wearing nothing but a pearl necklace?'

'No, not really. They'll regret that they ever met Blanchard now. I wouldn't be tempted to spend a night in his arms even if I was dripping with diamonds. I always keep my promises. I can't think of any circumstances in which I'd be unfaithful to my husband.'

'You're forgetting something.'

'Am I?'

'We're not married.'

She gave him a challenging smile. 'Not yet, anyway.'

Paul Blanchard was in a quandary. He resented Colbeck because the inspector knew the hideous truth about Giles Blanchard. At the same time, however, the son needed the inspector to solve the murder of his father. The one saving grace was that Colbeck was a discreet man, unlikely to spread details of the elder Blanchard's private life. He was in his father's study when he heard the front door of the house being opened. When Colbeck's voice filtered through to him, he got up and went into the hall. He was in time to see three visitors being invited into the house. Colbeck doffed his top hat then performed the introductions. Blanchard was not impressed by the sight of Leeming.

He led the visitors into the drawing room where they all sat down. Blanchard was hopeful.

'Has something happened?' he asked.

'Yes,' replied Colbeck. 'I despatched Sergeant Leeming and Constable Hinton to visit jewellery shops in different directions.'

'I had no success,' admitted Leeming.

'I had more luck,' said Hinton.

He went on to give an account of his visit to Wilfred Weekes's shop in Chichester and of his trip to Oving in search of its vicar. Blanchard was duly impressed by the way that he had checked on the man who sold the ring and the pocket watch to the jeweller.

'That was very enterprising of you,' he said.

'It's something that the inspector has drummed into me, sir,' said Hinton.

'And you have the stolen items with you?'

'I do.'

Since Hinton had found them, Colbeck had given him the honour of handing over the two items. Blanchard almost snatched the box from him and opened it. When he saw the ring and the pocket watch, he let out a gasp of delight, taking each one out in turn to examine it.

'I take it that you recognise these items,' said Colbeck.

'Oh, yes,' replied Blanchard. 'And I'm so pleased to have them back again. Mother will be thrilled to see the wedding ring again.' He turned to Hinton. 'I can't thank you enough for tracking these down. Your persistence was admirable.'

'All my detectives are schooled in persistence,' explained Colbeck. 'It's the reason that I know we will soon catch the man we are after – and his accomplice. We never give up, sir.'

'I find that reassuring.'

Colbeck stood up. 'Then we will leave you to pass on the good news to your family.'

'But what about the jeweller?' asked Blanchard. 'Assuming it to be a fair transaction, he will have paid this bogus clergyman a decent amount for the items. I will insist on paying him.'

'Mr Weekes will not hear of it, sir,' said Hinton. 'He chided himself for being so completely deceived and insisted that he will bear the cost himself.'

'I will at least send him a letter of thanks.'

'Then you will need his address,' said Hinton, producing a card from inside his coat. 'I took the trouble to ask for his business card and he gave me this.'

Blanchard took it from him. 'You seem to have thought of everything.'

Colbeck signalled his colleagues and they rose from their seats.

'We'll take our leave,' he said, 'and continue our search.'

'Are you sure that I can't offer you refreshments?'

'That's very kind of you, sir, but we have to be off.'

'Let me show you to the door,' said Blanchard, getting up. 'Having my father's wedding ring and pocket watch has cheered me immeasurably. I never thought to see them again.'

'You'll soon see the person who stole them,' promised Colbeck.

Emily Venn had stood outside the bank for several minutes to gather the strength to go into it. After taking a deep breath, she entered the building and went across to the counter. The clerk gave her a polite welcome then raised an eyebrow when he heard how much she wished to withdraw.

'I need to buy something for my husband's birthday,' she explained.

'Lucky man!'

Though she appeared calm, she squirmed inwardly. It was, however, the first hurdle and she had got over it satisfactorily. She knew, however, there would be many more hurdles in the future.

* * *

Having been invited to dinner at the Colbeck residence, Caleb Andrews had been able to listen to his granddaughter reciting the latest poem she had learnt by heart. Helena Rose had already eaten her meal so had retired to bed, leaving Andrews and Madeleine alone in the drawing room.

'She reminds me so much of you, Maddy,' he said. 'She's interested in everything.'

'I don't think that I was as clever as her.'

'Yes, you were. Your mother and I were amazed at how quickly you learnt things.'

'Then I must have slowed down,' said Madeleine. 'I find things more difficult to learn now.'

'So do I – it's a sign of old age . . .'

He tried to explain how his memory was failing him, but Madeleine was no longer there to listen to him. Having heard a key being inserted in the front door lock, she had leapt to her feet and run into the hall. The moment the door opened, she flung herself into her husband's arms.

'What a wonderful surprise!' she cried.

'And what a wonderful welcome!' said Colbeck.

'Why didn't you warn me that you'd be coming home this evening?'

'It was a decision taken on the spur of the moment.'

'What's going on, Maddy?' asked her father, coming into the hall. He saw Colbeck. 'Ah, you're back home at last. Have you made an arrest?'

'No,' said Colbeck, 'but we did take a significant

step towards one earlier on. I thought we could reward ourselves with a visit home. Apart from anything else, I'll be able to deliver a report in person to the superintendent first thing in the morning.'

'Did Victor come with you?' asked Madeleine.

'Yes, he'll probably be giving Estelle and the boys a nice surprise at this very moment.'

'What about Alan?'

'He stayed in Portsmouth to hold the fort.'

'You've timed it just right,' said Andrews. 'Grub will be served any moment.'

'There's something more important than food.' Colbeck glanced upwards. 'Is Helena Rose still awake?'

'I'm sure she is,' replied Madeleine. 'She'll be reading in bed. You might have to listen to her reciting poems at you, but she'll be delighted to see you.'

'Then I'll get up there at once.'

Colbeck ran to the staircase and raced up it. Andrews was impressed by his speed.

'Look at him, will you? He went up those steps like a mountain goat.'

Edward Tallis left his home early next morning and began his usual brisk walk to Scotland Yard. He had several things on his mind but the one at the forefront concerned Colbeck. The inspector had failed to send him a telegraph the previous day, giving him some idea of how the investigation was proceeding. It was a rare mistake on the inspector's part, and it deserved a stern reproach. When he reached his destination, Tallis went straight to his office and flung open the door.

'Good morning, sir,' said Colbeck, rising from his chair.

'What the devil are you doing here?' demanded Tallis, taken aback.

'I've come to report the latest development in the case, sir. It's the reason I did not send a telegraph yesterday. I wanted to give you a fuller account. I also wanted to thank you in person for sending Detective Constable Hinton to us.'

'You looked as if you could use help.'

'We did, sir, and Hinton has already proved his value.'

'In what way?'

'If you sit down,' said Colbeck, 'I'll tell you. Because he used his initiative, Hinton has recovered items stolen from the murder victim. Let me explain how . . .'

Having completed his tour of jewellery shops, Hinton had now been given a similar assignment.

Colbeck had now instructed him to call at various churches and theatres to see if any of them had had a cassock stolen. He began his search in Portsmouth. The person he spoke to at the Theatre Royal was the manager, Harold Tremayne, a small, animated, expressive individual with a well-trimmed beard that he kept stroking.

'You're the second person this week asking about thefts from our wardrobe,' he said. 'The first was an Inspector Colbeck.'

'It was the inspector sent me here, sir.'

'I told him the truth. We've had no naval uniforms stolen.'

'It's clerical garb I'm after this time, Mr Tremayne. We're on the trail of a man pretending to be the vicar of Oving.'

'Where on earth is that?'

'It's a small village not far from Chichester.'

'Well, the thief didn't get his cassock and bands from here.'

'Then I'll have to try somewhere else.' Hinton remembered something. 'Oh, I must tell you how much the inspector enjoyed the performance two nights ago. He and Sergeant Leeming could not stop talking about it.'

'Inspector Colbeck is a handsome man with a good voice. If he were not a detective,' said Tremayne, 'he could make a good living as an actor.'

'He loves the job that he already has, sir.'

'What about you?'

Hinton was startled. 'Me?'

'Yes,' said the manager, studying him. 'I can think of a dozen roles that you could play.

'Really?'

'You're a good-looking young man and you hold yourself well. Have you ever thought about a career on the stage?'

'No, I haven't.'

'It's a pity. My brother-in-law is an agent. He'd find work for you in no time.'

'I prefer the work I already do, Mr Tremayne. Besides, I'd go weak at the knees if I tried to act on a stage. I'll leave it to those who are born to it.'

Colbeck and Leeming met in London at the railway station. On the train journey back to Portsmouth, they were able to compare their nights at home.

'Estelle and the boys were so pleased,' said Leeming. 'It was lovely to have a meal with the family again. What about you, sir?'

'I dined with Madeleine and her father. Before that, I listened to the poems my daughter had memorised. They were about different animals.'

'I was hopeless at learning nursery rhymes.'

'Helena Rose has a wonderful memory. It's probably better than mine.'

'I doubt it, sir. You've got a mind like an encyclopaedia. How did you get on with the superintendent?'

'I think I cheered him up. I told him that his idea of sending Alan Hinton to us was a stroke of genius. For a few seconds, it removed that angry glare from his eyes.'

'Did you tell him that Sir Anthony Absolute reminded us of him?'

Colbeck grinned. 'I'm not that foolhardy.'

'He'd be shocked to learn that we spent an evening at a theatre.'

'It did us both good, Victor. You had a first taste of what a wonderful playwright Sheridan is, and I savoured the way that *The Rivals* was constructed. It was masterly.

However,' he added, 'all of our attention must shift back to the investigation now.'

'What's our next move?'

'Well, I'm hoping that we can get more and better help from Mr Blanchard. Now that we've recovered some of his father's possessions, he'll recognise the effort we're putting into this case. It might prompt him to be more open with us.'

'Do you think he's hiding something?'

'I think he's still dazed by the shock of what happened,' said Colbeck. 'And as a businessman he wants to read only heartening news about his father in the newspapers. He's terrified that the truth about Giles Blanchard's private life will be exposed.'

'I don't blame him.'

'His mother would learn the ugly truth then. At least he had something positive to report to her yesterday. Seeing her husband's wedding ring and pocket watch must have cheered her up a little. It would also have proved that we have picked up a scent. That should please her.'

It was the first time since the murder that Catherine Blanchard had a reason to wake up and face the world. Hitherto, she had been in such a state of apprehension that all she could do was to stay in her bed and mourn her husband. When her son knocked on the bedroom door before entering the room, he found her seated in an armchair with her dressing gown on. In her hands were the wedding ring and pocket watch belonging to her husband. Catherine seemed to draw strength from them.

'How do you feel now, Mother?' asked her son.

'As well as can be expected, I suppose.'

'Have you taken your medication?'

'No, I haven't,' said Catherine. 'Doctor Reynolds said that I should only have it when I felt the need.' She managed a tired smile. 'So far today, I haven't.'

'That's good to hear.'

'You and Verity have been wonderful to me.'

'I just wish we could do more, Mother.'

'Moving in here was an act of true kindness,' she said. 'You must miss the children terribly.'

'They're being looked after,' he said, 'Verity and I have both popped back to the house from time to time. The children always send their love to you.'

'I miss seeing them, Paul, but I'm . . . not in the right frame of mind yet.'

'They understand, Mother.'

She looked him in the eye. 'Tell me about the detectives.'

'There's no need for you to bother about them, I promise you.'

'I have a right to know. Do you have faith in them?'

'Yes, I do – especially after yesterday when they returned the stolen items.'

'The inspector sounds as if he is a clever man.'

'He's very clever and very understanding, Mother. I'm so grateful that we didn't have the local police in charge of the case. They would have trampled in here and shown no respect or consideration. Inspector Colbeck is a gentleman,' he said. 'He has also been releasing statements to the newspapers about the investigation, so that we are not bothered.'

'That is a relief.'

'Now, I came to see if there is anything that you want?'

'Nothing at all, thank you.'

'Refreshments, perhaps?'

'Nothing.'

'Then I'll leave you alone. Verity will come up to see you very soon. Like me, she will be so pleased to see how much you have improved. You've got colour in your cheeks again.'

He began to walk away but did not get far.

'Paul . . .' she called.

'Yes?' he replied, turning to face her.

She met his gaze. 'Your father and I were very happy.'

'I know, Mother. I saw it with my own eyes.'

'I want you to think well of him.'

'How could I not do so?' he asked. 'I idolised Father.'

'I hope that you will continue to do so. It means so much to me.'

'Why on earth are you talking like this?'

'Ignore me,' she advised. 'Dismiss what I said as the ramblings of an old woman.'

'You are not old, and you don't ramble.' He moved closer. 'What is going on, Mother?'

'Nothing,' she said, softly. 'Nothing whatsoever . . .'

* * *

Christina Falconbridge had promised that she would pay the money in a few days. The two people who were blackmailing her had no reason to doubt her. When they watched her house from a concealed position that morning, they did not have long to wait. She came out in a smart dress and a wide-brimmed hat that made it impossible to see her face. As she set off, they followed from a safe distance. Christina took the same route to the church. When she got there, she went into the building. The man was surprised.

'I thought she was going to hand it over outside the church,' he said.

'That was the arrangement.'

'Then what is she doing in there?'

'I daresay that she is praying,' said the woman. 'Her faith means a lot to her.'

'Mrs Falconbridge didn't pray before she went to bed with Blanchard. She gave in to a surge of lust. The woman must be tortured with guilt now. Luckily for us, her guilt has a price tag.'

'I warned her what would happen if we didn't get every penny of our demand.'

'Give her five minutes,' he suggested. 'If she is not out by then, go in after her.'

In fact, there was no need to wait. Almost immediately, Christina stepped out of the church and looked around nervously. The woman came out of her hiding place and strolled across to her.

'Good morning, Mrs Falconbridge,' she said.

'Who are you?' asked the other.

'I'm someone with your best interests at heart – as long as you do what I tell you.'

'It's blackmail!'

'I prefer to call it a form of insurance. You are protected from your husband's anger and I guarantee that he will never know what you did.'

'How did you find out?'

'I'll ask the questions.' She extended a hand. 'Where's the money?'

'It's here,' said Christina, taking some banknotes from her pocket and handing them over. 'You told me that I had to pay the same amount in a month's time.'

'The same amount in the same place, please.'

'It's not fair.'

'Were you being fair to Major Falconbridge when you slept with another man?'

'It was only that once.'

'That's enough to make your husband kick you out,' said the woman. 'Besides, there might have been other times if Mr Blanchard had still been alive. You cared for him, didn't you?'

Christina lowered her head. 'Yes, I did,' admitted the other.

'How did you meet him?'

'We bought the house from Giles . . . Mr Blanchard, that is.'

'Then he would have been aware of your husband's frequent absences.'

'Stop tormenting me!' protested Christina. 'You make it sound so sordid and it was not like that at all. He loved me. You're a woman. Can't you understand that?'

'I can never understand betrayal.'

'I was desperately lonely.'

'That's why he took advantage of you, Mrs Falconbridge.'

'He didn't "take advantage". We were friends. He saw the plight I was in.'

'Blanchard exploited you. Don't you realise that? You're only one of his victims. What you enjoyed only once, other women relished several times.'

Christina was horrified. 'I don't believe you.'

'He might have been special to you,' said the woman, 'but you were certainly not special to him. Whenever he wished, he could pick and choose someone to warm his bed. If he was not with you, he was taking advantage of some other poor, lonely, misguided fool. Good day to you, Mrs Falconbridge. I'll see you here on this very spot a month from today.'

Christina was in such distress that all she could do was to stand there with tears streaming down her face. The woman, meanwhile, had disappeared.

The train journey to Portsmouth gave them an opportunity to examine every aspect of the case. By the time they reached their destination, they were feeling more convinced that they would soon bring the investigation to a successful conclusion. Leeming was curious.

'Why was young Mr Blanchard so shocked by his discovery of those letters?'

'I think that most sons in that situation would be horrified,' said Colbeck.

'Yes, but the Blanchards worked so closely together. If he spent so much time with his father, you'd have thought that Paul would have seen the signs of his interest in women.'

'If he did, he chose to ignore them. What I do know is that he was badly shaken by the revelations. It wasn't only the fact that his father had befriended other women that upset him, it was the way that he kept a secret horde of letters from them. His father had wanted to gloat over his mistresses.'

'That was disgusting,' said Leeming.

'Those letters flattered his vanity.'

'No wonder his son lit a fire to destroy them.'

'He can't destroy the memory of what he found,' said Colbeck. 'It's a secret he'll carry for the rest of his life – and it's a very painful one.'

'I don't like the man, but I do feel sorry for him.'

'My sympathy is reserved for his mother.'

'Didn't she guess that . . . well, that her husband was not the happy family man he pretended to be?'

'I think it highly unlikely, Victor.'

'There must have been signs.'

'If there were, Mrs Blanchard chose to ignore them.'

'Don't some people have strange marriages?' asked Leeming. 'Estelle and I are completely honest with each other. It's the best way to be.'

'I agree.'

'I'd hate to go through life with dark secrets.'

'It would be alien to your character, Victor.'

'It would be wrong, sir – very wrong. I was brought up to know that.'

'There's another aspect to consider,' said Colbeck. 'The kind of life that Giles Blanchard lived was only possible because he was a rich man. He had the money to buy the affection of women who did not receive it at home.'

'Yes,' replied Leeming. 'He couldn't have done that if he earned the wages we do.'

Verity Blanchard had been sitting with her mother-in-law for the best part of an hour. The older woman was grateful for companionship. Now that she was slowly recovering from the shock of her husband's murder, Catherine felt that she was back in the real world again. She talked fondly about her twin grandchildren and longed for the time when she could see them again.

'How much do they understand about what happened?' she asked.

'We simply told them that grandfather had died suddenly. They're far too young to know the gruesome details. When they are old enough, we will tell them the truth.'

'It will be very painful for them, Verity.'

'We know. Paul is not looking forward to that conversation with the twins.'

Instead of replying, Catherine seemed to go off into a daydream. A sad smile appeared on her face and her eyes stared unseeingly at the ceiling. After a few minutes of silence, Verity touched her gently on the arm.

'Would you like me to go?' she asked.

'No, no, of course not.'

'But you looked as if you were about to go to sleep.'

'Then I apologise for being so rude,' said Catherine, turning to her. 'Memories keep flooding into my mind. Most of them are happy memories of good times.' She looked her daughter-in-law in the eye. 'Some are not, I'm afraid.'

CHAPTER FIFTEEN

When their train stopped at Brighton station, they were reminded once again of their association with the place. Over a decade earlier, they had been involved in a murder case relating to a fatal crash on the line that ended with the death of an engine driver. Colbeck had a good reason to remember the incident.

'My father-in-law knew the victim well,' he recalled. 'His name was Frank Pike and he was driving the Brighton Express for the very first time. When his train was derailed, he refused to leave it. Instead of jumping to safety, he remained on the footplate and was killed when his locomotive collided with a ballast train coming towards it.'

'I remember the case, sir. His fireman had leapt to safety.'

'I wouldn't call it safety, Victor. The fireman, John Heddle, has been tortured by the memory of the crash ever since. According to my father-in-law, he refused to travel on the footplate again. In fact, he soon left the railway altogether and now works as a coal merchant.'

'I don't blame him, sir. If I'd survived a crash like that, I'd have had nightmares about it for the rest of my life.'

'You've survived lots of other crises,' said Colbeck, 'but you don't lose sleep over those.'

'That's different. I love chasing villains. If it means that I pick up a few bruises along the way, so be it. The pain eases very quickly. Well, look at my face.'

Colbeck smiled. 'To be honest, I try not to.'

'The two men who attacked me fought like tigers, but one of them ended up with a broken nose and the other lost a few teeth. I had great pleasure putting handcuffs on them after I'd knocked the pair of them unconscious.'

'It serves them right. They were stupid enough to take you on, Victor.'

'I wear these scars with pride.'

They heard a whistle being blown and the train started to move. Out of the corner of his eye, Colbeck caught sight of someone on the platform, hurrying towards the exit. He seemed to recognise the man at first then changed his mind. Leeming saw the confusion on his face.

'Is something wrong, sir?'

'I made a mistake, that's all.'

'Then it's a very rare one.'

'I thought I recognised a man on the platform,' said Colbeck, 'but I was wrong.'

'Who did you think it was?'

'Nigel Buckmaster, that extraordinary actor-manager.'

Leeming laughed. 'Thank goodness it wasn't him.'

'Why do you say that?'

'Because we have our hands full with Giles Blanchard. We don't want to cope with Buckmaster as well. He caused us all sorts of trouble.'

'I have fonder memories of him,' said Colbeck. 'However, these's no cause for alarm. On reflection, I'm certain that it was not him.'

Tall, lean, and arresting, Nigel Buckmaster was wearing a black cloak that swirled about him as he strode out of the station. His face was half-hidden by a wide-brimmed black hat. Long, dark locks, now edged with grey, poked out from beneath the hat. Having strolled to the rank, he clambered into the waiting cab and gave a booming command.

'Theatre Royal!'

'Yes, sir,' said the cab driver, flicking the reins to set the horse in motion.

'And be quick about it!'

'I'll have you there in no time, sir.'

Buckmaster beamed, raising a regal hand and waving to an invisible crowd.

* * *

Verity Blanchard knew better than to interrupt her husband when he was busy. Work came first in their marriage. It was hours before he came into the drawing room and saw her sitting there.

'I thought that you were looking after Mother,' he said.

'She was very tired, Paul. She wanted to sleep.'

'Then you were right to let her do so.'

'Do you have a moment?' she asked, almost timidly.

'Only if it concerns a matter of importance.'

'Oh, it does.'

'Then I'll stay and listen.' He lowered himself into the chair opposite her. 'Well, what's the problem exactly?'

'I had a rather distressing conversation with your mother.'

'What do you mean?'

She was hesitant. 'I feel embarrassed to tell you.'

'Why?'

'Well, it was so unexpected. We were in the middle of a conversation when she suddenly went off into a trance. It was as if I wasn't there. I wondered if I should slip quietly out the room, so I touched her gently on the arm by way of farewell. Before I could leave, however, she came out of her trance and apologised to me for drifting off like that.'

'What was her explanation?'

'Your mother said that memories had suddenly flooded her mind.'

'That's hardly surprising in the circumstances.'

'Most of them were happy memories,' said Verity, 'but some were not.'

Blanchard winced. 'Did she tell you why?'

'No, it was just . . . left in the air.'

'Then I should forget all about it, my love. Those tablets she was given have made her rather confused. I've had strange conversations with her myself. Ignore what Mother said.'

'But she was telling me something important, Paul – something she felt that I should know.'

He stiffened. 'My parents had a very happy marriage, Verity.'

'That's not what your mother was trying to tell me.'

Paul was roused. 'Well, it might interest you to know that she told me something quite different. Mother told me, in so many words, that she and Father had been happy together. It was the reason his death had such a destructive effect on her. A marriage they both revelled in had been snuffed out in the compartment of a railway train late at night. She doted on him, Verity,' he said, raising his voice. 'Can't you hear what I'm telling you? It was a match made in heaven.'

'There's no need to shout.'

'I won't have you criticising my parents.'

'I'm not criticising anybody,' she responded. 'I'm just telling you what I was told. Don't you see? It may be that your mother felt impelled to hint that there had been . . . well, difficulties in their marriage.'

'Out of the question,' he said, angrily.

'It was not my place to ask her but perhaps you should do so.'

'What, in God's name, are you talking about?'

'If there were awkward times between them,' she argued, 'it might have had some bearing on what happened to him. It would explain why your father spent so much time away from here.'

'Say no more!' he ordered. 'This conversation is closed.'

'I'm only trying to help, Paul.'

'Do as you're told, woman!'

She reacted as if from a blow. It took her several moments to recover.

'There's something you should know,' she said at length.

'I've heard more than enough, thank you.'

'This is not about what your mother said. It's not about her at all.' She paused to gather her strength. 'It's about your father and me.'

He was appalled. 'What the devil do you mean?'

'Don't stare at me like that. It frightens me.'

'I'm sorry,' he said, trying to control his emotions. 'What's this about you and Father?'

'I could be wrong, of course, but his behaviour was disturbing.'

'Verity—'

'Let me finish, please,' she begged. 'I've kept this secret for so long that I simply must let it out. Not long after our engagement, you and your parents dined at our house. It was a lovely occasion. Until I had to go to my room to fetch a photograph album, that is. Your father suddenly appeared and stood in my way.'

'If you're making any of this up . . .' he warned.

'I'm not, I promise you.'

'Then why haven't you told me before?'

'It was because I was confused. Your father told me how pleased he was at our engagement. Then he suddenly enfolded me in his arms and held me close – very close, actually. I didn't know what to do. He was my future father-in-law, after all. He was entitled to embrace me. Except that it was much more than an embrace. I was young and innocent. I didn't realise what was happening.'

He raised a palm to silence her then moved to sit beside her and put an arm around her.

They held each other tightly. Verity was unaware of the tears forming in her husband's eyes.

Reunited with Alan Hinton, they listened to his report. Hinton had continued his search for the church from which a cassock had been stolen. Colbeck and Leeming were impressed by the number of places that he had visited. They were seated in the lounge at the Hope and Anchor. Leeming was amused.

'You've been on quite a pilgrimage, Alan,' he said.

'Not really,' Colbeck pointed out. 'Pilgrims go to shrines to pray at the grave of a saint.

'The man we are after is much more of a sinner than a saint.'

'I wonder if he'll turn up at Blanchard's funeral.'

'That's a rather bizarre suggestion, Victor.'

'He wouldn't be the first killer who did that.'

'True.'

'We don't even know that he's still in the area,' said Hinton.

'Oh, I know,' said Colbeck, firmly. 'This is the man's home territory. He's here somewhere, and he's probably looking for his next victim.'

'How do we find him, sir?'

'We keep knocking on doors until we catch him.'

'There must be an easier way,' ventured Leeming.

'There is, Victor. One of Mr Blanchard's conquests could give us priceless help. If my guess is right, one or more of those women has been approached by the killer and his accomplice. Blackmail can be a highly profitable business. Blanchard was probably careful to choose married women with absent or preoccupied husbands. It must have given him some kind of stimulus to cuckold other men by offering his victims pleasures they had been denied.'

'Where will we find these women?' asked Hinton.

'They're here or hereabout, Alan. We must look at three precise locations.'

'What are they?'

'Portsmouth, Chichester, and the Isle of Wight.'

'I'll take Chichester,' volunteered Leeming. 'We know for a fact that Blanchard found women in that area. Mr Collier confirmed that. I could speak to him again.'

'If you do,' warned Colbeck, 'refuse any offers of malt whisky.'

'Oh, I will, I promise you!'

'What about me, sir?' asked Hinton.

'Widen your search from Portsmouth,' said Colbeck. 'Every village has a church.'

'That leaves the Isle of Wight to you,' noted Leeming.

'I intend to go there very soon. First, I think, I need to have a serious talk with Paul Blanchard. It's high time that he gave us the help that we need.'

Gwendoline Cardus had served Queen Victoria through good times and bad ones, delighting in the happiness of Her Majesty's marriage and sharing her deep sadness after Prince Albert's death. As she approached the room, she heard the strains of Mendelssohn's music and knew that it had a special meaning for the Queen. Seated at the piano, she was playing a sonata written by her favourite composer. Gwendoline waited until the music eventually came to an end.

'That was exquisite, Your Majesty,' she said.

'Thank you,' replied the other, turning to her. 'But I could never do the piece full justice.

'Only the composer himself could do that. He was such a brilliant pianist.'

'Listening to him was an absolute joy.'

'Indeed, it was. But I have another absolute joy to report.'

'Do tell me what it is, Your Majesty.'

'I received a letter this morning from Mr Buckmaster. He is about to revive his acclaimed production of *Twelfth Night* and take it on tour. He will play Malvolio. Remembering that open invitation to visit us here again, he is offering to come here one Sunday afternoon during the run at the Theatre Royal in Brighton to entertain us.'

'That's wonderful news, Your Majesty!'

'I still remember his last visit when we were utterly captivated by his performance.'

'He is truly a master of his craft.'

'I had a delicious thought, Gwendoline. Wouldn't it be wonderful if, one day, we could see both Nigel Buckmaster and Mrs Scott-Siddons here at Osborne House together? What a theatrical treat that would be for all of us!'

Colbeck was surprised. When he got to the house on the Isle of Wight, he found Paul Blanchard in an uncharacteristically subdued mood. The latter could barely meet his eye. He took his visitor into the study and shut the door behind him.

'I suppose that it's foolish to hope you've brought us good news, Inspector.'

'I have nothing certain to report, sir,' said Colbeck, 'but I do sense that we are getting closer to an arrest – two arrests, in fact.'

'I wish that I could share your optimism.'

'We'll catch the pair of them, sir. There's no doubt

about that. What I need from you is a little more cooperation.'

'I've done nothing but cooperate,' protested Blanchard.

'That's not strictly true, sir. When you made a shocking discovery about your father, you sought to hide it from me. It was only because Sergeant Leeming was given similar information about your father's private life that we realised what might have happened.'

'Need we go over it again?'

'I'm afraid that we do, sir. It's imperative that we trace one or more of the women whose names are linked to your father. You were able to give me some names, but I've so far been unable to trace the individuals. There may be another way to do so.'

'How?'

'I need your permission to gain access to your sales records.'

'Why on earth do you want those?' asked Blanchard.

'They could well contain the information that we need, sir. Like you, your father was wedded to his work. His daily routine would have left him with little time to . . . go astray, so to speak. And yet we both know that he did.'

'So?'

'In all probability, the women with whom he had secret liaisons were the wives of men who had dealings with your estate agency. Christina, Marigold and Emily were the names you remembered. I venture to suggest,' Colbeck went on, 'that their surnames may be found in your records. It was through a business transaction with your agency that your father would have met these women.'

'That's true, I suppose,' said the other, reluctantly.

'May I have your permission, please?'

There was a long pause. Blanchard was in a quandary. He found a discussion of his father's adultery highly embarrassing and wanted to pretend that it had never actually happened. At the same time, however, he could understand why Colbeck needed to probe even deeper into the private life of Giles Blanchard. Tempted to refuse the request, he instead remembered the confession by his wife. Before they had married, Verity had had a brief but unsettling experience with her future father-in-law. He had made unwanted advances to her. She had been so confused and ashamed by it that she could not bring herself to confide in the man about to marry her. The memory of his conversation with Verity made her husband reach a decision.

'Yes, of course,' he said, firmly. 'I'll take you to the agency right away.'

'I was hoping that you would agree, sir,' said Colbeck. 'I took the liberty of sending Sergeant Leeming to your agency in Chichester. He will tell them that he has your permission to look through the sales records. While I am searching for a Christina, a Marigold and an Emily here, he will be hunting them in Chichester.'

Benedict Mottram had grave reservations about the request. When an ill-kempt man with facial wounds came into the agency and asked to see its sales records, the manager was suspicious. He threatened to call the police, only to be shown Leeming's warrant card and to realise that he was talking to one of the detectives investigating the murder of Mottram's former employer. The manager was a watchful man in his forties with dark hair combed back neatly. He was clearly proud to be working for such a successful agency.

'We've sold a lot of houses in this area,' he said, airily. 'How far back in our files do you wish to go?'

'Two or three years should be enough, sir.'

'May I know why you wish to institute a search?'

'I'm afraid not,' said Leeming. 'It's a very sensitive matter.'

'In what way?'

'Just do as I ask, please, or you will answer to young Mr Blanchard.'

Mottram unlocked the door of a cupboard and indicated the neatly stacked files.

Nigel Buckmaster had a reputation for leaving nothing to chance. It was weeks before he would be bringing his production of *Twelfth Night* to Brighton but he nevertheless paid a visit to the Theatre Royal to acquaint the backstage staff with his requirements. He had brought photographs of the London production together with sketches of the set designs. Ben Gillow, the stage manager, was duly impressed. He was a diminutive, dark-haired man in his fifties with decades of experience in the theatre. Since they were old friends, he was delighted to see Buckmaster again.

'I had the pleasure of seeing the production at the Haymarket,' he said. 'It was hilarious. And it goes without saying that you were magnificent as Malvolio.'

'Thank you, Benjamin,' said the actor-manager. 'It is always rewarding to hear praise from a fellow professional. You may not appear onstage but your work behind it is always flawless.'

'We do our best, sir.'

'It's because I love this theatre so much that I chose to begin our tour here. We always have such an educated audience in Brighton.'

'People still talk about your performance of *Macbeth*.'

'That's a play for darker nights and colder weather. It's quite unsuitable for summer. It's the reason I chose one of Shakespeare's finest comedies.'

'A good decision.'

'Right,' said Buckmaster, clapping his hands together. 'Let's get down to fine detail, shall we? I expect everything to be ready and waiting for our arrival here. I know that I can rely on you.'

They were spending the afternoon by walking together through the park, listening to the birds and watching the ducks on the lake. Under the eyes of their nannies, young children were playing on the grass and whooping with joy.

'Isn't this wonderful?' he said. 'For once in our lives, we have no worries about money.'

'It's a glorious feeling,' she agreed. 'All our problems have disappeared.'

'We deserve it, my love. It's time to enjoy ourselves.'

'How long can it last?'

'Don't worry yourself about that. Make the most of our luck. And be grateful that the last man lured by your charms was Giles Blanchard. Our other victims rarely yielded more than a few guineas each. Blanchard has given us access to a small fortune.'

She was suddenly anxious. 'What if one of those women loses her nerve?'

'There's no chance of that happening. They know what's at stake.'

'I suppose so.'

'And don't spare them one iota of sympathy. They betrayed their husbands, remember. And they did so with that appalling estate agent. They ought to be grateful that we rescued them from his clutches. He was taking advantage of them.'

'Not any more – those days are over.'

'And we are the beneficiaries,' he pointed out. 'We can lead a new life from now on, free from the dangers when you had to deceive overexcited men with false promises.' He stopped to kiss her on the lips. 'Welcome to a wonderful future!'

The manager at the estate agency was very cooperative. Colbeck had assured him that he had Paul Blanchard's permission to inspect the company's files. David Trinder sprang into action, giving Colbeck the use of his office and ordering a member of his staff to carry the relevant files into it. Trinder was a rather sleek, well-spoken man in his forties with an urge to help. When the inspector first stepped into the agency, the manager cast an admiring glance at his appearance. He was thrilled to be involved in the murder investigation.

'You may see anything you wish, Inspector,' he promised.

'Thank you, Mr Trinder.'

'If I can help in any way, you only have to summon me.'

'As it happens,' said Colbeck, 'there is something you could do for me.'

'What is it?'

'Tell me something about Mr Blanchard's daily routine.'

'To which Mr Blanchard do you refer?'

'The deceased.'

'In fact, we saw rather more of his son because he was based here. His father was always on the move, showing clients the more expensive properties and spending at least a day or two a week at our Chichester office. He was full of energy,' said Trinder. 'Always striving to increase the size of the company by expanding on to the mainland. The Blanchard name is a guarantee of quality.'

'Was he ever away for a night or two?'

'Very occasionally.'

'Where would he be?'

'He would either stay at his club in Chichester or, now and then, spend a night in London if he had been doing business there.'

'What about his son?'

'Oh, he was on the island more or less all the time.'

'I see,' said Colbeck, looking at the stack of files on the desk. 'It looks as if I'm going to be here for some time. If you'll excuse me, I'll make a start.'

'Yes, yes, of course,' said Trinder. 'I'll leave you to get on with it.'

After backing towards the door, he gave a deferential nod then left the room.

Colbeck reached the first of the boxes in which the files were kept. The transactions related to properties that had been sold three years ago. When he took out a sheaf of papers, he saw that he was dealing with a house sold to a Mr and Mrs Merriman. They had bought a five-bedroomed property on the Isle of Wight that stood in the middle of two acres of land. One of its main attractions, Colbeck decided, was that it had a wonderful view of the sea. There was also a delightful sense of space on the island. He pictured his daughter, running along the beach or dipping a tentative toe in the sea. Helena Rose would love the place.

But he had no time to dwell on the possibilities of taking a holiday there with his family.

Solving a murder took pride of place so he returned to his perusal of the documents in the boxes. They were a record of unalloyed success. Giles Blanchard was an astute businessman. It was clear from the steady flow of sales that the company must have made substantial profits. Berwyn Rees and his other business rivals had good cause to resent his pre-eminence in that part of the country.

There was a polite knock on the door and David Trinder entered the office.

'I apologise for disturbing you, Inspector,' he said, putting another box on the desk. 'This should have been brought in here earlier. One of my minions made a mistake. He's lucky that I was the person to admonish him.'

'Why do you say that?'

'The elder Mr Blanchard was a martinet. He expected perfection. If someone erred in any way, he would explode with anger. Younger employees were sometimes reduced to tears.'

'I'm glad that you are more understanding.'

'I never forget that I was young myself once.'

'Thank you for bringing the box in, Mr Trinder.'

'I'll hold you up no longer.'

The manager let himself out and closed the door. Colbeck immediately picked up the sheaf of documents on which he had been working and flicked through them. He was disappointed that he could not find the information that he sought. Putting all the documents back in the box, he reached for the one that Trinder had just delivered. He took the contents out and flicked through them at speed. Since he was looking for only one thing, his perusal did not take him long. Colbeck was disappointed at his apparent failure and began to wonder if he was wasting his time. The very last document, however, justified his decision to come to the agency. As he studied the record of a sale of property on the island, he felt elated.

His search might have been worthwhile, after all.

CHAPTER SIXTEEN

Alan Hinton pressed on doggedly. After a fruitless visit to the churches in Porchester, he made his way westward to Fareham, a town that had been an active port in medieval times. It centred on the high street and the church of St Peter and St Paul. Having been sent on a search, Hinton suddenly became a sightseer. He had never seen a more delightful and picturesque high street, filled, as it was, with splendid Georgian houses. Many of them featured red bricks that were a Fareham speciality. Hinton stood there and marvelled, enjoying the sheer pleasure of visiting a special place. It was only when he recalled why he was there that he stopped being a wide-eyed visitor and became a detective on a mission.

When he let himself into the church, it seemed at first to be empty, so he enjoyed looking at the way the sun was slanting in through the windows. A noise from the vestry made him realise that there was someone else there, after all. He walked swiftly down the aisle.

'Hello!' he called. 'Can you spare a moment, please!'

'Keep your voice down, please,' said a portly man in a cassock, appearing from the vestry. 'You're in a church, not in a marketplace.'

'I'm sorry,' said Hinton.

'My name is Desmond Ensor and I'm a curate here.'

Hinton introduced himself to the man. Ensor was surprised that a Scotland Yard detective was visiting the church.

'What could possibly have brought you here?' he asked.

'I am looking for a church which may have been the victim of a crime.'

'Then you have come to the wrong place, I'm afraid. The congregation at St Peter and St Paul is exceptionally law-abiding.'

'You must have stray visitors.'

'Like you, for instance?' asked Ensor, smiling.

'No, not at all like me, as it happens. I am employed to enforce the law. The person I am after has broken it. In short, we believe that he stole a cassock and other items so that he could pretend to be in holy orders.'

'Why would anyone do that?'

'He wanted to convince a jeweller that he was the vicar of a church in Oving.'

'Good gracious!'

'You don't need to know the full details, Mr Ensor. Suffice it to say that the man is both a murderer and a thief. We are making every effort to track him down.'

'Well, you certainly won't find him here.'

'Does that mean you've had nothing stolen from your vestry?'

'I think it highly unlikely,' said the curate. 'We keep everything locked up.'

'Is it possible to check that nothing has gone astray?'

'Yes, of course,' said Ensor, taking out a key. 'Let's go into the vestry. Everything of value is kept in there.'

Hinton sighed. 'I know. I've been into several vestries already today.'

'Well, you've wasted your time coming here, I'm afraid. We make sure everything is secure.'

'That may not be good enough to keep this man at bay.'

The curate led him to the vestry where there were three tall cupboards in a row. He used a key to open the first of them and counted the surplices that were there.

'Do you see?' he asked. 'Everything is here.'

'Where do you keep the cassocks?' Ensor pointed to the next cupboard. 'Could you open it, please?'

'I will do so gladly but I'm afraid that it will be a waste of time.'

Unlocking the door, he opened it wide then gaped.

'The spare cassock has disappeared,' he said.

'Then I suspect I know who stole it.'

'How could he possibly open the door without the key?'

'He's a man who knows how to get what he wants,' said Hinton. 'I don't think that lock will have presented much of a challenge.'

'This is alarming. We've never had a theft from this church before. If you find the thief, please make him return our property.'

'I fancy that he'll have got rid of it by now. He's probably wearing a very different disguise.'

Having failed to find anything significant in the files at the Chichester agency, Victor Leeming went on to the Haven Club. As he had anticipated, Douglas Collier was not there. Still grieving over the death of his close friend, he was staying at home. Leeming immediately took a cab to the house and was given a warm welcome by Collier.

'How wonderful to see you again, Sergeant!' he said, effusively. 'Dare I hope that you've brought me good news about the investigation?'

'There's been no arrest as yet, sir, but we have made definite progress.'

'Take a seat and tell me all about it.'

They settled down in armchairs in the drawing room. Collier offered him refreshments, but Leeming thanked him and declined. He was there with the express purpose of getting information. First, however, he told his host that they had picked up the scent of the killer.

'We're getting closer to him every day,' he insisted.

'That's encouraging news.'

'The information you gave me earlier was a great help to us. We're trying to find some of the women with whom Mr Blanchard . . . consorted.'

'You chose the perfect word,' said Collier. 'In essence, Giles was a romantic. He was drawn to members of the opposite sex. By the same token, the women were drawn to him. They trusted him implicitly because he treated them so well.'

'Were they aware that he was married?'

'I'm sure that they were – just as Giles was aware that they, too, had marital partners. He was able to offer them the excitement that their husbands failed to provide. Having been happily married for over fifty years myself, I suppose that I should have disapproved strongly of his behaviour,' said Collier, 'but I couldn't do that somehow. Giles made it sound as if he were rescuing those ladies from barren unions.'

'Can you remember any of their names?'

'Oh, no. He never mentioned names.'

'One or two must have slipped out, surely.'

'Giles protected their identity, Sergeant. That's the kind of person he was. He wanted them to feel perfectly safe.'

'Well, they are not perfectly safe any more, sir. We've reason to believe that the man who killed him may have gained access to the names and addresses of those women. In short, they are at the mercy of a killer.'

'Heavens!' exclaimed Collier. 'They could be in grave danger.'

'That's why we are so anxious to trace them.'

'Their friendship with Giles may have become a curse.'

'They need our protection, sir.'

'Yes, indeed. I appreciate that. You must go and find them at once.'

The address he had found took him to Yarmouth on the west coast, formerly the chief port of the island. Colbeck had tempered his earlier enthusiasm with caution. What he had been searching for in the files at the estate agency was the name of any woman involved in the purchase of a property. It might explain how Giles Blanchard had come to meet one of the women who had surrendered to his charms. On his way to the address he had discovered, Colbeck had to remind himself that there was no guarantee that he was about to find someone who had had an intimate relationship with the estate agent. Rose Cottage might well be owned by a woman who had no friendship with him at all. When he rang the bell outside the front door, it was opened by a pretty, young servant with dimpled cheeks. She was impressed to see such a commanding figure standing there.

'Good day to you!' he said, touching the brim of his hat. 'Is this the home of Mrs Cardus?'

'Yes, it is, sir.'

'Is it possible to speak to the lady?'

'Well, yes . . . May I tell her who is calling?'

'I am Inspector Colbeck of Scotland Yard. What has brought me to this part of the country is the murder of someone who lived on the Isle of Wight.'

'Oh, yes,' she said, nervously. 'Everyone here is talking about that, sir.'

'Who is it?' croaked a voice from within the house.

'It's a gentleman who wishes to speak to you, Mrs Cardus.'

'I was just about to have my nap. Ask him to come back later.'

'It's imperative that I speak to you now, Mrs Cardus,' said Colbeck, raising his voice. 'I'm here on police business. I won't keep you long.'

'Oh,' said the woman in some confusion. 'What's this about police business? I've done nothing wrong, have I?'

'No, of course not. May I come in and explain?'

'Yes, please. Show the gentleman in, Mary.'

'This way, sir,' said the servant, standing back.

Colbeck removed his top hat and ducked as he entered what was a charming cottage dating back to Elizabethan times. He was taken into the drawing room where the beams supporting the ceiling were so low that he had to keep his head down. Seated near the rear window so that she had a good view of the garden was Isobel Cardus, a shrunken, almost skeletal woman of uncertain age. She dismissed the servant with a wave of her hand and studied her visitor before suggesting that he sat down. Colbeck was relieved to do so.

'You don't look like a policeman,' she complained.

'I'm a detective inspector, Mrs Cardus, and I'm here to lead the investigation into the murder of Giles Blanchard, the estate agent.'

'What a terrible shame that was! I met him when we bought Rose Cottage. He was such a considerate gentleman.'

'I didn't have the pleasure of meeting him.'

She shuddered. 'Who would have thought he'd be strangled to death?' she asked. 'And for what possible reason? The killer must be caught and hanged, Inspector.'

'We are doing our best to track him down, Mrs Cardus.'

'We need more police on our railways.'

'I couldn't agree more.'

'If you want my opinion . . .'

She had a voice that belied her frailty, a strong, rasping, educated voice that rolled off a list of complaints about the inadequacy of policing on the island and beyond. Colbeck listened politely and gave the occasional nod. Isobel Cardus was an interesting woman, but he realised that she had nothing to do with the dead man beyond the fact that she had bought her home from him. His visit had somehow given her a fresh burst of energy. Having talked about taking a nap earlier on, she was now quite animated. She offered him refreshment.

'No, no,' he said. 'I must be on my way.'

'But you haven't told me why you came in the first place, Inspector.'

'It was an unfortunate mistake, Mrs Cardus. I'll trouble you no longer.'

'But how did you come to pick on Rose Cottage?'

'I was doing some research in Mr Blanchard's office and your name caught my eye. You may well be the only woman on the island who has bought a house of her own.'

'Oh, I didn't buy it, Inspector.'

'Really?' he said in surprise. 'Your name is in the files.'

'That may well be,' she admitted, 'but it was my daughter who actually paid for Rose Cottage and put it in my name. That's the kind of person she is.'

'Doesn't she live here herself?'

'No, Gwendoline has much better accommodation on the island.'

'But this is such a delightful cottage in every way, Mrs Cardus.'

'It can't compete with the place where my daughter lives,' said the other with a dry laugh. 'Gwendoline is one of Her Majesty's companions. She resides occasionally at Osborne House.'

Gwendoline Cardus was seated in the library, apparently poring over a book. In fact, she was looking at the bill of sale relating to the purchase of Rose Cottage. It marked the moment when she had first met Giles Blanchard, a man who had gone on to change her life in the most profound way. That precious friendship had been extinguished for ever in the compartment of a train. She was bereft.

Hearing someone approaching her, she closed the book so that the bill of sale was hidden inside it. When she rose to her feet, she saw that it was one of the servants.

'Hello, Anne,' she said.

'Good afternoon, Miss Cardus.' The woman peered at her. 'Has something upset you?' she said with concern. 'You haven't been crying, have you?'

Still in the park, they were sitting at a table in the little restaurant there. A parasol gave them shade from the sun. He had bought a copy of the local newspaper to see how the murder case was now being reported. She looked anxiously across at him.

'Well?' she asked.

'The police are still floundering,' he said.

'Is that what it says?'

'More or less. Inspector Colbeck is quoted as saying that they are making steady progress, but he gives no details of it. In other words, we are in the clear.'

'Our luck is bound to run out sooner or later.'

'Don't be so pessimistic,' he said. 'There's nothing to connect us with what happened that night on the train to Portsmouth.' He blew her a kiss. 'Stop worrying.'

'I'm wondering if we should move away from here.'

'That's a ridiculous idea. What happens to the three

women we've blackmailed into paying us money on a regular basis?'

'We could come back once a month to collect it.'

'We need to stay here,' he insisted. 'Also, there are other victims to approach. Two of them live in Chichester and another in Havant. Then there's the one at Osborne House.'

'We can't possibly get in touch with her.'

'Why not?'

'Osborne House is closely guarded.'

'I daresay that we can reach her by letter.'

'Don't even suggest it,' she begged. 'The others are much safer targets.' She paused to nibble at some food. 'I'm wondering how long we can squeeze money out of the three women we've already approached.'

'Our income should be safe indefinitely.'

'Only if they do as we tell them. What if their money runs out?'

'Why are you so anxious all of a sudden?' he asked, worriedly. 'We have those three women eating out of our hands. They're terrified of us.'

'It's bound to show. Before long, one of them will give the game away.'

'That's impossible. You've met all three of them face to face. They're scared stiff. To avoid a catastrophe in their marriages, they will do almost anything we tell them.'

'How can you be so certain about that?'

'Instinct,' he said with a smile. 'It's the same infallible

instinct that made me choose you as my partner in life. That's why I know that I can rely on it.' She gazed at him lovingly. 'I also know that we can rely on Mrs Venn. She will have done exactly what you told her to do.' He took out his watch and glanced at it. 'It will soon be time for us to go and collect the money we demanded.'

Having such a large amount of cash in her reticule had made Emily Venn nervous. Though she hated the idea of handing it over to a stranger, she consoled herself with the thought that it would dispel the nagging fear of being caught by her husband with so much money. She knew that she would have to go through the agony once more of drawing out money and handing it over to a stranger at the end of the month, but that was four weeks away. Emily would at least have had a respite. Before she could take advantage of it, there was the ordeal of paying off her blackmailer for the first time. She had been given instructions of where and when to do so. It had come with a grim warning. If she refused to cooperate, her husband would learn of her secret romance.

Emily was seated in the garden in the shade of an elm tree. In her lap was the book she had brought out to read. It was still unopened because she was in no mood to read anything. All that she wanted to do was to remember the snatched moments of joy she had shared with her lover. He not only sold houses. He had also rented out furnished properties. Whenever one was vacant, Blanchard would take Emily there under the pretext of showing the house to a prospective client. As a result, the two of them had shared memorable encounters on several different beds. The variety had added to the excitement.

She was still luxuriating in fond memories when a sharp voice brought them to an end.

'Emily!' called her husband. 'Where the devil are you?'

'I'm out here by the elm tree, Peter,' she replied, rising to her feet in surprise. 'What are you doing home at this time of the day?'

He came into view, face pale and brow wrinkled. 'I was not feeling well.'

'Not one of your headaches again, I hope.'

'I feel as if my brain is about to explode. Those tablets from the doctor have absolutely no effect. It was impossible for me to work so I came back home.'

'You did the right thing, Peter.'

He was a slight, ginger-haired man with a small moustache sprouting on his upper lip. Putting a hand to his forehead, he slumped into a chair beside her. It was not the first time that he had come home unexpectedly from the office where he worked as a solicitor. Occasional headaches had troubled him throughout their marriage. It was one of the reasons why the couple slept apart.

Emily was quietly alarmed to see him. She was due to hand over money to her blackmailer soon and she could hardly do that if she was tending her husband. Her mind was racing. She made a conscious effort to behave like a caring wife.

'Go straight to bed, Peter,' she suggested.

'I just want to sit down and relax.'

'Sleep is the best thing for you.'

'How can I sleep when my head is pounding like this?'

'Come on,' she said, taking him by the arm and guiding him gently back into the house. 'You need to get out of the sun. If I draw the blinds in the bedroom, you'll soon drop off.'

'Emily . . .'

'I know what's best for you, Peter. Now let me help you upstairs. Forget about the office. Your work is done for the day. You can have a nice, long, well-deserved rest.'

He surrendered. 'Very well, dear. If you insist.'

'I do insist.'

As they passed the grandfather clock in the hall, she noticed the time. In less than half an hour she was due to hand over money to the mysterious woman who had suddenly turned up. It was vital to get her husband asleep so that she could slip out of the house unseen.

When they had completed their individual assignments, Leeming and Hinton met up at the docks in Portsmouth and took the ferry to the Isle of Wight. They compared their experiences.

'So you did find a church from which the cassock was stolen,' said Leeming. 'Well done, Alan. It's a real triumph.'

'Hardly,' said Hinton. 'All I established was that the

theft had taken place. The curate had no idea who had stolen it or for what purpose.'

'It was to fool that jeweller who bought the wedding ring and the pocket watch from them. You tracked down those as well. You obviously have a gift as a retriever.'

'You managed to win the confidence of Mr Collier. Without the information he provided, we'd never have made the progress we have.'

'Yet we're no nearer an arrest,' complained Leeming.

'I think that we may be closer to that stage than you think.'

When they reached the island, they left the steamer and walked along the pier to the restaurant at the far end. Colbeck was waiting for them, sipping a cup of tea as he scanned a newspaper. He beckoned them over to his table. When they delivered their reports, he gave a nod of satisfaction. Colbeck then talked about his search through the files at the estate agency.

'Mrs Cardus was the only female buyer,' he explained. 'When I saw that Giles Blanchard had handled the sale of Rose Cottage, I assumed that a friendship might have grown up between the two of them. She was a lady of quality – but far too old for any romantic entanglement.'

'What about that daughter of hers?' asked Leeming.

'Miss Cardus spends all her time at Osborne House.'

'Didn't someone tell us that Blanchard and his wife were regular visitors?'

'That's right,' said Colbeck, thoughtfully. 'They were invited to functions there.'

'Maybe that was how this woman got to know him.'

'It's possible, Victor.'

'There's one simple way to find out, sir,' Leeming pointed out. 'You're too modest to remember that we were invited to the palace by Prince Albert so that he and Her Majesty could thank us in person for the way we'd saved them from being killed on the railway. They were indebted to you.'

'That was years ago.'

'People don't forget an attempt on their lives.'

'I agree,' added Hinton. 'Besides, if Blanchard was a familiar visitor at Osborne House, Her Majesty would be interested to know how the search for his killer was going.'

'I think she'd be more than interested, Alan,' said Colbeck.

'Then why not tell her?'

'You'd be welcomed with open arms,' said Leeming. 'What's more, you might have the opportunity of meeting Gwendoline Cardus there.'

Colbeck nodded. 'It would be the main reason for going, Victor. I'll take your advice.'

'Before you do that, can we order something to eat? I don't know about Alan but I'm absolutely starving.'

Madeleine Colbeck had been looking forward to her friend's visit all day. Lydia Quayle was not only coming to dinner, she had also promised to be there early enough to read a bedtime story to Helena Rose. When she arrived at the house, she had a surprise for Madeleine.

'Have you heard about the visit to a jeweller?' she asked.

'No,' admitted her friend. 'The letter I had from Robert today made no mention of it.'

'Then for once I have the advantage over you. Alan was so pleased to have recovered items that had been stolen from the victim that he wrote to tell me all about it.'

'I bet he was delighted to have an excuse to contact you, Lydia.'

'His letter was a delightful surprise.'

'I want to hear all the details,' insisted Madeleine.

'Then you'll have to wait your turn. Helena Rose comes first.'

'She's dying to see her Auntie Lydia.'

'How is she getting on with those poems about animals?'

'She's memorised almost half of them for you.'

'Excellent.'

'I'll give her a chance to prove it,' said Madeleine.

Picking up a small bell from the side table, she rang it. The response was immediate. Helena Rose came out of the nursery and ran down the stairs before throwing herself into Lydia's arms. They hugged each other.

Madeleine looked on with a smile. 'I told you that you'd get a warm welcome.'

* * *

One of the benefits of being such a tireless letter-writer was that Queen Victoria received shoals of missives in return. When she worked her way through the day's pile, she was watched by Gwendoline Cardus, always in attendance at that time of day. As one letter was discarded, another was picked up and opened. There was a cry of pleasure.

'What a lovely surprise!' said the Queen. 'It's a letter from Inspector Colbeck.'

'Oh,' said Gwendoline, quivering slightly.

'He's offering to come here.'

'For what purpose, Your Majesty?'

'He's been made aware of the fact that Mr Blanchard was a regular visitor here in the past. As a courtesy, he is offering to come to Osborne House to bring me up to date with the investigation. I daresay that he would like to hear more about the social events that Mr Blanchard attended. That's typical of the inspector. He gathers intelligence from every possible source.'

'Will you accept his invitation, Your Majesty?'

'I'll do so gladly.'

Gwendoline forced a smile. 'It will be good to see Inspector Colbeck again,' she said with as much enthusiasm as she could muster. 'I remember the time when he and Sergeant Leeming came to the palace to receive your thanks in person for preventing an attack on you and other members of the family.'

'It's a memory I often savour. The inspector is such a gentleman, and I'm unable to say that of every police officer. He stands out from the herd.'

'I'll leave you to compose a reply to his letter.'

'Thank you, Gwendoline.'

'I'll be within call, Your Majesty.'

She withdrew from the room with her usual dignity, but she was in complete turmoil. Once alone, she sank down on the first available chair. Her heart was pounding, and her mind was filled with apprehension. What was the real reason why Inspector Colbeck was coming to Osborne House? Was it simply a courtesy visit or did he have a more serious intention? During her friendship with Giles Blanchard, she had thrown caution to the wind in every sense. Desperate to keep in touch with her lover during times apart, she had written some letters to him, and he had told her how much he had treasured them. Could it be that the inspector had somehow found her letters?

Her life in royal service was suddenly in danger.

CHAPTER SEVENTEEN

The orders had been specific. Emily was to meet the woman a short distance from the house so that there was no danger of the servants catching sight of them together. She was to hand over the money as the woman brushed past her. No words would be spoken. Emily felt trapped. Because of her relationship with a man she loved, she was at the mercy of someone who was involved in Blanchard's death. Desperate to know how and why he had died, she would be denied the truth.

It meant that meeting the woman again – albeit for a matter of seconds – would be an ordeal. To make matters worse, her husband had suddenly turned up in need of help. Instead of being able to go to the designated place at the right time, she was seated beside the bed on which he was stretched out, putting a cold compress on his brow.

'Thank you, Emily,' he said.

'Be quiet,' she advised. 'Try to sleep.'

'I'll see the doctor in the morning.'

'Hush . . .'

She glanced at the clock on the bedside table. Time was quickly running out.

The two of them had got there early so that they could take up a position from which they could see her as she approached. They were confident that Emily Venn would obey her orders. As the minutes passed, however, the woman began to have doubts.

'She's not coming,' she decided.

'Give her time, my love.'

'She's late.'

'It's only a matter of minutes.'

'Mrs Venn has changed her mind.'

'She's far too scared to do that.'

'Then what could possibly have delayed her?'

'Calm down, will you?' he urged.

'I'm concerned. Perhaps she gave herself away somehow. What if her husband forced her to tell him the truth. Let's go,' she advised. 'We're not going to get a penny from her.'

'I'm not giving up so easily.'

'She promised to be here on the dot and there's no sign of her.'

They continued to argue about what to do. Certain that Mrs Venn was not coming, she began to feel unsafe. He kept trying to still her fears but with little success. Eventually, he agreed that they were wasting their time. As he led her away from their hiding place, however, he took one last look in the direction from which Emily Venn would come.

She was there at last, bustling along as fast as she could. He pointed her out.

'Here she comes,' he told his companion. 'She's all yours.'

'Thank goodness!' she said, turning to go back to her.

'I told you that she wouldn't let us down.'

He watched as his companion walked back to intercept the woman. There was no conversation between them. After handing something over, Emily turned on her heel and scurried away. The woman, meanwhile, strolled quickly back to the man. She held up a small package.

'You were right,' she admitted. 'Mrs Venn did pay up.'

'Remember that the next time.'

'I'm sorry that I mistrusted her.'

'Please don't get into a state like that again,' he said. 'You worried me.'

'If you think that I was upset, you should have seen her.'

'What do you mean?'

'She was shaking like a leaf,' said the woman. 'I almost felt sorry for her.

'Handing over the money was torture for her, but it's something she'll have to get used to.'

'Make that clear to her. If she's late again like this,' he warned, 'we'll put her payment up by an extra fifty pounds. That will teach her to be punctual.'

Because he had promised to keep the son abreast of every development in the case, Colbeck paid another visit to the house. Once again, he was invited in and taken straight to the study, the place where Paul Blanchard had made the devastating discovery of his father's private life. He was pleased to hear from Colbeck that Hinton had tracked down the cassock used by the killer when he sold the items stolen from the murder victim.

'He sounds like a cunning devil,' said Blanchard.

'Yes,' agreed Colbeck. 'He is as convincing as a vicar as he was as a naval officer. I wonder what his next disguise will be?'

'At least it proves that he is still in the area.'

'Still in the area and confident of his safety.'

'Was your visit to our agency a success, Inspector?' asked Blanchard.

'I think so, sir. It certainly gave me another line of enquiry.'

'Really?'

'Do you remember a client named Isobel Cardus?'

'Vaguely – my father dealt with her. He sold her Rose

Cottage here on the island – except that Mrs Cardus did not actually buy it. Her daughter did.'

'Yes, that's right.'

'Did you ever meet either of these ladies?'

'I may have caught a glimpse of them but that's as far as it went.'

'The daughter, Gwendoline Cardus, is a companion of the Queen.'

'Father mentioned that fact to me. He felt sorry for the mother.'

'Why?'

'Apparently, her husband had died in distressing circumstances, leaving his wife more or less isolated. The daughter rescued her mother from the place where she was living and brought her to Hampshire. She bought Rose Cottage for Mrs Cardus.'

'Your father took an especial interest in the sale, I fancy.'

Blanchard was startled. 'What are you implying?'

'He was an occasional visitor to Osborne House, I gather.'

'That's true. He took Mother there from time to time.'

'But he also had an excuse to go there without her,' suggested Colbeck. 'It's not impossible that he developed a friendship with Miss Cardus.'

Blanchard stiffened. 'Do you have any proof of that, Inspector?'

'No – but the possibility exists and that's the reason I'm here. Please think back to the moment when you made that . . . unfortunate discovery about your father's private life. I know that you were dismayed so much by the letters sent to him that you started a fire to burn them.'

'I couldn't bear to keep them,' confessed Blanchard.

'But you did force yourself to read them first.'

'I did – and it was a sickening experience.'

'You recalled two of the names you'd seen – Christina and Emily. Did you also read a letter sent by a Gwendoline?'

Blanchard shook his head. 'No, I don't believe that I did.'

'Think hard, please. She might not have signed her full name.'

Blanchard was perplexed. Willing to help, he was upset at the notion of having to recall correspondence that had offended him so much that he had destroyed it. Try as he may, however, he could not dismiss the letters from his mind – or the silver box containing locks of hair belonging to his father's mistresses.

Colbeck waited patiently. After several minutes, he had his reward.

'There was one letter . . .' recalled Blanchard.

'Go on, sir.'

'It stood out because of its beautiful calligraphy.'

'Who had signed it?'

'That was the strange thing. The name was no more than a squiggle. It was as if the person who signed it wanted to keep her name secret.'

'Can you at least remember the first letter of her name?'

'It was . . . well, I fancy that it might have been a "G" followed by a short wavy line.'

'Gwen,' said Colbeck, hopefully. 'I'll raise the matter with the lady herself.'

Gwendoline Cardus was alone in the chapel at Osborne House. Kneeling in a pew, she was praying furiously for help and guidance. In becoming involved with a married man, she accepted, she had committed a sin and deserved punishment. But the punishment she suffered was out of all proportion to the sin. She had not only lost the one man who had shown any serious interest in her, she had to cope with the horror of his murder. It had left a gaping hole in her life that could never be filled. All that was left for her was agony and regret.

Leeming and Hinton were conducting their own search. At Colbeck's suggestion, they had made their way to the estate agency owned by Berwyn Rees. The Welshman gave them a cordial welcome and ushered them into his office. There was no need to explain why they were there. Rees already knew.

'Inspector Colbeck asked me to do some research on his behalf,' he explained. 'He was searching for a woman with the name of Emily and another with the name of Christina.'

'Have you had any luck?' asked Leeming.

'With regard to the second woman, I've had no success at all. That means, I fancy, that nobody on the island bears the name of Christina.'

'What about Emily?' said Hinton.

'I've tracked down two of them.'

'How did you do that?'

Rees grinned. 'I have my spies.'

'Could we find these women?'

'There's no need to search for Emily Sutherland.'

'Why not?' said Leeming.

'Because she is only four years old, apparently. That rules her out.'

'What about the second Emily?'

'You may be on safer ground there, Sergeant. Emily Venn is a woman in her late thirties. She is married to Peter Venn, who is a solicitor. That is all I can tell you. I'm not accusing Mrs Venn of being in any way involved with Giles Blanchard. I just did what the inspector asked me and searched for someone who bore the name of Emily.'

'Do you have an address for her?' asked Hinton.

'I have it right here,' said Rees, picking up a piece of paper and handing it over. 'Two healthy detectives like you could walk there in little over twenty minutes. Let me stress that I'm not able to guarantee that this Emily is the one that you want.'

'It's a starting point, sir.'

'And we're very grateful to you,' added Leeming.

'Let me know how you get on,' said Rees. 'I'll be

tickled to death if Emily Venn turns out to be the person you're after. My detective work will not have been in vain.'

When she got back to her house, Emily Venn discovered that her husband was fast asleep upstairs. She therefore went into the drawing room and poured herself a glass of sherry from the decanter.

After taking a few sips, she felt marginally better. She lowered herself onto the sofa and realised how close she had come to disobeying her orders. Had she arrived a few minutes later at the meeting place, the woman would have disappeared and revealed Emily's secret to her husband by way of retaliation. As it was, she was just in time to hand over the money and appease her tormentor. She needed to ensure that that kind of panic did not exist the next time.

At least she could now afford to relax. Her husband's sudden return home had complicated the situation but she was equal to it. Emily congratulated herself on the way that she had behaved.

The whole process would be much easier next time. In the short term, her worries were over.

They had walked a couple of hundred yards before they stopped to count the money. He loved the feel of the crisp banknotes in his hands. The full amount was there. It meant that their first three victims had paid what was demanded. In time, they would add other names to their list, allowing them to enjoy a much higher monthly income than usual.

'This is so exciting,' she said. 'I'm really getting the hang of it.'

'That's why I wanted you to deal with them. You're less threatening than I would appear to be and you get the best possible results.'

'So much for your early fears,' she teased.

'What early fears?'

'When you saw that Inspector Colbeck was leading the murder investigation, you told me to take extra care, yet we haven't had the slightest trouble from him.'

'It's true.'

'He doesn't have a clue who we are or where we are.'

'Let's keep it that way.'

'This is one case he will never be able to solve.'

'Don't underestimate him, my love. Others have done that and have ended up with a rope around their necks. We will only escape the same fate if we move with extreme care. Understood?'

She kissed him on the lips. 'Understood.'

No matter how many times Colbeck assured him that they were making progress, Paul Blanchard remained sceptical. The only thing that would satisfy him were two significant arrests.

'They will come in due course, sir,' said Colbeck.

'When?'

'When we have amassed enough evidence to identify the killer and his accomplice.'

'Why is it taking so much time?'

'Every scintilla of evidence has to be checked and re-checked.'

'Can't you simply arrest the suspects and beat a confession out of them?'

'No, sir, we can't.'

They were still in the study in Giles Blanchard's house, going through the evidence so far gathered and assessing its usefulness. Blanchard's son was increasingly impatient.

'I still believe that Berwyn Rees is implicated somehow.'

'There's no proof whatsoever to that effect.'

'Just look at the man, will you? He hated my father.'

'He also respected him for his achievements, sir.'

'Rees should be behind bars.'

'Well, he couldn't stay there for long,' said Colbeck. 'I'm sure that he would retain the best solicitor on the island. We'd have to release him immediately. Besides, we need him to help us.'

'He's far more likely to bamboozle you, Inspector.'

'Mr Rees is a man with a lot of contacts on this island. That's why I sought his help. I have every reason to believe that he will not let me down.'

Victor Leeming and Alan Hinton felt that they might be getting somewhere at last. Thanks to the address given to them by Berwyn Rees, they had walked quickly towards the house. When they got within sight of the property, Leeming came to a halt.

'Why are we stopping?' asked Hinton.

'This is where we part company, Alan.'

'For what reason?'

'I'll stay here and watch from a distance,' said Leeming. 'Mrs Venn, I hope, will be at home alone. Who would she prefer to see on her doorstep? A handsome young detective with a polite manner or a battle-scarred veteran like me whose face would probably frighten her?'

'Do you trust me to go in there on my own?' asked Hinton, pleased at the idea.

'She's a woman in a delicate frame of mind, Alan. Handle her with consideration.'

'I'll try.'

'Then what are you waiting for?' He shoved Hinton. 'Off you go, man!'

Emily Venn was seated in the drawing room when she first caught sight of him through the window. He was over a hundred yards away when he began to stride in the direction of the house. It never occurred to her that he might be coming to speak to her. When he got much closer, however, she could see the determination in his face and discern his sense of purpose. He was coming to the house. Emily flew into a panic. With her husband at home, she felt extremely vulnerable and prayed that he would stay asleep. Running into the hall, she opened the front door before any of the servants got there first.

She could tell from Hinton's manner that he had come on serious business. When he had introduced himself, she hustled him into the drawing room before anyone else realised that he was inside the house. Perching on the edge of the sofa, she waved him to an armchair.

'It is Mrs Venn, isn't it?' he said, taking out his notebook.

'Yes,' she murmured.

'Emily Venn?'

'That's me.'

'You were, I believe, acquainted with Giles Blanchard.'

'I . . . did know him by sight,' she conceded, 'but we were not close.'

'I understood that you were . . . friends.'

'You must be thinking of another Emily. I am not the only one on the island.'

'I was given your name and this address, Mrs Venn.'

'Then I'm sorry to disappoint you.'

'I was told to pass on a warning. The man who killed Mr Blanchard also stole everything that he was carrying. We believe that it included an address book with your name in it.'

'How can that be?' she gasped. 'I was not a close friend.'

'We think that the killer will make use of that notebook. It contains the names of women who may or may not have been close to Mr Blanchard. Can you understand, Mrs Venn?'

'I can understand only too well,' she said, voice

trembling. 'He might try to blackmail some of those women friends. How my name came to be among them, I have no idea. But I can assure you that I have not been approached for money by . . . whoever killed Mr Blanchard.'

'Are you certain of that, Mrs Venn?'

'Yes, I am – very certain.'

'But if you were . . .'

'There's no reason why anyone should bother me,' she insisted. 'I did know Mr Blanchard but I only ever saw him when he was with his wife. I'm sorry that you've come on a fool's errand.'

'It seems that I was misinformed,' he said, getting up. 'I'm sorry to trouble you.'

'I hope that you catch this dreadful man very soon.'

'We will, I can assure you.'

Emily heard sounds from the room above and realised that her husband had woken up.

Getting the visitor out of the house became her priority. Taking him by the arm, she escorted him to the front door and opened it wide. After another apology, Hinton put his notebook away and headed back in the direction from which he came. Emily closed the door with relief.

'Who was that?' asked her husband, appearing at the top of the stairs.

'Someone asking for directions,' she said. 'He was hopelessly lost.'

* * *

When they got back to their house in Portsmouth, they were in high spirits. Like Agnes Lenham and Christina Falconbridge, they had Emily Venn under their control. What struck the woman who had taken money from them was how different the three victims were.

'They had nothing in common with each other,' she said.

'Oh, yes they did.'

'You never got close to any of them.'

'I didn't need to, my love. My guess is that all three of them led lives that lacked excitement. It made them available. Blanchard sensed their need and picked them off one by one.'

'He was a predator.'

'None of them realised that. He clearly had charm and confidence. Also, of course, he was wealthy. That gave him a certain lustre. He made each of his victims feel special.'

'Well, he didn't make me feel special,' she complained. 'He just lunged at me on the train as if he was about to take me by force.'

'Luckily, you had me at hand.'

'I've never been so grateful.'

He reached out to kiss her. She responded willingly.

'I've just thought of something,' he said as they parted. 'Now that we have a comfortable income, we might think of starting a family. How does that sound?'

'It sounds wonderful.'

'If the money keeps rolling in, we can do anything we wish.'

'It's such an exciting thought.'.'

'Isn't a family what you've always wanted?'

'Yes, it is,' she said. 'There's something else I've always wanted as well.'

'You'll have to be patient.'

'We've been together for so long now.'

'I've told you before. I'm not ready to hurry into marriage.'

'Then I'll have to change your mind, won't I?'

He smiled. 'And how do you propose to do that?'

'I will make myself indispensable.'

'You already are indispensable to me,' he told her.

'In that case,' she replied, 'I'll have to become less available.'

When he met the two of them at the wharf, Colbeck was intrigued to hear about the discovery of one of the women who had been seduced by Giles Blanchard. It showed the inspector that his decision to ask for help from Berwyn Rees had been justified. He listened carefully to Hinton's account of his visit to the woman's house.

'What made you think that she lied to you?' he asked.

'I could see it in her eyes, sir,' replied Hinton. 'Her gaze kept flicking upwards as if there was someone in the room above.'

'Her husband, perhaps?'

'It's possible. What was obvious was her desperation

to get me out of there quickly.'

'You'd already made an important discovery, Alan.'

'Yes, sir. Although she denied it hotly, Mrs Venn had been one of his lovers. When I warned her that Blanchard's killer might well try to extort money from her and others, a look of sheer terror came into her eyes.'

'What did you make of her reaction?'

'She'd already been approached.'

'The killer is not wasting any time,' said Leeming. 'The moment he saw that notebook of Blanchard's, he realised that he had a hold over those women and wants to exploit it to the full.'

'I agree, Victor,' said Colbeck. 'And, by the way, you were wise not to go to the house yourself. Mrs Venn would certainly not have invited you in.'

'I know, sir. When I look in a mirror, I sometimes scare myself.'

'It was a good test for Alan, and he came through it with flying colours.'

'Thank you,' said Hinton. 'I just wish that I had put more pressure on the woman, but I was not in the house long enough. Effectively, she threw me out.'

'That, in itself, was significant,' said Colbeck.

'I've never seen anyone so nervous.'

'She must have been horrified to learn that you knew her secret.'

'I certainly knew that she'd been Blanchard's victim. It was written all over her face.'

'I'd make another assumption,' said Colbeck. 'A

financial demand was made, and she had no choice but to pay the money.'

'How much would that be?' asked Leeming.

'A substantial amount, I'd say, Victor.'

'Five pounds would be a substantial amount for me, but Mrs Venn could afford a lot more than that. Judging by the size of that house, she has a rich husband.'

'I daresay that she has money of her own as well,' said Colbeck. 'She could hardly ask her husband for the cash because he'd insist on knowing what it was for.'

'And she couldn't possibly have told him the truth,' said Hinton.

'Quite right. Well done, Alan. This is the evidence we've been waiting for.'

'Is it?' asked Leeming.

'Yes, Victor. In my opinion, Mrs Venn is the victim of blackmail. She has paid up at once.'

'But how does that help us, sir?'

'It puts a weapon in our hands.'

'We can challenge her about being at the mercy of blackmailers,' said Hinton.

'Oh, I think we can do better than that, Alan,' said Colbeck.

'I don't follow, sir.'

'Neither do I,' added Leeming.

'Use your imaginations,' advised Colbeck. 'When I meet her myself, I will not only be certain that she has paid the money demanded, I'll know the exact amount that she handed over.'

'How can you possibly do that?' asked Leeming.

'Wait and see.'

Gwendoline Cardus had been extraordinarily lucky. Having begun her career in royal service at Buckingham Palace, she had established a reputation for working hard, being very patient and showing unusual intelligence. As time passed, she moved gradually closer and closer to Her Majesty, the Queen. She was now a trusted advisor to the monarch, someone who moved around Osborne House as if it were her home. When she was able to bring her widowed mother to the Isle of Wight, she felt that her life was complete. She had never been so happy. It was then that Giles Blanchard showed an interest in her.

He was kind, attentive, and always finding ways of praising her. What began as a formal relationship soon changed into something far deeper. When he won her trust, Gwendoline was almost delirious with joy. For the first time in her life, she surrendered to a man and realised what she had been missing. Their moments together had been rare, but that only served to increase their intensity. She was realistic enough to know that he would never be exclusively hers and that she gained far more from the friendship than he did. But he had awakened her to possibilities she had never dreamt of before. He had made her blossom into a real woman.

At a stroke, her dreams had been shattered. Her lover had not only died, he had been killed in a brutal way. Whenever she pictured the scene in the train, she felt sick. Gwendoline had been in mourning ever since. She could still perform her duties as well as before but there was no longer the same sense of satisfaction. Something precious was missing from her life and the loss was increasingly unbearable. When she had discharged her duties that afternoon, she felt the need to get away from Osborne House, and went to visit her mother. Rose Cottage was beautiful at that time of year and her heart lifted when she saw its floral abundance.

Her mother was in the garden, seated beneath a shade with a cup of tea on the table. Isobel Cardus looked serene and happy. The very sight of her mother gave Gwendoline a surge of pleasure. She was proud of being able to rescue the old woman from a lonely house and a lonelier life. Since she had moved to the island, Isobel had improved in every way.

'Hello, Mother,' said Gwendoline, moving in to place a kiss on her cheek. 'Are you being looked after properly?'

'Yes, I am,' replied Isobel, 'and it's all because of your kindness.'

'I've only done what any daughter would do for a mother.'

'You did far more. You brought me back to life again. But what a lovely surprise to see you! I thought you'd be too busy to see me.'

'I can always make time for you, Mother.'

'Thank you,' said Isobel, squeezing her daughter's

arm. 'You are truly a blessing. And I'm glad that you came here today.'

'Why is that?'

'A letter came for you. It's on the table in the hallway.'

'Did you recognise the handwriting?'

'Oh, no. My old eyes are no longer as good as they used to be.'

'Would you like some more tea?'

'Yes, please.'

'Then I'll order another pot and collect my letter while I'm in the house.'

After going into the kitchen to place the order with a servant, Gwendoline picked up the letter from the hall table and glanced at it. The handwriting was unfamiliar. Opening the missive, she read the terse message.

'Blanchard is dead. We know your secret. It will cost you money to suppress it.'

Overcome with fear, Gwendoline promptly fainted.

CHAPTER EIGHTEEN

On the short trip back to the mainland, Leeming was delighted to see Brendan Mulryne again. The two of them immediately began to talk about days when they both wore police uniforms. Each of them had come a long way since then.

'Don't forget me, Victor,' said Mulryne.

'I could never do that. We shared too many good times together.'

'I'm talking about now. Just because I'm no longer in the Metropolitan Police Force, it doesn't mean I've lost the instincts I had. I can still tell the difference between right and wrong. Also, I miss having so many chances to enjoy a brawl.'

'You may well get an opportunity for a fight, Brendan. The man we're after strangled someone to death so he must be strong. When we finally corner him, we might need you.'

Mulryne grinned. 'I'm counting on it.'

When the steamer docked in Portsmouth, they bade farewell to the Irishman and walked swiftly to the Hope and Anchor. Messages awaited them. A letter for Leeming had been sent by his wife, and one from Lydia Quayle brought a huge smile to Hinton's face. But it was Colbeck who had the greatest delight. He waved the invitation in front of his colleagues.

'You'll never guess who sent this,' he declared.

'Was it Superintendent Tallis?' asked Leeming.

'No – his orders always come by means of a telegraph.'

'Is it a letter from your dear wife?' suggested Hinton.

'That would be the only thing more wonderful than this invitation,' said Colbeck. 'Because I made contact with Her Majesty, I have been asked to join her tomorrow morning at Osborne House.'

'Does the invitation include us?' asked Leeming, hopefully.

'Unfortunately, it does not, Victor.'

'That's a pity. I'd love to see inside that house.'

'I won't be expecting a grand tour of the place. When I get there, two tasks will await me.'

'What are they, sir?'

'First and foremost, I need to reassure Her Majesty

that our investigation will soon begin to bear fruit. Since she befriended Giles Blanchard, she will be eager to hear about developments in the case. He was a regular guest at Osborne House.'

'What is your second task?' asked Hinton.

'I want to have a private conference with Miss Gwendoline Cardus. She was very close to Her Majesty. When I spoke to Paul Blanchard earlier, he had come round to the idea that the woman might be one of the people his father had . . . developed an interest in.'

'What will we be doing tomorrow?' wondered Leeming.

'You will be trying to find a woman named Christina something or other. Since she does not live on the island, she might well reside in another area familiar to the elder Mr Blanchard.'

'Chichester, for instance?'

'The very place, Victor.'

'Am I to accompany Sergeant Leeming?' said Hinton.

'No, Alan, you will be paying a second visit to Mrs Venn – but this time you'll be armed with more information than you had today.'

Hinton was confused. 'Information?'

'Yes,' said Colbeck. 'Since you had the feeling that the woman was being blackmailed, I will do my best to find out how much money she had to pay.'

'You can't expect her to volunteer that information, sir.'

'I'll get it from another source, Alan – her bank. Before

I go to Osborne House, you and I will visit the banks on the island to establish which one holds an account in the name of Mrs Emily Venn. Ordinarily, they would never release such information, but I will impress upon them that, in a murder investigation, we need access to private accounts.'

'I'd never have thought of doing that,' confessed Hinton.

'Nor me,' said Leeming.

'Treat the woman with great sympathy,' said Colbeck. 'She will no doubt be terrified that her husband will find out about her . . . friendship with the estate agent. Assure her that we will be very discreet.'

'Leave it to me, Inspector.'

'We know what Mrs Venn is like,' said Leeming, 'but what sort of a woman is Gwendoline Cardus? How will she respond to a blackmail demand?'

'I hope to find out tomorrow,' said Colbeck.

Queen Victoria's days were always filled with routine tasks. From the moment that she got up, there were jobs to do, people to see, requests to consider and, inevitably, letters to read and to respond to. Even though she was caught up in continuous activity, she was not unaware of the needs of people close to her. It was the reason she sought a private moment with one of her closest companions.

'What is the problem, Gwendoline?' she asked.

'There is no problem, Your Majesty.'

'Then why are you behaving so oddly?'

'I was not aware that I was,' said Gwendoline, blushing slightly.

'Is it something to do with your mother?'

'Well, yes, I suppose that it is. I am happy to have her so close to me, but I worry that she is cut off from everybody in her social circle. I hoped that she would soon make friends here, but it simply has not happened. Mother is too old, I fear.'

'Is it anxiety over her that has made you so preoccupied?'

'I believe that it is, Your Majesty.'

'Then I disagree. I know you too well, Gwendoline. There's something else that is on your mind, something more serious than concern for your mother's welfare.'

'There is nothing else, I assure you.'

'Then why have other people noticed the same lapses that I have spotted? Are you ill in some way? Is that the problem?'

'I feel as if I'm glowing with health, Your Majesty.'

'Well, you certainly don't look it.'

'Oh . . .'

'Would you like a doctor to examine you?'

'No, no,' said Gwendoline in alarm. 'There's no need for that.'

'But he might be able to prescribe something that will make you feel better. You are a precious part of my household – and I want you back as the faithful servant you have always been.'

'I'm sorry that my behaviour has troubled you, Your

Majesty,' said Gwendoline, writhing in discomfort. 'Serving you has been the most pleasurable and rewarding thing that I have ever done. If I have erred in some way, I apologise. I will do my utmost to make sure that it never happens again.'

'I want the old Gwendoline back.'

'Then you shall have her, I promise.'

'And are you sure that there is no . . . medical problem?'

'I am certain of it, Your Majesty. I'm in the rudest health.'

'Apart from your mother, there is no other problem weighing on your mind?'

'None at all,' replied Gwendoline, conjuring up a smile. 'I remain ready to do my job to the very best of my abilities.'

'Good,' said the Queen, visibly relaxing. 'Thank you for reassuring me.'

Caleb Andrews arrived early at the house that morning. He had promised to take his granddaughter to the park and was pleased that the weather was ideal for such an outing. Madeleine let him into the house and gave him a welcoming kiss.

'Any word from Robert?' he asked.

'It's far too early for the post.'

'What is taking him so long this time?'

'You can't expect immediate results in a case like this, Father,' she said. 'When he found a moment to come home for a night, Robert warned that it might take weeks to solve the crime.'

'I expect results, Maddy.'

'Then you'll have to be patient.'

'He's built his reputation on the speed at which he works.'

'You're wrong,' she said. 'Robert never rushes things. It's because he's so meticulous that he gets the successes that he does. Besides, he is not going to make arrests simply to please you.'

'More's the pity!'

She laughed. 'Robert would never dare to tell you how to drive a train.'

'He'd better not, Maddy.'

'So why are you telling him how to catch a killer?'

'What happened is a terrible advertisement for travelling by train,' he argued. 'If you buy a ticket – especially for first-class travel – you have a right to expect a safe and comfortable journey. When someone gets strangled to death on a train, it makes people think twice about travelling that way. I love railways. I don't want them getting a bad name.'

'Murders during train journeys are very rare,' she reminded him. 'When they do occur, Robert is often called in to investigate.'

'And he usually gets a move on.'

'Father!'

'Well, he does, Maddy.'

'I won't hear another word,' she said, sternly. 'But I

can assure you of one thing. Robert is working hard on this case, and he will solve it in due course. Even as we speak, he will be searching for evidence.'

After visiting two banks without success, Colbeck and Hinton found one that had both Peter and Emily Venn as customers. Howard Ewing, the manager, a fleshy man with a gleaming bald head, was hesitant at first. He did not like the idea of giving private information about his clients to the police.

When Colbeck explained to him how vital it was for them to have access to Emily Venn's account, the manager changed his mind.

'What exactly is the problem, Inspector?' he asked.

'We have reason to believe that Mrs Venn is at risk, sir,' said Colbeck.

Ewing was alarmed. 'What sort of risk?'

'I can't go into details, I'm afraid.'

'The reason I ask is that Mrs Venn's husband is a solicitor. If we are at fault, he will certainly seek legal redress. I'd hate that to happen.'

'It won't, sir. Now, may I have details of Mrs Venn's account?'

'Yes, of course.'

Ewing took a ledger from one of the bookshelves that lined his office. After flicking through it, he came to the most recent transaction regarding the account. When he showed the details to Colbeck, the latter gave a sigh of satisfaction.

'Thank you, Mr Ewing,' he said. 'This is exactly what

I was hoping to find. I must now ask another favour from you.'

'What is it?'

'I'd like to speak to the clerk who dealt with Mrs Venn.'

Ewing was surprised. 'Is that necessary?'

'I'm afraid that it is, sir.'

'Very well. I'll fetch him at once.'

When the manager had left the room, Hinton looked around and shivered.

'I'd hate to work in a place like this,' he said. 'It's so dull and uninteresting.'

'I disagree. Looking after a large amount of money is very interesting. What it lacks is the excitement you get from being a detective.'

'How discreet is the manager?'

'Very discreet, Alan. That's why I impressed upon him that our enquiries relate to Mrs Venn only. There's no need for her husband to know about our visit here.'

'Why did you ask to speak to the clerk who handled the last transaction?'

'You'll soon see.'

There was not long to wait. The door opened and the manager ushered in Stanley Race, a nervous man who clearly thought that he was in trouble. After being introduced to him, Colbeck tried to allay his fears.

'You've done nothing wrong, Mr Race,' he said. 'As it happens, you may be able to help us in our latest investigation. Are you happy to do that?'

'Yes, Inspector, I am.'

'Do you remember dealing with Mrs Emily Venn recently?'

'I remember it well.'

'Does she come into the bank often?'

'No, it's quite a rare event.'

'Were you surprised by the amount of money she sought to withdraw?'

'Yes, I was, Inspector. It was quite unusual.'

'How did Mrs Venn seem?' asked Colbeck.

'Seem?'

'Was she relaxed? Tense? Troubled in any way?'

'The lady was certainly uneasy,' said Race. 'I've dealt with her before and we always have a pleasant conversation. Not on the last occasion. Mrs Venn seemed . . . very nervous.'

'Did she say why she wanted an unusually large amount of money?'

'Yes, she wished to buy her husband a birthday present.'

'Thank you, sir,' said Colbeck. 'That will be all.'

Race glanced at the manager who gave him a curt nod. The clerk left the office at once.

'Is there anything else we can do for you, Inspector?' asked Ewing.

'No, thank you, sir. You've provided invaluable service. We will now be able to act on what we have learnt here this morning.'

* * *

A new day had brought Emily Venn some relief from her fears. Her husband had woken up feeling much better and – although he still intended to visit the doctor – he set off for work with a spring in his step. Emily could now feel certain that he would not be coming home unexpectedly from work as he had done so the previous day. She could feel safe.

As it was such a glorious day, she decided to have a long walk in the hope that it would give her an opportunity to consider her problems. The most immediate one concerned the situation she was in. Someone was blackmailing her. The only way that they could do that was if they had been party to the murder of a man who had brought such joy into her life. She was being forced to pay for all the pleasure they had shared together. It could well be a life sentence. Yet there was no obvious way to escape from the commitment. Confession to her husband would mean the end of the marriage and certain eviction from the house.

Another problem loomed large. How could she pay her respects to Giles Blanchard? No details had yet been released about his funeral. Since he been a leading businessman on the island, the occasion would be a grand affair. Emily was desperate to be among the mourners outside the church but would it be altogether sensible for her to attend? If she went as an observer, she might be spotted and questions might be asked about her reason for being there. If she did not go, she would feel that she was letting her lover down. He had earned the right to be mourned by her. Emily decided that she simply had to be there.

A fresh anxiety brought her to a halt. What if Detective Constable Hinton came back?

When he was shown into the room, Gwendoline Cardus felt a stab of guilt. Since she had been close to Giles Blanchard, she had information that might be of use to the police, but she had no desire to pass it on. Though she had met him once before, she had no wish to be in Colbeck's presence. She knew that he was an elegant man with a natural grace. Nobody meeting him could imagine that he was a detective inspector at Scotland Yard. Unsettled by his appearance, Gwendoline could not take her eyes off him. When he met the Queen, she noticed, he gave her a polite nod and a dutiful smile.

Colbeck seemed surprisingly at ease in the presence of the monarch.

Gwendoline was only one of three royal companions present. When she saw that the Queen had decided to introduce each one of them to the newcomer, she felt a sudden rush of fear. She wished that she had a legitimate excuse to leave the room, but none existed. She was the last of the three to be introduced to the visitor. Colbeck greeted each woman in turn, exchanging a brief handshake and a few words. When it was Gwendoline's turn, she had to force herself to look at his eyes. While his handshake was warm, hers was cold and timid.

'It's good to see you again, Miss Cardus.'

'Thank you.'

'I visited Rose Cottage,' he told her. 'It is delightful.'

'Oh,' she murmured. 'Thank you . . .'

'It's you who deserve the thanks, Miss Cardus. Buying that cottage for your mother was an act of generosity and love.'

She was too surprised to reply, and, in any case, the Queen had conducted him towards the next room. All that she could see of him was his long, dark hair and immaculate frock coat. She stood there for minutes, tortured by an amalgam of fear and guilt.

Having failed to track down a woman on an earlier visit, Victor Leeming tried something different.

Instead of going to the Chichester estate agency, he called at the police station. Explaining the nature of his search, he asked if they could suggest any way in which he could track down a married woman whose first name was Christina. The duty sergeant, a grizzled veteran with a broken nose, scratched his head.

'Might that be Christina Wragg?' he asked.

'It might,' said Leeming.

'Would she be in her late thirties?'

'It's more than possible.'

'What colour is her hair – brown, black or fair?'

'I haven't a clue, Sergeant.'

'The Christina I have in mind is a redhead.'

'That's a possibility, I suppose.'

'Then it's your lucky day, Detective Sergeant Leeming,' said the other.

'Is it?'

'Yes, I fancy that Christina Wragg might be just the person you're looking for.'

'Wonderful! How will I find her?'

'I'll take you there myself,' said the other, reaching for a set of keys. 'Follow me.'

Unlocking a door, the duty sergeant led Leeming down a long corridor with cells either side of it. When he came to the last one, he inserted the key in the lock and twisted it. He opened the cell door wide and indicated the drunken woman curled up in a corner in a tattered dress.

'Here she is,' he announced. 'Christina Wragg. Is this the lady you're after?'

Leeming had been tricked. Joined by the other policeman there, the duty sergeant had a long, gleeful laugh at their visitor's expense. Leeming took it in his stride.

'Right,' he said. 'Now that you've had your fun at my expense, you can do some real police work for a change. Find this woman for me or I'll report you for wasting the time of a Scotland Yard detective who is engaged in a murder investigation. My guess is that most of you will be drummed out of the police force – and good riddance to you!'

The policemen stood there shamefaced.

* * *

On his first visit to the house, Alan Hinton had been hurried out of the front door. He was determined that he would not be ejected so unceremoniously again. The servant who answered his knock invited him in and asked him to wait in the hall while she reported his arrival to her employer. A reluctant Emily Venn soon came out and invited him into the drawing room.

When they sat down, she was patently ill at ease.

'The last time I was here,' he reminded her, 'you were anxious to get rid of me.'

'I didn't mean to be so rude,' she said.

'Your behaviour meant that you had something to hide.'

'That's not true at all. I was grateful that you came to warn me.'

'Then let me give you another warning, Mrs Venn,' he said. 'Before you start lying to me again, you ought to know that Inspector Colbeck and I visited your bank earlier today. We were given access to your account.'

'How dare you!' she exclaimed. 'You had no right.'

'In a case like this, we had every right.'

'This is insupportable,' she cried. 'I will move my account from that bank immediately.'

'I wouldn't advise that, Mrs Venn. Apart from anything else, you would have to explain to your husband why you had taken such impulsive action – and I don't think you'd dare to do that.'

She stood up. 'I'd like you to leave immediately.'

'I can't do that, I'm afraid. You forget that we are

involved in a murder investigation. That dictates what we do. Catching the killer means that we will stop at nothing. Instead of helping us, you think only of yourself.'

She slumped down on the sofa again. 'What did Mr Ewing tell you?'

'He showed us how much money you withdrew recently from your account.'

'There's nothing illegal in that. I can have access to cash whenever I wish.'

'But this was not a normal transaction,' he told her. 'We talked to Mr Race, the clerk who dealt with your request. He remembers how nervous you were.'

'It's none of his business!'

'I'm afraid that it is.' He lowered his voice. 'I'm here to help you, Mrs Venn, but you must help us in return. We believe that someone is blackmailing you. The money withdrawn from the bank was a first instalment. Do you want to go on paying the same amount time and again?'

'No, I don't,' she said, anxiously.

'As a result of Mr Blanchard's death, your name somehow came into the hands of his killer. He has seized on the opportunity of making a lot of money. You are one of his victims.' Her head sank to her chest. 'We're not making moral judgements. Your private life is your own. But we simply must catch this man before he bleeds you and the other women dry.'

She was stunned. 'How many others are there?' she asked, forlornly.

'We don't know, Mrs Venn, but you are certainly not alone.'

'He swore to me that—'

'It's irrelevant to us. We need your help to arrest the man who is blackmailing you.' She put her head in her hands. 'Tell me how he approached you, and what threats he made. If you do that, you will never have to pay him another penny.' When she looked up at him, he saw the despair in her eyes. 'Your husband need never know,' he assured her.

It was minutes before she felt able to speak. The words came out slowly.

'I was approached by a woman,' she admitted.

'Did you pay her the money she demanded?'

'Yes, I did.'

He took out his notebook and pencil. 'Right,' he said. 'Describe this woman in as much detail as you can. And remember that she was probably involved in the murder.'

Colbeck enjoyed his visit to Osborne House. He was not only seeing the interior of the building, he was also doing so in the presence of the Queen. Left alone with her, he gave a brief account of the progress on the investigation, stressing that he was confident of making arrests before too long.

After asking him to clarify some aspects of his report, she smiled at him.

'I am sorry for the circumstances that brought you here,' she said, 'but I am glad to see you again, Inspector.

I will never forget the wonderful service you rendered years ago.'

'I was only doing my job, Your Majesty.'

'You are always so modest about your achievements. That puts you in sharp contrast with another old friend who has been in contact with me recently. I speak of Nigel Buckmaster, the famous actor-manager.'

'I know him well and have admired his performances over the years. But you are quite right. Modesty is not part of an actor's stock-in-trade. Of necessity, he must crave attention.'

'He is soon bringing his company to the Theatre Royal in Brighton,' she explained, 'and offered his services on a Sunday during his stay there. He has entertained us superbly in the past.'

'Royal approval will be music to his ears, Your Majesty.'

'Did you say that you knew him?'

'I regard him as an old friend,' said Colbeck. 'During an investigation that took us to Cardiff, I had the good fortune to meet Mr Buckmaster and to see his performance as Macbeth. It was masterly. However,' he added, dismissively, 'enough of my memories. I was very grateful for the opportunity to visit you in this splendid house and to discuss the case in hand. Since I know how fiendishly busy you keep yourself, Your Majesty, I will not take up any more of your time. What I would ask before I go is the opportunity to speak to one of your companions.'

'Yes, of course,' she said. 'To whom do you wish to speak?'

'Miss Gwendoline Cardus.'

From the moment she met him again, Gwendoline was uneasy. Inspector Colbeck had not only visited her mother at Rose Cottage, he had looked deep into Gwendoline's eyes as if he was aware of her situation. She was now on edge. Gone was the air of serenity she had cultivated. Because she sensed danger ahead, she was almost dithering. The inspector's arrival came hard on the heels of the anonymous letter she had received. Someone not only knew of her friendship with Giles Blanchard, he or she was demanding money that she simply did not have. She was horrified.

Her days in royal service were clearly numbered. When her secret was out, she would face instant dismissal and the strong disapproval of her friends. Most harrowing of all was the confession she would have to make to her mother. Living in Rose Cottage with her would be a penance.

Alan Hinton had filled several pages of his notebook. Once Emily Venn began to talk, the words poured out in a torrent. She not only gave him a detailed description of the woman to whom she had paid money, she described how she and Giles Blanchard had developed such a close friendship.

Hinton felt sorry for her. Having been made to feel

that she had a special place in his heart, she now knew the truth about her lover. There were other women in his life.

Adding to the discomfort was the fact that she was forced to confess what had happened to a detective who was much younger than her. Emily was grateful for his understanding.

'Thank you for being so sympathetic,' she said.

'You need help, Mrs Venn. We will provide it.'

'That's very reassuring.'

'Is there anything else – however trivial – that you can tell me about the woman who took the money from you? Every detail is valuable.'

'There is one thing,' she recalled, uncertainly.

'What is it?'

'Well . . .'

'Take your time. There's no hurry.'

Emily searched her memory. It was over a minute before she spoke.

'I had a strange feeling that I'd seen the woman before,' she said. 'I don't know where or when but she . . . stirred a memory. My husband and I used to go to the theatre occasionally. I'm wondering if that's where I may have seen her – on stage.'

For some part of every year, Osborne House was Gwendoline Cardus's home. It was a joy to live there. She always felt supremely safe. That safety was now under threat. As she was summoned to a private room to be questioned by Inspector Colbeck, she was trembling. He sensed her discomfort immediately and, after indicating a chair, he waited until she had sat down before sitting opposite her. He asked her if she enjoyed her time at Osborne House and let her talk about the honour she felt at being able to serve Queen Victoria. The more she talked, the more relaxed she became. When he felt that Gwendoline had calmed down sufficiently, he introduced the subject that he really wanted to discuss.

'I believe that Giles Blanchard handled the sale of Rose Cottage. Is that correct?'

'Yes, it is, Inspector.'

'May I ask how he behaved towards you?'

'He was polite and considerate.'

'I gather that you'd met him at functions held here.'

'That's true. He and Mrs Blanchard were often guests at Osborne House.'

'Did he ever come without his wife?'

'Once or twice,' she admitted.

'When did you pay your first visit to Rose Cottage?'

'Oh, it was months ago.'

'And how did you get to the property?'

There was a long pause. 'Mr Blanchard drove me there in his trap.'

'Was anyone living at the house?'

'No, Inspector. The previous owners had already left.'

'So you were able to look around at will.'

'Yes, I was. Mr Blanchard was kind enough to point

302

out repairs needed to be done before a new owner moved in.'

'Not all estate agents would have done that,' suggested Colbeck. 'They would have tried to disguise some of the defects. Mr Blanchard was clearly honest with you.'

'He was one of the most honest people I ever met,' said Gwendoline with sudden passion. 'I trusted him completely.'

'Let me come to a more delicate matter, Miss Cardus. In the wake of his father's death, Paul Blanchard discovered some letters of a private nature. As it happened, he destroyed them. I am of the opinion that you may have written some of those letters.'

'That's not true,' she denied, cheeks reddening.

'Let me finish, please. Whoever killed him stole everything that he had on him. We believe that it included names and addresses of . . . female friends close to him. One of them has already been the victim of blackmail. We know that she was forced to take money from her bank to pay the killer and his accomplice.' He saw her look of dismay. 'Other women may also have been approached. May I ask if you have been one of them?'

'Certainly not!' she snapped. 'I find that question insulting!'

'I apologise for having to ask it, Miss Cardus. We are anxious to trace the person who has sent the demands. We can only do that with the cooperation of the victims. Otherwise, those who are targeted will spend the rest of their lives paying money to complete strangers in order to conceal aspects of their friendship with Mr Blanchard. It's a dreadful position to be in.'

Gwendoline remained silent but he could see the anguish in her eyes.

'We have the greatest sympathy for the victims,' he said, 'and will do everything we can to safeguard their privacy. If they help us, their secrets will not be revealed in any way. When the fear is lifted from them, they can resume a normal life and put the past behind them.' He lowered his voice. 'Do you understand what I am telling you, Miss Cardus?'

'No, Inspector,' she said with an attempt at defiance. 'I don't. My relationship with Mr Blanchard was entirely respectable, and I resent the suggestion that I behaved improperly with him. Frankly, it is insulting.'

'Miss Cardus—'

'I'm sorry but I have duties to attend to,' she said, rising to her feet. 'Please excuse me.'

And before he could stop her, she flounced out of the room.

CHAPTER NINETEEN

When they met at the Hope and Anchor, they discussed their contrasting fortunes. Alan Hinton felt that he had made a giant step forward in the investigation, whereas Victor Leeming had come back from his travels with nothing to show for his efforts. He felt thwarted.

'First,' he complained, 'the police in Chichester had a joke at my expense. I made them pay dearly for that. Then I had a pointless search of various addresses in the area. I must have met ten or more women by the name of Christina. The oldest was in her eighties. None of them was the person I was after, so I gave up in despair.'

'I'm sorry to hear that.'

'Thank goodness that one of us had some success.'

'Mrs Venn was very helpful,' said Hinton. 'Once she realised that I was not shocked by what she had done, she decided to tell me the truth.'

'How did she react to the news that she was not the only one?'

'It really upset her.'

'I can imagine.'

'Blanchard managed to convince each of those women that they were very special to him.

'He was so clever – and so cruel.'

'I struggle to have any sympathy for the way he was killed,' said Leeming. 'I'm usually sorry for any murder victim but not in this case. He not only tricked a succession of women, he left them in a perilous situation.'

'Mrs Venn was at the end of her tether.'

'I'm glad that you persuaded her to help us, Alan.'

'She was helping herself, really.'

'Yes, I suppose so. It was the only way to escape from being blackmailed.'

'I'm not sure that this description is going to help us,' said Hinton, flipping open the pages of his notebook. 'It may be accurate, but I've already seen three or four women it would fit. How do we find the right one?'

'Leave that to the inspector.'

'He can't perform miracles.'

'Oh, yes he can,' said Leeming with a chuckle. 'I've seen him do it so many times.'

* * *

Edward Tallis had had a busy morning that included a long discussion with the commissioner. When he got back to his office, the superintendent hoped for a letter from Colbeck with details of how the investigation was progressing. Instead of a letter, all that he got was a telegraph bearing the information that Colbeck had been invited to Osborne House.

'Why on earth are you going there?' demanded Tallis, tossing the telegraph onto his desk. 'The one person who definitely did not commit murder on that train was Her Majesty, Queen Victoria!'

Gwendoline Cardus had some time alone to compose herself before she felt able to join the Queen. When she did so, she found her reading a batch of letters delivered that morning. Gwendoline stood quietly nearby and wondered why she had behaved so badly in front of Inspector Colbeck. The simple fact was that she was the victim both of a man she had loved and of the people responsible for his murder. Though she had a reasonable amount of money in the bank, it would not last long if she had to pay out a tidy sum on a regular basis. And how could she trust the blackmailer not to reveal her secret? When Gwendoline's money ran out, he or she might expose her shame out of sheer spite.

There was no escape. She either had to help the police or suffer the horror of being at the mercy of strangers almost indefinitely. It was a frightening dilemma. If she turned to the police, she would be admitting that she had yielded up her virginity to Giles Blanchard and committed adultery with him on subsequent occasions. She had done so in the foolish belief that he loved her as much as she adored him. Now that she realised that she was one of a group of women he had duped, she felt deeply wounded. The whole experience had left her bewildered.

What could she possibly do to retain some semblance of dignity?

Colbeck was in a hurry. When he got back to Portsmouth, the first thing he did was to listen to reports from Hinton and Leeming. Pleased by Hinton's news, he jotted down the description that had been given to the detective constable by Emily Venn.

'That's a start, at last,' he said.

'Mrs Venn was in a terrible state,' explained Hinton. 'It took me some time to get all that information out of her.'

'You did well, Alan.'

'Unlike me,' groaned Leeming.

'Nobody could fault your persistence, Victor.'

'It just didn't yield any results, sir.'

'Then you'll have to go back to Chichester and try again,' said Colbeck. 'Alan will go with you this time. He might bring you luck.' He stood up. 'I've checked the train times. If we can get to the station in twenty minutes' time, we'll catch the fast train to London.'

'We?' repeated Leeming. 'Are you coming with us?'

'No, Victor. You'll get off at Chichester, but I'll go on to London.'

'Are you going to see the superintendent?'

'I hope not,' said Colbeck.

'Then what's the reason for your visit?'

'I want to pass on the description that Mrs Venn gave Alan to someone who might recognise the woman in question. It would save us a lot of time.'

'Who are you going to see?' asked Hinton.

'Malvolio.'

Leeming gaped. 'Who?'

'You know him best as Nigel Buckmaster. He's busy rehearsing his role in *Twelfth Night*.'

'No, no, no!' howled Buckmaster. 'The play must be heard as well as seen. How many times must I tell you? Follow my example. Open your lungs and project those wonderful words. Reach every pair of ears in the theatre. Those in the back row of the upper circle deserve to hear what they have paid to hear. Give them their money's worth!'

Cowed by his deafening criticism, the cast muttered their apologies and went back to the beginning of the scene. When they performed it again, they did so with clearer diction and greater volume. Buckmaster nodded his approval. The next scene featured Malvolio, so he took his place onstage and arranged the actors in their correct positions. None of them dared to pretend that they might catch the attention of an audience. Whenever he stepped onstage, Buckmaster was a commanding figure. He dwarfed everyone around him.

During the train journey, Colbeck was able to describe what had happened when he visited Osborne House earlier that morning. He was disappointed that he had been unable to get cooperation from Gwendoline Cardus. Though it was plainly in her interests to trust the police, she preferred to ignore Colbeck's offer of help, claiming instead that her friendship with Giles Blanchard had been entirely innocent and that a potential blackmailer would have no reason to threaten her.

'That was a blatant lie,' said Leeming.

'Yes,' agreed Colbeck, 'and Miss Cardus knows it only too well.'

'Is she in imminent danger?' asked Hinton.

'She could well be, Alan. I sensed that she was quietly terrified, and yet unable to admit the truth to herself. Her greatest fear, of course, is that the Queen will learn the truth about her. It would astound Her Majesty and lead to dismissal for Miss Cardus.'

'It was stupid of her to reject your offer of help.'

'Yes, Alan. It was. I can only hope that she will come to her senses and cooperate with us.'

'Mrs Venn was far more sensible.'

'There may be other victims,' Colbeck reminded him. 'Paul Blanchard recalls eight or nine women who wrote to his father in secret. It's a pity that he can't remember every name. He did remember Christina.

'Do your best to find her, please.'

'We will, sir,' said Leeming.

'How will you find this actor-manager?' asked Hinton.

'Mr Buckmaster will have hired a rehearsal room and will be putting his cast through their paces. He's a stern taskmaster. He makes his actors work until they drop.'

'His productions always get good reviews,' said Leeming.

'That's because he has immense talent, Victor. And, of course, he appears in the plays himself – usually in the leading role. He has a huge following.'

'Especially among ladies.'

'The main reason I'm approaching him,' said Colbeck, 'is that he has an extraordinary memory. He's either met, worked with, or watched every actor and actress of consequence in the British theatre over the last thirty years. If the woman we are after really has worked on the boards, I guarantee that Mr Buckmaster will know who she is.'

Paul Blanchard had arrived at the agency that morning in time to open it up. Even though he had many other things on his mind, he persisted in going through the routine that his father had taught him. He had to accept that every customer who came in wanted to pass on their condolences, and he took that in his stride. Other businesses had closed when the owner had died suddenly. Paul knew that his father would have insisted that he kept the agency open and working at full stretch.

After a busy morning, he was about to take time off for refreshment when he heard the approach of a horse and glanced through the front window. A trap pulled up outside and his wife climbed out of it. Paul rushed out into the street to take her in his arms. Verity was almost out of breath. She needed a few moments to compose herself.

'What's wrong?' he asked.

'It's your mother, Paul.'

Panic seized him. 'You don't mean that—'

'No, no, she's still alive as far as we know but she's disappeared.'

'Have you organised a search for her?'

'Yes, of course but to no avail.'

'Come into my office and tell me exactly what happened,' he said.

With an arm around her, he escorted her into the building and past the curious eyes of his employees. Once they were in the privacy of the office, he lowered her gently into a chair.

'Who discovered that she had gone?'

'It was Marion. She went into your mother's bedroom to clean it and it was empty. There was no sign of your mother.'

'Perhaps she was in the garden somewhere,' he suggested.

'We searched every inch of it,' she explained, 'but she was not there. When we looked in the immediate surroundings of the house, we couldn't find any trace of her.'

'Do you have any idea what she was wearing?'

'As far as we know, your mother must still be in her nightdress.'

Paul was alarmed. 'Where, in the name of God, can she be?'

'I think we should go to the police and get them to organise a proper search.'

'We can certainly do that, Verity,' he said, 'but I want to be there when she's found. It's my duty as a son.' He clicked his tongue in irritation. 'We have enough on our plates without having a scare like this. Where are you, Mother?'

'Let's drive to the police station.'

'I want every man available to join in the search,' he insisted. 'We simply must find her.'

Flinging open the door of his office, he hustled his wife out.

Gwendoline Cardus was in despair. Desperate to be alone, she had to perform her duties and talk to the other women who waited on the Queen. The fact that Her Majesty was entertaining visitors meant that Gwendoline was not under royal scrutiny, and that was a relief. But there would be a time when she and the Queen would be alone together. Questions would be asked of her, and she was not sure that she could find answers that would keep the Queen at arm's length.

Another thought stung her like the bite of an insect. In her handbag was the anonymous letter sent to her. It would be the first of many, giving her orders, making threats, demanding money, and robbing her of her freedom to do what she pleased. Hopelessly enslaved, she would be forced to do the bidding of a stranger.

'Ah, there you are,' said the Queen, sweeping into view.

'Did you want me, Your Majesty?' replied Gwendoline, startled.

'Yes, I'd like a private conversation with you.'

It sounded like a threat.

When he found the rehearsal room, Colbeck was in time to see the last scene of *Twelfth Night*. The powerful hand of Nigel Buckmaster had everything completely under control. In the role of Malvolio, the pompous steward at Olivia's house, he limped into view in a dreadful state. He had been locked up, teased, tormented, and deprived of his former dignity. Olivia was shocked to see him so pitilessly abused. Alone of those onstage, she had sympathy for him.

Alas, poor fool, how have they baffled thee!

Feste, the clown, added further mockery of Malvolio, goading him into a wild threat.

I'll be revenged on the whole pack of you!

His howl of pain and humiliation rang around the rehearsal room. When he stormed off stage, it was left to Feste to bring the play to a close with a song. As the only member of the audience, Colbeck clapped his hands enthusiastically. Buckmaster rounded on him.

'This is a private rehearsal,' he snarled. 'You have no right to be here, sir.'

'I was hoping for a word with you, Mr Buckmaster,' said Colbeck.

'I have no time for conversation with strangers. Please depart immediately, Mr . . .'

'Colbeck – Inspector Robert Colbeck.'

'Then I'm delighted to see you,' said Buckmaster, spreading his arms wide and moving forward to enfold his visitor in a warm embrace. He turned to the cast. 'We will have a break for thirty minutes,' he announced. 'Come back on time or there will be consequences.'

The actors drifted away, allowing him to turn his attention to his old friend.

'It's wonderful to see you again, Inspector,' he said, pumping his hand.

'I could say the same of you.'

'What brings you here?'

Colbeck smiled. 'I'm hoping that you may be able to help me.'

When he saw how distressed his wife was, Paul Blanchard did his best to calm her down, assuring her that she was not to blame for his mother's disappearance. He then helped her into the waiting trap. Climbing in beside her, he snapped the reins and set the horse off. Verity kept apologising.

'It was not your fault,' he told her. 'You can't watch Mother twenty-four hours a day.'

'Then why do I feel so guilty?' she asked.

'I don't know. Had she been behaving oddly?'

'No, Paul, I sat with her for hours. Then she asked to be left alone because she was tired.'

'When did Marion discover that she was no longer in the house?'

'It was about half an hour later.'

'How could she sneak out without being noticed?'

'That's what we kept asking ourselves,' said Verity.

Because of the pace at which he was driving, they soon reached the police station. After helping his wife to the ground, Blanchard led the way into the building. Inspector Ruggles was on duty. He looked up from his desk.

'We have an emergency,' said Blanchard. 'My mother has left the house on foot, and we have no idea where she is. We need every officer you've got, Inspector Ruggles.'

'No, you don't, sir,' replied the other.

'Do as I say, man!'

'There's no need to shout at me, sir.'

'Then do as you're told – or there'll be repercussions.'

'I can understand your anxiety but there's really no need for it. A report came in some time ago of an elderly

316

woman in a nightdress, wandering alone near Bembridge Windmill.'

'What on earth is she doing there?' demanded Blanchard.

'You'll have to ask her, sir.'

'Is she safe and well?' asked Verity.

'Yes,' said Ruggles. 'As far as I know, anyway. The problem is that she's refusing to leave the spot or one of my officers would have driven her home. People of that age do behave strangely at times,' he went on. 'In fact . . .'

He got no further. Grabbing his wife's hand, Blanchard ran out of the police station. They got back into the trap and rode away.

Gwendoline Cardus was the victim of her own sense of guilt. Taken aside by the Queen, she feared that she might be sternly reprimanded or even summarily dismissed. In fact, she found the older woman remarkably sympathetic. Gwendoline was taken by surprise.

'Will you take my advice?' asked the Queen.

'Of course, Your Majesty.'

'It may be that you have been pushing yourself too hard.'

'You deserve the finest support and that is what I've always strived to give you.'

'Indeed, you have. Your commitment has been extraordinary. Until,' added the Queen, 'recently, that is. Your mind has wandered, you've made mistakes and you're clearly upset about something. Since you won't explain what it is, I'm suggesting that you take some time off.'

'No!' cried Gwendoline. 'I don't want to let you down, Your Majesty.'

'Frankly, you're no use to me at the moment.'

'Then I apologise deeply. I'll make amends.'

'Only after you've had a rest from your duties.'

'But it's my work here that has helped to keep me sane.'

'Take a week off,' counselled the other. 'A fortnight, if necessary. Forget about us and enjoy your mother's company instead. She's a virtual newcomer here. Isn't it high time that you took her on a tour of the island?'

'Well, yes, I suppose that it is.'

'That's settled then.'

'But I don't want to leave Osborne House, Your Majesty.'

'You're little use to me in your present state of mind, Gwendoline. Since you've no wish to confide in me properly – and that is your right – you are better off confronting your demons somewhere else. When you have done that, you will be welcomed back with open arms.'

Colbeck was patient. Before he could explain why he had come in search of the actor-manager, he had to wait while Nigel Buckmaster boasted about the theatrical triumphs he had had since they last met. Sitting back in his chair, he then gestured for his friend to speak. Colbeck gave him a summary of the murder investigation, stressing the facts that the killer had been able to pass as a naval officer and as a clergyman without arousing suspicion.

'In short,' he said, 'I think that he may be in the same profession as yourself.'

'That may well be so – except that he is no longer able to find work as an actor, and has turned to crime instead. But he is of less interest to me than his female accomplice.'

'Why is that?'

'She is the real performer,' explained Buckmaster. 'The man may have strangled someone to death, but the woman is the key figure in what happened afterwards. She has established a link with these poor women who were deceived and exploited by this latter-day Don Giovanni. Each of those victims was different in character. The person who approached them would have had to make subtle adjustments to the way she spoke to each one. That is why she was entrusted with the role.'

'I see what you mean.'

'Of the two of them,' concluded Buckmaster, 'my guess is that the woman is the true thespian.'

'But do you have any idea whom she might be?' asked Colbeck.

'I can think of half-a-dozen actresses who would lower themselves to such a crime.'

'May I have their names?'

'Don't rush me, my friend. I need to concentrate. Let me go back to the murder on that train. You think that there were three people in that compartment?'

'Yes, I do. The woman might somehow have enticed Mr Blanchard to follow her on to the train. He clearly had an eye for a beautiful woman. Before he could take advantage of her – this is guesswork on my part – they were interrupted by the arrival of another passenger.'

'This naval officer – pretending to be drunk, perhaps, and going off to sleep.'

'A good suggestion. It would explain why Blanchard felt able to assault the woman. My theory is that things got out of hand and the woman was in genuine distress.'

'That was when her friend strangled the fellow,' said Buckmaster. 'After he'd been killed, they emptied his pockets and realised they had found a very different source of money.'

'It was safer, involved no violence and gave them great power over the women.'

'So they started to fleece their victims.'

'One of whom has admitted how she was blackmailed,' said Colbeck. 'Can you think of a former actress ruthless enough to frighten those women into paying her money on a regular basis?'

'I can think of two or three capable of that.'

'Who are they?'

'Wait, Inspector. I need time to think this through.'

Buckmaster went off into a long, brooding silence. All that Colbeck could do was to wait quietly. While he admired the man's extraordinary gifts as an actor, he was acutely conscious of his reputation among women in his profession. Every time they met, Buckmaster had had a different actress on his arm – and they seemed to get younger each time.

At length, the actor sat up abruptly and snapped his fingers.

'Bethany Drake,' he declared.

'Who?' asked Colbeck.

'She was a young, talented actress I met some years ago. Bethany had all the skills needed to reach the upper tier of the profession, but she had a besetting sin.'

'What was it?'

'She had criminal tendencies,' said Buckmaster. 'I hardly need to tell you what they are, do I? You must be an expert on the ways that a criminal tendency can corrupt the mind of weaker vessels. When I engaged Bethany Drake to play the part of Desdemona on tour, we were bedevilled by crime. Money disappeared, personal belongings went astray, and bickering broke out among the cast. It was only when I had the sense to dismiss her from the company that the whole mood improved instantly. We all realised why,' he said. 'Bethany was the culprit.'

'Why didn't you hand her over to the police?'

'She disappeared before I could do so. Naturally, I spread the word and no management would touch her with a bargepole. She had to resort exclusively to crime.'

'What about the man who is her associate?'

'At a guess, he's another outlaw from the profession. Bethany was very desirable. She could pick and choose her lovers.' He sighed. 'To be honest, I always envied them.'

It was Leeming's turn to come up with a good idea. Hitherto, Hinton had garnered the praise. He had traced items stolen from the murder victim to a jewellery shop in Chichester, and he had also found the church from which clerical garb worn by the killer had been taken. Having failed in an earlier search for a woman named Christina, he thought of another way to find her.

'We could go to church, Alan,' he suggested.

'Whatever for – it's not Sunday.'

'The information we need is there seven days a week.'

'Stop talking in riddles.'

'What happens when you get married?'

'It's no use asking me,' said Hinton with a laugh. 'I'm still a bachelor.'

'Your time will come. When the ceremony is over, bride and bridegroom retire to the vestry to sign their names. Think of Mrs Venn.'

'What about her?'

'How old would you say she was?'

'Oh, I'm not sure – no older than forty, I'd say.'

'Then the woman named Christina will be roughly the same age. Blanchard was attracted to experienced married women in their thirties. If we visit the churches here in Chichester, we can go through the records of weddings that took place ten or fifteen years ago. Who knows?' said Leeming with a grin. 'A Christina might just pop up.'

Hinton was dubious. 'It's a bit of a long shot.'

'I've explored most of the obvious avenues. Let's at least have a try.'

'If it's that important to you, I'm happy to search church records.'

'It'll be good experience for you, Alan,' said Leeming, winking at him. 'When you finally get married, you'll know exactly what you need to do in the vestry.'

'I'm happy being a bachelor.'

'That's what I thought until I met Estelle.'

'I'm not looking for a wife at the moment.'

'Wait until you meet a woman looking for a husband,' said Leeming with a grin. 'When that happens, you'll start to think differently.'

Bembridge was on the east coast of the island. Having been built over a hundred and fifty years earlier, its windmill had withstood the test of time and was still in good, if noisy, working order. The sails were turning in the wind when Paul Blanchard and his wife arrived in the trap. Standing close by were two uniformed policemen, talking to an elderly woman with a blanket wrapped around her. Bringing the horse to a halt, Paul jumped out of the trap, helped his wife to the ground then ran across to the three figures. 'What are you doing here, Mother?' he asked.

'Oh, hello, Paul,' she said, turning to him. 'I told these gentlemen that you would come to get me. I wasn't going to move from here until I saw you.'

'Mrs Blanchard refused to let us take her home,' said one of the policemen.

'That's what Inspector Ruggles told us,' recalled Blanchard. 'Thank you for looking after her. I'm very grateful to you. My wife and I will take over now.'

'Very good, sir.'

'Where did this blanket come from?'

'One of the neighbours kindly brought it out. They saw your mother shivering in this breeze.'

'We'll return it,' said Blanchard.

He waved the policemen off then turned his attention to his mother. Verity had already put an arm around the older woman and was talking quietly to her. Catherine was pleased to see her son and daughter-in-law. She showed no sign of distress.

'I knew that you'd find me,' said Catherine.

'But why did you come here in the first place?' asked her son.

'Yes,' added Verity. 'When I realised that you were no longer in the house, I was alarmed. I drove to the office to tell Paul what had happened.'

'You caused us a lot of distress,' he said.

'I just went for a walk, that's all,' explained Catherine. 'I'm entitled to do that, surely.'

'Not in your nightdress, Mother.'

'And why did you come here?' asked Verity.

'Ah, well,' said Catherine. 'I had a good reason.'

'If you'd told me what it was, I'd have come with you.'

'I had to be alone, Verity. Don't you realise that?'

'Frankly, Mother, we don't,' said Blanchard. 'You scared us.'

'I didn't mean to, Paul. I just had this urge and so I came.'

'But why here?'

Catherine smiled. 'This place is very special to me.'

'It's just a creaky old windmill.'

'It's much more than that to me – and to your father. This is where he proposed to me, you see, so it holds wonderful memories. That's why I had to come.'

'But you didn't have to do so alone,' argued Verity. 'If it was that important to you, I would have been happy to bring you here.'

'I had to be on my own. Don't you understand?'

'Frankly, I don't.'

'And neither do I,' added Blanchard.

'My whole life changed in the shadow of this windmill,' said his mother.

'That doesn't mean you have to sneak out of the house to come here, Mother.'

'No, it doesn't and I'm sorry if I upset anyone, Paul.'

'You scared us unnecessarily,' he chided.

'I didn't mean to, honestly. I just had this urge to see the windmill once again and bask in some happy memories.' Catherine gave a hopeless shrug. 'Since your father died, memories are all that I have left.'

CHAPTER TWENTY

Robert Colbeck had found his brief reunion with the actor-manager exhilarating. It not only brought back happy memories of the time when they first met, he was also reminded of the fact that Nigel Buckmaster was a true titan of the stage. Even in polite conversation, the man was a master of gesture and speech. He made the most insignificant sentences sound as if they had been extracted from a well-known play. Where words were insufficient on their own, his eyes took over, flashing, glaring, narrowing, and widening dramatically whenever necessary.

Colbeck had felt as if he had a front-row seat in a London theatre.

Buckmaster had been so confident when he identified the woman who had been in the same compartment as Giles Blanchard on the night in question that Colbeck's hopes had been raised. At least he now knew the name of one of the people he was after. Finding out who her male companion was would, however, be more difficult. At the time he had employed the actress, Buckmaster remembered that Bethany Drake had always courted male attention. She had a string of actors vying for her favours. He had recalled the names of three of them. Colbeck wrote the names in his notebook. Bethany Drake might have lured a man into a first-class compartment, but it was her companion who had committed the murder. Who was he?

On the train journey back to Portsmouth, he had ample time to review the information he had gathered. When Colbeck had mentioned his visit to Osborne House, he had been forced to listen to accounts of when Buckmaster had been there, entertaining selected guests by declaiming famous speeches from Shakespeare's plays. It occurred to Colbeck that it was highly likely that Giles Blanchard might have been present at some of those occasions – and so had Gwendoline Cardus. Coincidences were starting to build up.

Having already explored several churches, Alan Hinton was not looking forward to doing so again, but he soon changed his mind. The churchwardens they met were universally helpful. When they heard that their records might contain information relating to a murder investigation, they allowed immediate access to the list of marriages in their respective churches. The detectives learnt that, since the reign of Henry VIII, parish records of births, marriages and deaths were to be kept by law, turning churches into a rich source of information.

Their initial enthusiasm soon disappeared. Though they searched diligently, they found no record of a marriage that involved a bride by the name of Christina. When they came to the last church and met with failure yet again, Hinton began to lose heart.

'It was a good idea of yours,' he said, 'but I'm afraid that it didn't get us what we wanted.'

'Don't give up hope, Alan.'

'But we've been to every church in Chichester.'

'Except the most important one,' noted Leeming. 'The cathedral.'

'There's no point in going to that.'

'Why not?'

'Well,' said Hinton, 'only people of importance get married there.'

'How do you know that Christina was not important?'

'I don't, I suppose.'

'Then let's go to the cathedral,' said Leeming, 'and keep our fingers crossed.'

When his mother felt ready to go home, Paul Blanchard sent her off in the trap with Verity. Because there was no room in the vehicle for him, he followed on foot, striding out purposefully. His mother's behaviour was disturbing. She would clearly need to be watched more carefully in future. That might be relatively easy to do during the day, but more problematical after dark. What if his mother let herself out of the house at midnight? She might encounter all sorts of dangers. Yet they could hardly keep the woman under lock and key. It was, after all, her house and she had a right to come and go. For her own protection, however, there had to be some constraints. A plan had to be devised. It would require careful thought.

Of more concern to Blanchard was his mother's attitude to her husband. She seemed to view him in a romantic light. What else could have propelled her out of her bedroom and all the way to a windmill? Because of its associations, the place had a special meaning for her. Catherine had pushed the horror of her husband's murder out of her mind and remembered him as a young man in love with her. She had already hinted to her son that she was not entirely unaware of his behaviour in more recent years, but Catherine preferred to recall the man that her husband had been many years ago. That was her reality.

'What are you doing here, Gwen?'

'Well, that's a fine welcome!' teased her daughter. 'Aren't you pleased to see me?'

'Of course, I am,' said Isobel Cardus.

'I'm having some time off from work, Mother.'

The old woman was anxious. 'You've not been dismissed from royal service, have you?'

'Not at all,' said Gwendoline. 'It was Her Majesty's idea that I deserved a rest. She also pointed out that I haven't really shown you most of the island.'

'I'm perfectly happy here, Gwen.'

'But there's so much else to see.'

'There's no hurry.'

'I'll introduce you to some of the friends I've made here.'

'That will be nice,' said her mother. 'Oh, what a lovely surprise it is to see you!'

She got up from the garden bench to embrace her daughter. Gwendoline kept a smile on her face but her emotions were churning. In effect, she had been laid off because she was no longer performing her duties satisfactorily. Being told to take a rest had been a real blow to her pride.

Much as she loved her mother, there was no kudos in sharing Rose Cottage with her. Instead of living in the finest house on the island, she had moved into a quaint little cottage. Gwendoline was forced to accept the harsh truth. Temporarily, she had been demoted.

'How do you feel?' asked her mother.

'I feel fine,' said Gwendoline.

'Well, you don't look it, I must say. You've put on too much weight, for a start. It's not good for you, Gwen. Mark my words. You need some long walks.'

'We'll go together.'

'That would be lovely.'

'We can't waste this wonderful weather.'

'Will you take me to Osborne House?' asked Isobel, excitedly.

'Of course – I know where we can get the best view of it.'

'I'd like to see inside, Gwen.'

Her daughter was uneasy. 'That . . . may not be possible, Mother.'

'Why not? You work there, don't you?'

'Yes, of course, but Her Majesty is very busy. There are lots of visitors at the house and the prime minister will be staying there over the weekend with his wife.'

Her mother was deflated. 'Oh, I see.'

'But I'll find a time . . . in due course. You'll have to be patient, I'm afraid.'

'If you say so, Gwen.'

'And there are lots of other places to visit.'

'We can make a list,' said her mother, beaming. 'Fetch a pen and some paper.'

'Let's go into the drawing room. That's the best place to do it.'

After another embrace, they went arm in arm into the house.

When they walked to the cathedral, they stood outside it for some time, admiring its sheer size. It had a relatively plain exterior, free from the excessive decoration of other cathedrals. Its most striking feature was its noble spire, climbing to a height of three hundred feet.

Leeming was impressed. 'How long did it take to build that?'

'Too long,' said Hinton. 'Stonemasons who started working on it originally must have died long before it was finished.'

'Well, they could take pride in what they did, Alan.'

'Just like us.'

'Oh, I'm not feeling very proud – quite the opposite, in fact.'

'Why do you say that?'

'We seem to be marking time in this investigation.'

'I disagree. We've made real progress.'

'But we're no nearer an arrest.'

'Yes, we are. I sense that we're getting close.'

'This cathedral may be our last resort,' moaned Leeming. 'Let's go inside and pray for help.'

Hinton laughed. 'Stop teasing!'

'I'm deadly serious.'

They went into the cathedral and paused to marvel at its cavernous interior. The verger gave them a warm welcome and, when he knew the reason for their visit, took them to meet the dean, an elderly man with an air of nobility about him. The dean spoke in a reverential whisper. He hardly seemed to notice the sergeant's facial wounds. Leeming explained why they had come and received instant cooperation from him.

'I remember reading about that case in the newspaper,'

said the dean. 'There's a famous detective involved, isn't there?'

'That's right – Detective Inspector Colbeck.'

'They're very fortunate to have him.'

'We agree, sir,' said Leeming.

The dean took them into the vestry and produced a ring to which several keys were attached. After selecting one, he walked across to a large cupboard and inserted the key into the lock. The door swung open to reveal a collection of documents, including a large, leatherbound volume. Reaching it out, the dean placed it on the table in the middle of the vestry.

'Handle this with great care,' he warned. 'It's very precious.'

'How far back does it go?' asked Hinton.

'Far longer than you'll need.'

'We're only interested in the last ten years or so.'

'Fifteen at most,' added Leeming.

'Then I'll leave you to it,' said the dean.

When the man had left, Leeming opened the cover very gently and read the inscription inside. He then turned the pages slowly and carefully until he reached details of marriages in 1851. They both marvelled at the quality of the calligraphy.

'I could never write like that,' admitted Hinton.

'You'll have to learn how to do it, Alan.'

'Why?'

'Because you'll be putting your signature in a book just like this one day.'

Hinton came close to blushing, but Leeming did not notice. He was too busy studying the names of the long succession of brides who had been joined in holy matrimony in the cathedral.

Year followed year but there was no sign of the name they sought. After working his way through five years without success, Leeming came close to desperation.

'This is a waste of time. She's not here.'

'Don't give up,' urged Hinton. 'Keep going.'

'My arm is starting to ache.'

'Then let me take over.'

'No, no, I'll force myself to carry on but it's a forlorn hope.'

He turned a page to reveal another marriage certificate. Hinton pointed a finger.

'There she is,' he cried. 'Christina Lindsey Powell.'

'She's Mrs Falconbridge now – she married Charles Daniel Falconbridge.'

'We've found her at last!'

'Don't be so hasty, Alan,' warned Leeming. 'All that we've found is a woman by the name of Christina. She may not be the person we're after.'

'She is,' insisted Hinton. 'And we found her because you had the sense to bring us here.'

'That's true.'

After recording the details of the wedding in his notebook, Leeming closed the volume gently and carried it across to the safe. He then left the vestry with Hinton.

Halfway down the main aisle, they were intercepted by the dean.

'Did you find what you wanted?' he asked.

'We hope so,' replied Leeming. 'Thank you for your help.'

'Oh, I can take no credit. I prefer to believe that the help came from above . . .'

Christina Falconbridge was in a quandary. She had received a letter that morning from her husband with the news that he would be coming home on leave in a week's time. Ordinarily, it would have raised her spirits and filled her with anticipatory delight. Their reunions were always occasions for joy. At least, they had been in the past. It was different now. Instead of coming home to a loving wife, her husband would be returning to the arms of a woman who had betrayed him. Christina feared that she might be unable to hide the truth from him. Horrified at what she had done, he would be aghast at the thought that she was paying money to someone to conceal her disgrace. Her marriage might well end up in ruins.

She was tempted to blame Giles Blanchard for what had happened, but the truth was that she had to take an equal share of the blame. There had been a moment when she and the estate agent had been alone together in the house before she had actually moved into it. Christina and Blanchard discussed possible improvements to the property. Without warning, he had smiled at her with undisguised affection. Shocked at first, she began to feel attracted. By the time their tour of the house had ended, she had forgotten all about her marriage vows.

'Nobody will ever find out,' he had whispered in her ear.

Yet they had, and she was now the victim of blackmail. Her lover had been murdered and her life had been changed beyond recall. The future was bleak. Continuous pain and remorse beckoned.

When she had taken her mother-in-law home, Verity Blanchard had driven the trap towards Bembridge so that she could collect her husband. He took over the reins.

'Thank you for saving me a long walk,' he said.

'It's the least I could do, Paul.'

'Where is Mother?'

'She went straight to bed.'

'We must find out who put that blanket around her and return it to them.'

'There's no hurry for that,' said Verity. 'The most important thing to do is to calm your mother down. I had the most terrible fright when I learnt that she'd wandered off.'

'We found her – that's the main thing.'

'But how do we stop her from doing it again? I'm worried, Paul. She might wander off in the middle of the night.'

'We'll find a way somehow,' he promised. 'I don't think there is any immediate danger.

'Mother had what she wanted most. She revived a happy memory in Bembridge.'

'I'm not sure I'd have wanted a proposal of marriage in the shadow of a windmill.'

'That's why I chose the summer house instead,' he recalled.

She smiled dreamily. 'It was a lovely moment.'

'There'll be a lot more of those when this business is done. Meanwhile, we have a funeral to organise and a killer to find. When that's over,' he promised, putting an arm around her shoulders, 'we can start to live a normal life once again.'

As soon as he arrived in Portsmouth, Colbeck left the railway station and walked to the theatre. After renewing his acquaintance with the manager, Harold Tremayne, he asked if he kept programmes of the plays that had been performed there over the years.

'Of course,' said the manager. 'They're part of our heritage. We have a complete set of programmes, going back to the very first production staged here. Since then, as you can imagine, we've collected a sizeable number.'

'Including the programme for the current offering,' said Colbeck. '*The Rivals*.'

'It's the third time Sheridan's play has been staged here, Inspector. Its appeal remains as great as ever. Let me show you our collection,' said the manager, crossing to the large cupboard in his office. 'I must ask you to handle them with great care. They're worthless to you but priceless to us.' He used a key to unlock the door and revealed sets of boxes. 'Where would you like to start?'

'Fifteen years ago, please.'

'That takes us back to 1851. This theatre did not exist then. Its predecessor was variously known as Portsmouth Theatre, Portsmouth and Portsea Theatre, and the Theatre Royal. It was first opened in 1761 and entertained generations of playgoers until 1854 when the building was sold to the War Office. Our present theatre dates from that time – though I do have a good selection of programmes that go back into the previous century.'

'If you have anything for 1855,' suggested Colbeck, 'we'll begin there. The actress I'm after might well have started her career by then.'

'May I know her name?'

'Only if you give me your solemn promise that you won't mention it to anyone else.'

'You can count on me, Inspector. I'm very discreet.'

'The actress's name is Bethany Drake,'

The manager frowned. 'That name rings a bell. She was in Buckmaster's troupe, I fancy. I certainly can't put a face to her – but I'm certain that she has appeared on our stage.'

'Excellent.'

'Sit down behind the desk and I'll bring the relevant boxes over to you.'

'Thank you,' said Colbeck, lowering himself into the chair.

'Nothing is quite so fascinating as theatrical history,' said the manager.

'I agree,' said Colbeck, 'and I'm very grateful. You could save me a great deal of time and help to move our investigation forward.'

Gwendoline Cardus and her mother were enjoying a cup of tea in the cosy drawing room at Rose Cottage. Isobel was still adjusting to her new life. The house was smaller than the one where she had been living, but it had considerably more charm. It also had the two servants she had brought with her. They were aware of her needs and looked after her attentively.

'It's a real treat to have you here for a while, Gwen,' she said.

'Thank you, Mother. I thought that Rose Cottage would suit you.'

'It's delightful – in spring and summer, anyway. I daresay that it may be different here in the dead of winter.' She sipped her tea. 'I've noticed that the garden shed is filled with logs. I love sitting beside a roaring fire. Christmas here will be a delight.'

'I'm sure it will.'

'Though I daresay you won't be able to spend it with me,' said Isobel. 'As usual, you'll be celebrating it with the Royal Family. You won't have time to spare for me.'

'I'll make time, Mother. That's a promise.'

'Thank you.'

Isobel finished her tea and set the cup in the saucer.

She then yawned involuntarily and apologised at once. Gwendoline was understanding. She knew that her mother liked to enjoy an afternoon nap. When Isobel's eyelids began to flutter, it was only a matter of minutes before she drifted off to sleep. Gwendoline got up quietly and went out into the garden. Before she could settle down in a chair, she saw a woman in summer attire and a straw hat admiring the flowers.

'Your roses are beautiful,' said the visitor.

'They give us so much pleasure.'

'It must be a joy to live here – but then you spend most of your time at Osborne House, don't you? I do envy you, I must say.'

Gwendoline tensed. 'Who are you?'

'You don't need to know my name.'

'What are you doing here?'

'I just came to see if you had read my message.'

Gwendoline gasped. 'Did you send it?'

'Yes,' said the other, smiling. 'We have your best interests at heart, Miss Cardus.'

'Who are you?'

'I suppose you could call me a benefactor.'

'You threatened me.'

'That was only a means of getting your attention,' said the other. 'We know your secret, Miss Cardus. This cottage holds a special memory for you, doesn't it? Mr Blanchard showed you every room, didn't he?' Her eyes twinkled. 'Including the main bedroom, I daresay.'

'Keep your voice down,' begged Gwendoline, looking

over her shoulder. 'You'll wake Mother.'

'What would she say if she knew the truth about her daughter? For that matter, what would Her Majesty the Queen, say if she realised that one of the women closest to her had behaved in the way that you did?'

'Who are you – and how do you know about me and Mr . . . the estate agent?'

'I'll ask the questions. The first one is this. How soon can you get the money for me?'

Gwendoline was flustered. 'I don't know. How much do you want?'

'This is the figure we think is reasonable,' said the woman, handing her a slip of paper. 'We will expect payment sometime tomorrow. Agreed?'

'I can't get this amount easily,' said Gwendoline, gibbering. 'It's cruel of you to ask. And you still haven't told me your name and address. Where do you live?'

'We live close enough to keep an eye on you, Miss Cardus. It was good meeting you. You're intelligent enough to know that you have no choice. I'll be back tomorrow at noon to collect the money from you. That's a promise.'

'No,' said Gwendoline. 'Don't come here. Let's meet outside my bank here on the Isle of Wight. That's where I'll have to withdraw the money.'

'Which bank is it?'

'Emsley's Bank in Ryde.'

'I'll meet you outside at noon tomorrow,' said the woman. 'Don't you dare let us down.'

'I won't – I promise.'

'That means you're safe for a whole month. Then we'll have a second instalment. Otherwise . . .'

The woman disappeared, leaving the threat hanging in the air.

Left alone in the manager's office, Colbeck was leafing through programmes that told the story of British theatre over several years. He was fascinated. Searching for the name of Bethany Drake, he first came upon Nigel Buckmaster's name. In a production of *Romeo and Juliet*, the actor-manager had taken the role of Romeo. There was no sign in the cast list of the actress Colbeck was after. Evidently, her career had not begun at that point. It was nearly eight years before she made an appearance. It was in a touring production of *The Merchant of Venice*. Once again, Buckmaster had cast himself in the title role. Bethany Drake had played the part of Nerissa, waiting-gentlewoman to Portia, the play's heroine.

Colbeck not only made a note of her debut, but also recorded the names of two actors in the play because they had been mentioned by Buckmaster as particular friends of Bethany Drake. When she next appeared in a programme, she had left Buckmaster's company and belonged to another troupe. Her progress was steady. They visited Portsmouth on tour in 1856 and she had an important role in Dion Boucicault's play, *London Assurance*. Colbeck noticed that the two actors named earlier by Buckmaster were not in the cast but the third one – Jack Harrity – was. Harrity also appeared in the next play in which Bethany Drake was featured.

What struck Colbeck was the way that railways had been such a boon to the acting profession, allowing companies to travel with comparative ease to provincial theatres. During her career, Bethany Drake would have been using trains regularly. As an experienced actress, she could practise her art on other travellers in her compartment. An audience, however small, was always welcome. It was a means of honing her craft.

The last mention of her in the programmes was in 1864. Reunited with Nigel Buckmaster's company, she had been promoted. In the touring production of *The Merchant of Venice*, she had been playing Portia this time. Interestingly, the actor-manager himself had appeared as Shylock, setting himself a difficult challenge. It was Jack Harrity who had been given the title role.

After that production, Bethany Drake had disappeared. There was no sign of her – or of Harrity – in any subsequent productions. Colbeck decided that Buckmaster had spread the word about her criminal inclinations. Managements had paid attention to such a powerful voice as his and the actress's career in the theatre had ended abruptly. She would have been angry and vengeful. Since she had been shunned by theatres, Colbeck reasoned, she had sought to use her gifts in a different way and developed an alternative career – perhaps in conjunction with Harrity.

Colbeck was putting the programmes away when the

manager came back into the office.

'Did you find what you were looking for, Inspector?' he asked.

'I found more than I expected.'

'I'm glad that your visit was worthwhile.'

'It was very worthwhile,' said Colbeck. 'I feel that I am on the right track at last.'

'Good – and thank you for tidying everything away.'

'It's the least I can do.'

'Those programmes are like the Crown Jewels to me.'

'They're very precious to me as well,' said Colbeck with a smile.

Concern over his mother remained. As a precaution, Paul Blanchard had sent for the doctor to ask him if he would examine her in the wake of her strange behaviour. By the time that he arrived at the house, Catherine had woken up and was sitting in a chair in her bedroom, lost in thought. When her son brought the doctor in, she was surprised but not offended. Blanchard had left them alone.

It was a long time before the doctor reappeared. His demeanour was solemn. After declining the offer of refreshment, he told Paul that there were no ill effects from his mother's disappearance.

'Her physical condition is exactly what I would expect of a woman of that age,' he said.

'It's her mind that worries us,' admitted Blanchard.

'That's where the problem lies. Mrs Blanchard seems to have regressed to a time over thirty years ago. She talked about incidents from those days as if they occurred yesterday.'

'I daresay that she'll have told you why she felt the need to go to Bembridge Windmill.'

'Yes,' said the doctor, 'she quoted your father's proposal to her word for word.'

Blanchard was anxious. 'Do you think that she's . . . not of sound mind?'

'I think that she's behaving as many elderly people do in the wake of a profound shock. Your father meant everything to her. To lose him in such a distressing way has robbed her of all the certainties in her life. Mrs Blanchard is so fearful of her future that she has gone back into the past when everything was safe and predictable.'

'Will she ever adjust to . . . my father's death?'

'Not for a long time,' replied the doctor. 'Your mother needs care and support. I can prescribe some stronger medication for her but it's not a guaranteed cure. What she needs most is the love and help of her family.'

'She'll certainly get that.'

'For as long as they last, you'll have to tolerate her . . . eccentricities.'

'We'll do anything necessary,' vowed Blanchard.

'I'm sure that you will. By moving in here with your mother, you did the best possible thing. You and your wife have been a tremendous support to her. Your mother recognises that. But there's another phase ahead,' he warned. 'The real pain of her loss will come when the funeral takes place. Mrs Blanchard will be forced to face a life without the man who meant everything to her. That realisation will be very painful. It's the moment when you and your wife will be needed most.'

Blanchard nodded. 'We'll be ready, Doctor.'

Victor Leeming and Alan Hinton travelled back to Portsmouth by train. They felt proud of what they had discovered and were keen to pass on the information to Colbeck. When they got back to the Hope and Anchor, they found the inspector waiting for them in the lounge. They sat down beside him with smiles on their faces.

'Well?' he asked. 'Success or failure?'

'A bit of both, sir,' replied Hinton.

'Spare me the latter. Just tell me what you achieved.'

'We found Christina.'

'Well done!' said Colbeck.

'Her full name is Christina Falconbridge. To be honest, I'd given up hope, but Sergeant Leeming insisted that we went to the cathedral. We searched the records of marriages there.'

'It was Alan who deserves the credit,' insisted Leeming. 'Once we found her name, I was ready to come back here but he pointed out that our job was only half done.'

'Yet you found the name you were after,' said Colbeck.

'But we had no idea where she lived.'

'I suggested that we went back to the cathedral,' explained Hinton. 'The dean who helped us was quite old. It may well be that he was involved in that particular wedding. And he was! He not only remembered the bride, he remembered the man she married – Captain Falconbridge.'

'Captain?' repeated Colbeck. 'Army or navy?'

'He's in the army, sir. And he's been promoted to the rank of major.'

'The dean was a godsend to you.'

'He even gave us Major and Mrs Falconbridge's address.'

'Except that the husband is rarely there,' added Leeming. 'He's based in Wiltshire.'

Colbeck understood at once how relevant that piece of news was. Delighted with the work of his detectives, he complimented them. They were anxious to know about his search.

'Oh, I didn't find anything of great interest,' said Colbeck, feigning disappointment.

Leeming was downcast. 'You must have discovered something.'

'I discovered that Nigel Buckmaster was as ebullient as ever, Victor. He interrupted a rehearsal to talk to me and gave me the name of a former actress who might possibly have been in that compartment with the killer.'

'A name!' cried Hinton. 'That's wonderful.'

'One name led to another. I may also have discovered her accomplice.'

'Do you have any idea where they live?'

'I've believed all along that their home is here in Portsmouth.'

'Then let's go and arrest the pair of them,' said Leeming, getting up.

'There's just one problem, Victor.'

'What is it?'

'We have no address for them. When I gave the names to the city police, they had no record of them. That didn't surprise me. Actors very often change their real names for ones that have more of a ring to them. The culprits whom I identified as Bethany Drake and Jack Harrity might well be using other aliases by now,' said Colbeck. 'Our task is to find out what they are.'

CHAPTER TWENTY-ONE

'The head is much too big,' said Caleb Andrews, clicking his tongue.

'Never disturb an artist at work, Father,' advised his daughter.

'But she's not an artist, Maddy.'

'Yes, she is. Look at that portrait of you that she drew.'

'It's nothing like me.'

'Helena Rose thinks so,' said Madeleine.

During the increasingly warm weather, the garden at the Colbeck residence came into its own. They spent a lot of time there. Madeleine was now seated at a table in a shaded corner with her father and her daughter. Andrews was looking over the shoulder of his granddaughter at the portraits she was trying to draw. The latest was of her father.

'Robert will be upset if he sees that,' warned Andrews.

'Don't be so critical,' said Madeleine. 'Helena Rose is doing very well.'

'I hoped that she might have your skill as an artist.'

'She is still young, Father. There's plenty of time for her to develop. Besides, I may be an artist but the only talent I have is for painting steam engines. I'm hopeless at portraits. It's the reason people rarely appear in my work.'

'I always hoped that I might do so one day,' he complained.

'It's because of you that I fell in love with the whole world of railways,' she reminded him. 'In that sense, you're in everything I produce. Well done, darling,' she went on as the child sat back to admire her latest portrait. 'Daddy will love it.'

'But it makes Robert looks so . . . enormous.'

'It's how children see their fathers. When I was her age, you looked enormous to me. What makes Robert so tall is that top hat she's drawn. It's three times as big as the real one.'

'If I'd worn a top hat at work, I'd have been laughed at.'

'Nobody laughed at the way you drove a steam engine.'

He smiled proudly. 'I loved doing it, Maddy, that's why.'

'Well, Helena Rose loves drawing and painting, so let's encourage her in every way we can. I can't wait to see what Robert makes of his portrait.'

'I can't wait to see Robert,' he muttered. 'When is he coming home?'

When she paid her visit to Rose Cottage to demand money, she had been on her own. Her partner, however, had been hidden within earshot so he heard the conversation between the two women. After what they felt was a profitable visit, they had headed for the coast and were now walking together along a beach. They had to raise their voices above the excited yells of the holidaymakers nearby. He looked around with a smile.

'They're having a wonderful time,' he observed. 'If they can play on the sand or walk barefoot in the sea, they think they're in Elysium. We have more sophisticated tastes.'

'Yes,' she agreed. 'Our pleasure comes from making money.'

'Are you sure that Miss Cardus will do as she is told?'

'I'm certain of it. She's terrified that we'll reveal her secret. Her position in royal service would disappear instantly. The Queen would be horrified at the disclosure. Miss Cardus would also lose most of her former friends. Imagine the kind of life she'd be forced to live.'

'I'm more interested in the kind of life we can now

enjoy,' he said. 'If those women were stupid enough to let themselves be seduced by Giles Blanchard, they deserve no sympathy.'

'I agree. I only had a fleeting acquaintance with him in the compartment of a train, but I found him repulsive.'

'Forget him. He's dead.'

'He's still very much alive for the women he seduced. Each one of them obviously found him irresistible. I daresay that they'll be weeping on the day of his funeral.'

'Whereas you and I will be cheering.'

They laughed harshly. After walking a few more yards, they came to a stop.

'Do you miss the life we used to have in the theatre?' he asked.

'I do and I don't.'

'What do you mean?'

'Well,' she said, 'I miss the sheer thrill of performing in front of an audience. There's nothing like an ovation to make the blood race. You feel so . . . special.'

'You are special,' he assured her.

'But there's another side to that life. After the ovation, you usually trudge off to cheap accommodation and begin the following day with a dreadful breakfast. It's a life of sacrifices. That's why I was ready to leave it.'

'I helped you to make that decision, my love.'

'And I'm eternally grateful. I'll never again have to endure the agony of wondering if a management will employ me again.'

'No chance of that, I'm afraid. Nigel Buckmaster brought your career to an end.'

'He was such a help to me at the start – and he never let me forget it.'

'I don't miss working with him,' he admitted. 'Whatever role I took, I was always in his shadow. Nobody ever noticed me.'

'I did,' she said, squeezing his hand. 'And I have no regrets.'

He kissed her on the cheek. 'That makes two of us.'

It was Victor Leeming's suggestion that had proved vital. In taking Hinton to Chichester Cathedral, he had led the way to the identification of Christina Falconbridge. As another possible victim of blackmail, Colbeck decided, she had to be contacted at once and it was a task he took upon himself. It was early evening by the time he arrived by train in Chichester. He took a cab to the address provided by the dean at the cathedral.

When he rang the bell, the door was opened by a maidservant. After giving his name and rank, he was invited into the hall and asked to wait while the woman went into the drawing room.

Shortly afterwards, Christina Falconbridge came out to see him. She was visibly shaking. When she invited him into the drawing room, her voice was full of dread. Once alone with her, Colbeck sought to calm her down and get her cooperation.

'I am leading the investigation into the death of Giles

Blanchard,' he told her. 'I believe that he sold this house to you and your husband.'

'That's right,' she murmured.

'I understand that you and Mr Blanchard became . . . close friends.'

'No,' she snapped, 'that's quite untrue.'

'I appreciate your need to deny any association with him,' said Colbeck, gently, 'but it's only fair to warn you that Paul Blanchard – his son – found letters from you, hidden away in his father's desk. Do you deny that you ever wrote such letters?'

'Oh, my God!' she exclaimed, burying her face in her hands.

'Let me assure you that those letters have been destroyed. That might bring you some comfort. Let me also assure you that nobody else need ever know the contents of those missives. In effect, they no longer exist.' She removed her hands to look at him. 'I'm not making any moral judgements on what happened. My priority is to find the man who killed Mr Blanchard.'

'How can I possibly help you?' she said.

'Having murdered him, the killer and his accomplice stole his wallet and everything else that he was carrying. We believe that one of the items was an address book containing your name and those of . . . other women he befriended.'

She was mortified. 'Others? He swore to me that I was the only—'

'He lied to you, Mrs Falconbridge. We have already

been in contact with some of the other close female friends to warn them that they may be approached by someone trying to blackmail them. One of them has already confessed to handing over a substantial amount.' He looked her in the eye. 'If we can arrest the blackmailer and her partner, we can rescue the victims from a dreadful fate. You may already be one of them. I'm here to get confirmation of that.'

Christina was in despair. She could hardly speak.

'Were you approached by a woman with a demand for money? We have a good description of her. She is beautiful, well-spoken, and in her late thirties.' Colbeck watched her carefully. 'You've met this person, haven't you?'

After a long pause, she nodded.

'Good,' he said with relief. 'Please tell me what happened.'

Leeming and Hinton had been sent to the Isle of Wight to find Gwendoline Cardus. During the crossing, they had a lively chat with Brendan Mulryne. The Irishman was still hoping that he might be called upon to provide help.

'Where exactly are you going, Victor?' he asked.

'It's a secret,' replied Leeming.

'You could tell me, surely.'

'I could, Brendan, but I have to obey orders.'

Mulryne's eyes glinted. 'That means you're close to an arrest.'

'If only we were!' sighed Leeming.

When they left the steamer, they took a cab to Rose Cottage and asked the driver to wait. Because Leeming feared that his facial injuries might startle the woman, Alan Hinton went to the cottage on his own. In response to his knock, Gwendoline opened the door to him. The moment that he explained who he was, she was almost panic-stricken. Closing the door behind her, she took him into the front garden.

'As I explained to Inspector Colbeck,' she said, 'I was not a friend of . . . Mr Blanchard.'

'The inspector thinks otherwise, Miss Cardus.'

'Then he has no right to do so.'

'He has every right,' said Hinton, 'because we are hunting a killer. You lied to him when he told you that we had evidence of your friendship with Mr Blanchard. As you know, letters sent by you to him were found by his son – then promptly destroyed.' Gwendoline's jaw dropped. 'They are evidence of a close – a very close – friendship. Do you admit that?'

Lowering her head, she nodded in agreement.

'And do you also admit that you misled Inspector Colbeck?'

'Yes – and I'm sorry I did that.'

'We know of someone else who was . . . close to Mr Blanchard. As a result, she received a dire warning. If she did not pay a sizeable amount of money to the people responsible for his death, her husband would be told of her deceit.'

'What did she do?'

'She handed over the money,' said Hinton. 'And she must do so again next month.'

'I've had a similar demand,' confessed Gwendoline.

'And was it made by the woman I described to you?'

'Yes, it was.'

'Do you want to spend the rest of your life at her mercy?'

'No!' cried Gwendoline. 'The very idea makes my blood run cold.'

'Then help us to catch this woman and her accomplice.'

'What can I possibly do?' she whined.

'You can be completely honest with me, Miss Cardus. You need to tell me how you were approached and how much money was demanded of you. Most important of all, we need to know the exact time when you must hand the money over?' He softened his voice. 'If you refuse our help, there's nobody else to call on. Do you understand?'

Paul Blanchard was alone in his father's study, wondering if it contained any more unpleasant secrets about a man he had admired. Everything about their relationship seemed to have been built on falsehood. In opening the branch in Chichester, he now realised, his father had not simply been extending the business. He had enjoyed an alternative life that revolved around The Haven. A husband who treated his wife with such respect betrayed her shamelessly when he was alone with one of his women friends. The tributes that would be paid to him at the funeral would embarrass his son. He knew the ugly truth.

There was a knock on the door then it opened to admit his wife, Verity. She looked weary.

'How is Mother?' he asked.

'She's finally gone to sleep.'

'It was so kind of you to sit with her for so long.'

'It was no trouble. She wanted to talk about her earlier life with your father. Did you know that she was never allowed to come in here?'

'Father hated being interrupted, that's why.'

'Did you ever come into the study when you were a boy?'

'No, I didn't,' he admitted. 'Father valued his privacy.'

'I think there was more to it than that, Paul.'

'How would you know?' he challenged, glaring at her.

Shocked and hurt, Verity backed away. He was immediately apologetic.

'I'm so sorry,' he said, getting up to put his arms around her. 'I didn't mean to shout like that. The truth is that father's murder has put me under immense pressure. Until the funeral is over, I'm unable to think straight. But that's no reason to turn on you, Verity. You've been a saint.'

'I've tried my best.'

'We can't really get back to leading a normal life until they catch the man who strangled my father. I'll be so glad when that happens.'

'So will I, Paul.'

Having listened carefully to her account, Colbeck put his notebook away and looked up at her. He had profound sympathy for the woman.

'Thank you, Mrs Falconbridge,' he said. 'You've been very honest.'

'I've also been very stupid,' she confessed. 'I see that now. I was . . . flattered.'

'What you've told me has been very instructive.'

'Will it help you to catch the man who . . . ?'

'I hope so,' said Colbeck. 'We are getting closer to him all the time.'

'May I ask you a question, Inspector?'

'Yes, of course.'

'Are you married?'

'Yes, I am,' he replied.

'What will your wife be doing now that she's home alone?'

'Madeleine won't be alone, Mrs Falconbridge. She will either be talking to her father who calls most days to see our daughter, or she will be upstairs in her studio.'

Christina was taken aback. 'Studio?'

'My wife is a talented artist. She loves to paint pictures. It started as a hobby, but she is now able to sell whatever she paints.'

'How clever of her!'

'There's not just cleverness involved,' he said. 'Madeleine relies on hard work and endless patience.

Before she gives a painting to the art dealer, she will work on it obsessively until she gets it exactly right. It sometimes takes ages.'

'Your wife must be very committed,' she said. 'She's obviously found something that gives her pleasure and occupies her time. I envy her. Living here without my husband, I was restless and bored. I had no children to look after. Inevitably, I suppose, I felt very lonely. That's not an excuse,' she added, quickly. 'But it did mean that I had . . . time on my hands.'

'I understand, Mrs Falconbridge.'

'It won't happen again, I promise.' She looked at him. 'If you catch this man . . .'

'Oh, there's no question about that. We'll arrest him soon.'

'Is there any way that he – or that woman I met – will carry out their threat?'

'No, they won't. They'll be locked up behind bars and unable to harm you – or anyone else who might be in your situation. I give you my word on that.'

'Thank you.'

'As for the money you were forced to pay them,' he told her, 'I can't guarantee that it will be repaid in full.'

'I don't want a single penny of it, Inspector,' she said with conviction. 'Whatever is recovered can be donated to a good cause. I did something unforgivable and I'm more than ready to bear the cost of being so foolishly led astray.'

* * *

Having criticised his granddaughter's attempt at being a portrait artist, Caleb Andrews was challenged to show if he could do better. He started with great confidence but soon became aware of his many weaknesses. His hand shook nervously, he had no sense of proportion and – worst of all – his poor eyesight meant that he could not see either his daughter or granddaughter well enough to draw them with any accuracy. Andrews did, however, persist. When he had finished, he took a measure of pride in what he had produced.

'That's good,' he said, studying the portraits.

'Let me see,' asked Madeleine.

He handed one of them over. 'You've got another artist in the family.' After a glance at the drawing, she burst out laughing. 'What's so funny?'

'This portrait of me is ridiculous.'

'You're holding the one of Helena Rose,' he pointed out.

'That's even worse.' She handed it to her daughter. 'What do you think, darling?'

Helena Rose giggled. 'It's funny. I've got bigger ears than a rabbit.'

'Show us the one of me,' Madeleine asked him.

'Not if you're going to laugh at me, Maddy,' he said, huffily.

'I'm sorry, Father – and so is Helena Rose.'

'Yes,' said the child, taking her cue from her mother. 'I'm sorry, Grandfather.'

'My old hands are too gnarled to draw properly,' he

confessed, holding them out. 'The portraits are useless, I know – but you must admit I was brave enough to try.'

Colbeck opened the package carefully and took out the sheet of cartridge paper. He was delighted with what he saw. After studying the face for a long time, he put it away. Within minutes, Leeming and Hinton came into the Hope and Anchor. They were bubbling with excitement.

'It looks as if you had a successful visit,' said Colbeck.

'We did, sir,' said Leeming. 'Alan succeeded where you failed.'

'Oh?'

'Miss Cardus told you that nobody had tried to blackmail her.'

'She was insulted that I'd even suggested the idea,' recalled Colbeck.

'Alan squeezed the truth out of her.'

'That's not quite true,' explained Hinton. 'When they sent her a warning letter, she tried to ignore it. Then someone turned up at Rose Cottage.'

'And?' pressed Colbeck.

'The threat was more explicit.'

'Pay up or we'll destroy your life,' said Leeming.

'It wasn't as crude as that. The demand was made by a woman.'

'How did Miss Cardus respond?' asked Colbeck.

'She had no choice, sir,' replied Hinton. 'If she refused, the Queen would be told the truth about her and Blanchard – and so would Miss Cardus's mother. That threat rattled her.'

'So she agreed to pay the money demanded,' said Leeming, taking over. 'What's more, we know when and where that will take place. It's tomorrow at noon outside Emsley's Bank in Ryde.'

'That's splendid news,' said Colbeck. 'Well done, Alan!'

'I persuaded Miss Cardus to trust me, sir.'

'It's that kind face of his,' teased Leeming. 'She told him that the woman was beautiful.'

Colbeck smiled. 'I agree wholeheartedly.'

'What do you mean, sir?' asked Hinton.

'See for yourself.'

Colbeck took out the sheet of cartridge paper and held it up so that they could see the portrait on it. Drawn by an artist with an eye for detail, it made the two detectives blink in astonishment.

'Is that her?' asked Hinton. 'She doesn't look like a criminal.'

'Well, that's what she is, Alan. We'll arrest her along with the killer. This portrait of Bethany Drake was drawn by a member of Buckmaster's company when she was still in it. Apparently, it was a good likeness of her. That,' said Colbeck, 'is what Mr Buckmaster said in the letter that came with his portrait.'

'How did it get here?' asked Hinton.

'It was sent by courier. Realising how interested I was in finding this actress, Mr Buckmaster retrieved this portrait of her from his files and sent it to me in the hope that it might be of use.'

'Of use?' echoed Leeming, gleefully. 'I'll say it is.'

'It's a pity we don't have a drawing of her accomplice,' said Hinton.

'He'll be outside that bank with her tomorrow. You can have the pleasure of arresting him, Alan. I'd prefer to put handcuffs on the lady.'

'You may both be needed to overpower the fellow,' Colbeck warned. 'He's strong enough to strangle a man to death, remember. We must not underestimate him.'

'There's three of us to one of him, sir,' said Leeming. 'He doesn't stand a chance.'

'Yes, he does, Victor. What if he is carrying a pistol? Then there's the woman herself. She might also have a concealed weapon.'

'Ah, I see what you mean.'

'We may need extra support.'

'Do you think that the police will supply it?' asked Hinton.

'I wasn't thinking of asking them,' said Colbeck. 'I'd rather recruit a man who works on the steamer going to Ryde.'

'Are you talking about that mad Irishman?'

'That's the fellow, Alan – Brendan Mulryne.'

'He'll be more than happy to help us,' said Leeming, confidently. 'And all he'll want by way of payment is a barrel of beer.'

* * *

When the steamer docked in Ryde, the passengers waited until the vessel had been secured then they surged ashore. Two young men tried to manoeuvre a large chest towards the gangplank. A member of the crew came to their aid.

'Let me show you how it's done, lads,' he volunteered.

Tipping the chest on its side, Mulryne put his arms around it in a bear hug and lifted it effortlessly from the deck. The men watched as he took it safely along the gangplank and put it gently on the wharf.

'There you are,' said the Irishman, cheerily. 'That's the way to carry it.'

At the end of a long, tiring day, Edward Tallis stubbed out his cigar in the ashtray on his desk and stood to his feet. He picked up the telegraph sent by Colbeck and read it again.

'Arrests are imminent, are they?' he cried. 'I certainly hope so! If you don't have the villains in handcuffs by this time tomorrow, Colbeck, I'll come to Portsmouth and take charge of the investigation myself.'

Gwendoline Cardus had a very bad night. Unable to sleep for hours on end, she finally dropped off and found herself in the middle of a nightmare. She was naked in bed with Giles Blanchard on top of her when the door burst open, and a succession of people came into the room, disgusted in turn by the grotesque spectacle. Gwendoline's mother led the way and gaped in horror at her daughter. Other members of the wider family came to express their surprise and contempt. Last in line was Her Majesty, the Queen, waddling to the bedside and staring in disbelief at what was going on. She dismissed Gwendoline from royal service on the spot.

It was enough to bring her suddenly awake, screaming aloud. When she sat up in bed, she found that she was covered in perspiration. Moments later, her mother came hurrying into the bedroom in a state of alarm.

'What happened, Gwen?' she asked.

'It's nothing, Mother,' she said. 'I had a bad dream, that's all.'

Word arrived early next morning that the body of Giles Blanchard would be released to the family. It meant that his son could complete the funeral arrangements. He had already discussed the event with a local printer. Now that he could provide the man with a definite date, invitations could be printed and sent out. Paul felt a huge sense of relief. It was not long now before his father – and his secrets – were buried in the earth.

Excitement had brought them both awake early that morning. The thought of collecting a large amount of money from Gwendoline Cardus was almost intoxicating. Once they had set up a regular monthly meeting with her – wherever she might be – they would have complete control over the woman. They intended to make full use of it.

'What are you going to wear?' he asked her.

'It's time to put on my new dress for the first time – and my new bonnet.'

'You'll get many admiring glances, if you do.'

'Well, they won't come from Miss Cardus,' she predicted with a laugh.

He had a momentary doubt. 'Are you quite sure that she will turn up?'

'Yes, of course – she wouldn't dare to disobey her orders. She knows only too well what the consequences would be. Have no worries about her.'

'She'd be drummed out of royal service immediately.'

'It's a threat we can hold over her head for years,' she said. 'Miss Cardus looks so prim and proper, but we've had a glimpse of her true character. Underneath that respectable exterior is a fully fledged woman. Blanchard brought her alive. She will be outside her bank at noon today – and she'll hand over the money.'

'All that we need to do,' he said, 'is to decide how to spend it.'

They laughed heartily.

Gwendoline Cardus sat opposite her mother at the table without saying a word. Lost in thought, she was jerked out of her silence by the sound of plates being removed by a servant.

'Oh,' she said to the woman. 'Thank you.'

'You hardly ate a thing, Gwen,' said her mother.

'I'm not hungry.'

'But you must have something. Breakfast is the most

important meal of all. It gives you the energy you need for the rest of the day.'

'I just don't have any appetite, Mother.'

'That's not like you at all,' said Isobel. 'Are you feeling unwell?'

'No, I just feel . . . weary, that's all.'

'It's that nightmare you had, isn't it? You never had a proper sleep.'

Gwendoline nodded her head. 'I was awake for ages.'

'Why? Is there something on your mind?'

'Not really,' replied her daughter. 'All I need is a long walk. The fresh air will wake me up.'

'That's a wonderful idea,' said Isobel. 'I'll come with you.'

Gwendoline was anxious. 'No, no, I need to go on my own.'

'But you were saying only yesterday that you would show me more of the island. What's wrong with having a proper look at it today?'

'I have shopping to do, Mother.'

'Then I can help to carry it.'

'Don't you understand?' snapped her daughter. 'I have appointments in Ryde.'

'What sort of appointments?'

'Well . . . I need to speak to the bank manager.'

'Can't I come with you?'

'I could be there for some time,' lied Gwendoline. 'However, I will keep my promise to show you around the island. We can go this afternoon. Will that suit you?'

Isobel eyed her with concern. 'Yes, I suppose so . . .'

Over breakfast that morning, Colbeck outlined his plan to his two companions. Hinton nodded in appreciation of all that was said, but Leeming was critical.

'You told us yesterday that the man may be armed,' he said.

Colbeck nodded. 'It's a strong possibility, Victor.'

'Then shouldn't we have firearms ourselves?'

'I don't think so.'

'We'll be at a disadvantage.'

'No, we won't. We'll have the advantage of surprise. That's priceless.'

'I agree,' said Hinton.

'In case of a problem,' Colbeck reminded them, 'we have some support – Mulryne.'

'Did his boss mind losing him for a whole morning?'

'I daresay that he did, Alan. But when I spoke to him yesterday evening, Mulryne was so pleased to be involved that he assured me he'd get time off somehow.'

'Will he be armed?'

Leeming laughed. 'When you're as big and strong as Brendan,' he said, 'you don't need to be armed. I've seen him stop a riot in a public house simply by walking in there.'

'His other advantage,' Colbeck pointed out, 'is that he doesn't look like one of us. To that woman and her accomplice, he'll seem to be no more than a casual bystander.'

'There's nothing casual about Brendan!' said Leeming. 'He just loves a fight.'

'With luck, it may not come to that.'

'I hope you're right, sir.'

'We'll soon find out,' said Colbeck, taking out his watch to check the time. 'We leave here in an hour and a half.'

'But that's far too early,' protested Leeming.

'No, it isn't, Victor. We need to familiarise ourselves with the location – and we need to do it before they arrive to do the same thing. My belief is that the woman will loiter near the bank while the man watches from a distance.'

'What about Miss Cardus, sir?' asked Hinton. 'Do you think she'll turn up?'

'I'm certain of it, Alan. There's far too much at stake.'

Having travelled on the steamer together, they split up when they reached the island. The woman went on ahead, taking a cab to Union Street and arriving there well before noon. Her accomplice favoured a slower approach, electing to walk. By the time he reached Emsley's Bank, he was feeling refreshed and happy. He caught a first glimpse of his partner, pretending to look in the windows of various shops. In a new dress and straw bonnet, she looked beautiful. He felt a surge of desire.

* * *

Gwendoline got herself ready and waited for the cab to arrive at Rose Cottage. Her mother hovered, feeling neglected and increasingly worried about her daughter's behaviour. What was so special about the appointment with the bank manager? Isobel would have been happy to wait an hour or more while Gwendoline completed whatever business she had. As it was, she was about to be left alone in the cottage on a glorious summer's day. The cab soon arrived.

'I hope that your visit to the bank goes well,' said Isobel.

'Thank you, Mother.'

'A meal will be waiting for you when you get back.'

Tense and haunted, Gwendoline gave her a brittle smile then climbed into the cab.

Colbeck had first deployed his detectives then gone into the bank. He introduced himself to the manager and explained why he was there. Sidney Morton, the obliging manager, offered him whatever he needed.

'A lady will come in to draw a large amount of money,' explained Colbeck. 'As soon as she leaves, it will be handed over to a woman who is blackmailing her.'

'Will you step in and arrest the woman, Inspector?'

'I will do so when we have identified her male accomplice.'

'And where will he be?'

'That is what my detectives are trying to find out.'

* * *

Victor Leeming was inside a toy shop, pretending to examine the items on display in the window while keeping one eye on the bank opposite. He picked up a wooden steam engine to examine it. While Colbeck loved trains, Leeming had always hated rail travel. But one of the sergeant's sons was now employed by a railway company. The lad was too old to play with a wooden toy, so he put it down again. Almost immediately, he saw a woman alight from a cab outside the bank and enter the building.

Alan Hinton was farther down the street, seated on a bench and apparently reading a newspaper. He, too, could see the bank clearly and watch people going in and coming out. When he saw Leeming emerge from the toy shop, he took a close look at pedestrians on both sides of the road. The woman he had seen going into the bank was Gwendoline Cardus. He was alerted.

Because he had met Gwendoline before, Colbeck took care to keep out of sight inside the bank. He watched her approach a clerk, explain what she wanted and pass her bank book to him under the grille. After opening it up, the man checked details of the account then opened a drawer to take out the money. Colbeck noticed how tense and uncomfortable she was.

When she left the bank, Colbeck waited a moment before following her. He came out in time to see her on the other side of the road, holding a bag in her hand and glancing nervously up and down the street. Pedestrians went past her in both directions, sometimes obscuring her for a second or two. A female pedestrian stopped to talk to her. Gwendoline handed the bag over then stood there watching the woman walk quickly away.

Leeming and Hinton came towards the woman from opposite directions, intercepting her and making the arrest. When the woman fought to escape, Leeming overpowered her while Hinton took out his handcuffs. Before she could be subdued, a man appeared from the crowd with a gun in his hand. Demanding the release of the prisoner, he made them walk several yards backwards before turning to run towards the waiting cab. He and the woman dived into it. Colbeck tried to get to the vehicle, but its sudden departure left him stranded.

He was soon joined by his detectives. Hinton was distressed.

'They've got away!' he cried.

'No, they haven't,' said Colbeck, breaking into a run. 'Let's get after them.'

Brendan Mulryne was perfectly placed to see the commotion. Hearing the clatter of hooves, he stepped into the middle of the road. The cab and its occupants were speeding towards him. Taking off his cap, he waved it so wildly at the oncoming horse that the animal flew into a panic, trying vainly to stop and sliding noisily on its hooves. The cab, meanwhile, was rocking uncontrollably. Screams came from the woman inside it. Struggling to bring the horse to a halt, the driver was thrown from his seat and hurled uncaringly to the ground. The horse itself reared up, neighing in fear. People nearby backed away from the animal, but Mulryne stood his ground. To the amazement of everyone nearby, he started to talk to the horse.

When they reached the cab, Colbeck saw that the animal was slowly calming down. Mulryne kept talking to it until it allowed him to step in and seize the bridle. Now that the cab was no longer swinging wildly to and fro, the occupants jumped out and tried to make a run for it. Hinton managed to grab the woman and – despite being kicked and spat at – held her tight. The man took to his heels with Leeming in close pursuit. Colbeck stepped in to take the bag from the woman's hands.

'That doesn't belong to you, Miss Drake,' he said.

'Who are you?' she demanded.

'We are detectives from Scotland Yard, here to end your little spree as blackmailers.'

Taking out a pair of handcuffs, Colbeck clipped them on to her wrists.

Leeming, meanwhile, was racing after her accomplice, undeterred by the fact that the man was armed. Hampered by the crowd, he was unable to run at full tilt. Every so often, he had to push people out of the way and dodge oncoming cabs. Leeming's top hat was blown off by the stiff breeze, but he did not stop to retrieve it. Ahead of him was the man who had committed murder then helped to terrorise a series of vulnerable women. Gun or not, he simply had to be caught. Determination put extra strength into Leeming's legs. He lengthened his stride and began to close the gap between himself and the killer.

The fugitive was armed but Leeming had one advantage over him. The man did not realise that he was being chased. Having abandoned the woman, he thought only of saving his own life. His escape attempt was cut rudely short. Making a final spurt, Leeming hurled himself at the man and knocked him to the ground, forcing him to hit the road hard and bang his head. Before the man knew what was happening, Leeming pulled his hands behind his back and snapped handcuffs on him. He then grabbed the gun from its holster.

Turning his quarry over, Leeming saw blood streaming down the man's face.

'You're under arrest, sir,' he gasped.

Alan Hinton, meanwhile, was holding his prisoner firmly. The woman was snarling abuse at him but she had no means of escape. Having been given her money back, Gwendoline Cardus was deeply grateful. Thanks to the detectives, her nightmare was over. Colbeck, meanwhile, was congratulating Mulryne on the way that the Irishman had calmed the horse down.

'The animal might have injured you with those flashing hooves, Brendan,' he said.

'Ah, no,' replied Mulryne, stroking the horse's neck. 'Horses know a friend when they see one. During my years in the circus, I worked with animals of all kinds – including a dozen horses. I learnt how to calm them down by talking to them. I was glad that I hadn't lost my touch.'

'The same can be said of Victor,' said Colbeck, as he saw Leeming approaching with his prisoner. 'When it comes to a chase, he always gets his man – even if it costs him his top hat.'

The telegraph that arrived that afternoon brought a rare smile to the superintendent's face. It told him that both suspects had been arrested and were in custody. Tallis noted with pleasure that Colbeck had also thought to send a telegraph to Captain Forrest, the Chief Constable of Hampshire. A notorious crime on the railway had finally been solved, allowing residents of the county to travel by train with far more confidence.

'Good work, Colbeck!' said Tallis. 'And the same to you, Leeming and Hinton!' He recalled his own visit to Portsmouth. 'The more I think about it,' he added, 'the more convinced I am that the person I saw on the steamer that day really was Brendan Mulryne. Whatever is that Irish scoundrel doing with his useless life these days?'

The three of them found an empty compartment in the train and sat back contentedly as it left Portsmouth railway station. Hinton felt a wave of sadness wash over him.

'To be honest,' he admitted, 'I'm sorry to leave. I really enjoyed our time on the Isle of Wight. I'd love to see far more of it.'

'It's a nice place to live,' said Leeming. 'It's much healthier than London and far safer. A house near the sea would be ideal for me and the family.'

'You'd be bored stiff after a week,' argued Colbeck. 'You thrive on action and the best place to get that is in the hurly-burly of the capital.'

'We had too much action there earlier today. I've never run so fast in my life.'

'You were a hero, Victor. Your name will be on the front page of the newspapers tomorrow.'

'So will yours, sir. You devised that plan to catch the pair of them.'

'Miss Cardus was central to that,' said Colbeck. 'When she visited her bank to get the money demanded, she flushed the couple out of their hiding place. In doing so, she not only helped herself, she came to the rescue of the other victims of blackmail. Their respective ordeals are over.'

'Ours will soon begin,' moaned Leeming. 'When we get back to Scotland Yard, we'll be grilled by the superintendent until we drop with fatigue.'

'Do we tell him about Mulryne's contribution?' asked Hinton.

'No,' said Colbeck. 'I think not.'

'But he brought that wild horse under control.'

'Yes, I know. Brendan is a man of many gifts. If it were left to me, I'd have him back in uniform as a constable in the Metropolitan Police Force.'

'So would I, sir,' said Leeming.

'It will never happen, I'm afraid. The superintendent regards him as more of a criminal than a policeman. We know his true worth. The next time we see a horse going berserk, we send for Brendan Mulryne. When he was in the circus, he told me, he once calmed down a rampaging elephant.'

Leeming grinned. 'Then we'll need him beside us when we see the superintendent.'

They laughed for the next ten minutes.

Edward Marston has written well over a hundred books, including some non-fiction. He is best known for his hugely successful Railway Detective series and he also writes the Bow Street Rivals series featuring twin detectives set during the Regency; the Home Front Detective novels set during the First World War; and the Ocean Liner mysteries.

edwardmarston.com

If you enjoyed *Murder in Transit*,
look out for more books by Edward Marston . . .

To discover more great fiction and to place an order
visit our website
www.allisonandbusby.com
or call us on
020 3950 7834